A Bridge to Somewhere

A WORLD WAR II CHRISTIAN FICTION NOVEL

Lorena M. Estep

Also by Author Lorena Estep

OUT OF THE MIST
HE RODE A PALOMINO
PUDDLES ON THE FLOOR

Copyright © 2016 by Lorena M. Estep
ALL RIGHTS RESERVED.

No part of this book may be reproduced in any form or by electronic means, including information storage and retrieval systems, without written permission from the publisher, except by a reviewer, who may quote passages in a review.

Published by Lorena M. Estep c/o Crescent Renewal, P.O. Box 581, Amissville, VA 20106. Email lestep@crescentrenewal.com

Cover and interior design by Tamira Ci Thayne, tami@tamiracithayne.com

ISBN-13: 978-1530632459
ISBN-10: 1530632455

Printed in the United States of America

First Edition

To my husband Chuck, with love

- and -

In memory of my brother Claire Montgomery,
who was one of the many injured while serving in World War II

Chapter One

Carter knocked hesitantly on the door of Allie's home. There were no lights anywhere, which was strange. He had been invited for supper, but the family car wasn't even in the driveway. He slowly opened the door, which they never locked.

"Allie?" There was no answer. He stepped from the mudroom into the kitchen.

Suddenly a light flashed on overhead, and he jumped back when he heard shouts of "Surprise!" He glanced around, confused, at the friends, relatives and neighbors who filled the room. A giant banner, with the words "GOOD LUCK CARTER," was strung on the wall, and flags hung in advantageous spots.

Grinning, Carter shook the hands of the men and accepted hugs from the women and girls, even though his shy nature rebelled against being the center of attention.

When he gripped his father's calloused hand, he was pulled into a fierce embrace, and was amazed to see tears in his dad's blue eyes. He couldn't remember his father ever crying, except when Grandma died; and, had his dad ever hugged him? Maybe when he was little.

But the news of the war that drifted back wasn't good. Two men from the area had been shipped home in boxes, and been awarded the Purple Heart posthumously. It would make the heart of any parent quake at the thought of a child going off to fight.

Then Allie stepped up and smiled teasingly at him. "Were you surprised, Carter?"

He picked her up and swung her around, eliciting hoots and whistles from the men and boys. "Totally! I can't believe you didn't let the cat out of the bag."

She pouted. "Carter, I *can* keep a secret when it's important."

He glanced around at all the people again. "Where are your cars and trucks? Did all of you walk here?" He grinned as the others laughed.

"They're either hidden behind the barn or next door at the neighbor's farm," Allie's father said. "We worked hard to keep it a surprise until you walked in the door."

"Alice Marie," her mother called to her, "Reverend Joshua will say grace, then you can take our guest-of-honor into the dining room to start the chow line."

Carter realized how hungry he was when he faced the food-laden table. These farm people knew how to cook. Everything appeared even more appetizing after eating in mess halls over the past months.

When he'd graduated from high school, he had gone to work at the Ford plant. When the Japanese bombed Pearl Harbor the past December, he'd joined the young men all around him who flocked to enlist.

Then came Basic Training in the Army Signal Corps, and following that, radio school. Now, a week from today, he'd leave for his assignment and could be thrown into the midst of the horrors that presently seemed so distant. Hopefully, working in communications would be a little safer than being in the midst of the battles.

Reaching to squeeze Allie's hand, he smiled into her blue eyes. The diamond he had bought for her was burning a hole in his pocket. He appreciated his relatives and friends gathering to give him a send-off, but he just wanted to get Allie alone and watch the joy on her face when he gave her the ring and asked her to wait for him.

Toward the end of their senior year he had finally gained the courage to ask her on a date, though he'd been eying her up for quite some time. She had promptly said, "Sure! What took you so long to ask me?" and she'd offered that glorious smile of hers. From then on, they'd been together as often as possible, until she started school at Moody Bible Institute in Chicago after graduation.

Carrying their plates and glasses of cider, they sought seats at the far end of the parlor where the noise and confusion were slightly less intrusive. From the other end of the room, the radio blared out, "I'll be seeing you in all the old familiar places." Some of the younger crowd sang loudly along with it.

With their plates empty, Carter put his arm around Allie's shoulder, pulling her closer to his side and whispering in her ear. "I suppose we have to wait until everyone leaves before we can get out of here ourselves."

She playfully slapped his leg. "Carter! Of course we do. You're the guest of honor. It would be rude to leave in the middle of your party. If you're done eating, you need to mingle and talk to everyone."

He glanced around at the people of all ages, and knew the kitchen and dining room were also full. A baby cried somewhere, and small children chased through the rooms. He scowled. "Okay, if I have to. But I wanted this to be our special night."

"It will be, Carter. Now give me your plate, and go make the rounds."

He stood reluctantly and forced a smile, turning to his best buddy who sat on his right. "Hey, Jesse, how's fatherhood going?"

Jesse smiled tiredly. "Ask me in a few months when Nathan starts sleeping all night. He has Annie and me worn out. She's in the kitchen, and that baby you heard wailing a bit ago was ours. It's what he does best. Doc says he has colic."

Carter clapped his friend on the shoulder. "Sorry you're not getting much sleep. I hear it gets better, not that I'm a firsthand expert."

Jesse stood and hugged Carter fiercely. "You take care, buddy, okay? I've been talking about joining up myself, but Annie panics every time I mention it."

"It's hard to leave families behind. Why don't you wait till the draft gets you?"

"That's what I'm planning to do."

Carter grinned. "You don't get much sleep in the service either." He patted Jesse's arm and moved on to the next guest.

He visited with everyone, but always keeping track of Allie's whereabouts. He finally caught her eye and motioned with his head toward the back door. He slipped outside, and she soon joined him. Pulling her close, he whispered, "I missed you, darlin'."

Leaning back in his arms, she smiled up at him. "I can't believe how many people came." She grinned impishly. "I didn't realize how popular you are, for a quiet guy."

"Hey, you know what they say: 'Still water runs deep.'"

"I discovered that early in our dating. When the other girls said you were boring, I just smiled, not wanting to let them in on the truth."

"Hey, what girls say I'm boring?" He started tickling her. "Boring, huh?"

Laughing uncontrollably, she grabbed his hands. "Stop it, Carter! You know I can't stand to be tickled."

"I won't stop till you tell me which girls are talking bad about me." Then he jumped back, sniffing.

"Is that smoke I smell?" He glanced toward the barn door that was lit by the pole light above it. "It's coming from the barn! Call the other men!" He sped toward the building where smoke now rolled from the windows.

Chapter Two

When Carter reached the barn door, it burst open and a string of teen boys came streaming out. He grabbed two of them. "What happened? Were you kids smoking in the haymow?"

The one boy nodded fearfully. "Someone must have dropped a match on one of the bales."

"Was Joey with you?"

"Yes, b-but he was trying to put the fire out and f-fell."

Carter shoved the two away. Calling for his kid brother, he ran into the barn. "Joey! Where are you?" The smoke burned his eyes and throat, but he found his way to one of the water barrels he knew Henry Preston kept in the barn. So far there was only smoke and no visible flames, but he needed to find Joey.

He dipped out a bucket of water and, finding the source of the smoke, flung the water over the area. It hissed, causing thick smoke to roll up. Coughing, he called again.

He heard the other men shouting and was grateful when he heard his dad's voice.

"Carter? You in here?"

"Over here, Dad. Tell them to bring buckets of water. I found where it's smoldering. We should be able to get it out. But I have to find Joey. Sammy said he fell trying to put out the fire."

His dad tossed the water he was carrying onto the source of the smoke and some embers sparked up. "Over here, Henry. I think we caught it in time," his dad shouted back toward the door. "Carter and I have to find Joey. Sammy said he's still in here." He ran after Carter, shouting Joey's name as he went.

Carter almost tripped over an inert form on the floor. "Joey!" He knelt and put a finger on the vein on the side of his brother's neck. "I found him, Dad. He's unconscious, but he's breathing. I'm afraid to move him without a solid support."

His dad appeared out of the haze and knelt by his younger son's side. He ran his hands over the youngster's body and head. "There's a knot on the back of his head." He pulled his hand up close to his face and noted the blood. "He's got a bleeding head wound." Turning back in the direction of the clamor the men were making, he yelled, "Henry, did Doc Wilson leave yet?"

"I'm right here, Amos. What's going on?"

"It's Joey. He fell and hit his head. Can you check him out before we move him?"

Doc Wilson soon knelt beside them, checking the boy over. He looked up at the two men looming above. "It's a possible concussion. If you're able to carry him, Carter, I think we can safely move him. My car is in front of the house; let's take him to my office where I can examine him more thoroughly."

Carter stooped to pick up his brother's limp form, but his father pushed him aside. "I'm not old and feeble yet, boy. I can carry him. He's my son."

Carter heard the pathos in his dad's voice and stepped back to give him space. His father was a large, muscular man in his late forties, and Carter knew he was well able to handle Joey's slight body.

His mother ran over when they stepped outside. "What happened to Joey?"

Carter caught the panic in her voice and hastened to reassure her. "He fell in the barn and hit his head, Mom. Doc Wilson thinks he may have a concussion. We're taking him to Doc's office so he can examine him."

She caressed her unconscious son's arm. "Joey. Always in some kind of trouble."

Carter was aware of Allie walking close by his side as he followed the men and his mom to Doc Wilson's late model Ford. Carter helped his dad into the back seat as he cradled Joey in his arms. "I'll drive my car over, Dad." Assisting his mom into the front seat with Doc, he closed both doors and turned to Allie.

"If he's okay, I'll be back later, sweetheart." He gave her a quick hug.

"We can wait till tomorrow for our time together, Carter. Just call and let me know how he is."

He searched her eyes briefly. "Okay. I'll phone you."

※

Three hours later, Joey groaned. His parents and Carter rushed to his side.

"Joey, can you hear me?" Doc Wilson asked as he bent over the boy on the examining table in his office.

The youngster slowly opened his eyes and blinked rapidly as he looked around. "My head hurts. Where am I?"

"You're in my office, Joey. You know me, Doc Wilson. You've had an accident. Do you remember anything about it?"

Joey was silent for a moment with closed eyes, and Carter was afraid he had slipped into unconsciousness again.

"Yes! I remember now. We were in the barn, and some of the guys were smoking. Someone must have dropped a match, or a lit cigarette, and the next thing we knew, smoke was rolling all around us. I was trying to put the fire out, but that's all I remember. Did the barn burn down?"

"No, son," his dad answered. "We managed to douse it before it got out of hand, but you must have fallen and hit your head."

"I remember tripping, but that's all." He looked around. "Where's Mom?"

"I'm right here." She moved over and took his hand.

"I need to check your eyes again, Joey," Doc said. He flashed a light on the boy's face. "Now open your eyes wide and follow the light." After a moment, Doc snapped the light off with a satisfied "Hmmph." "He definitely has a mild concussion," he addressed the adults, then turned to Joey.

"You'll need to take it easy for a few days. No climbing trees, no running. Just lots of rest."

He turned to the parents. "You can take him home and get him settled in for the night. I'll be over in the morning to check on him again."

With his father's assistance, Joey managed to walk to Carter's car. When they reached their farmhouse, Mr. Benton suggested to Carter, "How about waiting while we get Joey upstairs, then you can run me over to the Prestons' to pick up my truck."

"No problem, Dad. Take your time." Carter turned on the interior light and checked his watch. Midnight. *Would Allie still be up?* It was a mild night, and the moon was almost full. He longed to walk with her to the bench by her family's pond. He pictured kneeling beside her while the moon shone across the water. He would open the box with the diamond and ask her to marry him when the war was over.

He jumped when his dad opened the passenger door and slid in beside him. "That was quick. Did Joey have any trouble making it up the steps?"

"I half-carried him, and he flopped onto the bed and was instantly asleep. Your mother was worried that he shouldn't be sleeping so much that soon after a concussion."

"I've heard that some doctors have that opinion, but Doc Wilson seemed to think sleep would be good for him," Carter said.

"Yeah, and I trust old Doc. He's taken good care of a lot of people around here over the years."

When they pulled in front of the Prestons' home, Allie was sitting on the front porch swing, her blonde hair gleaming in the moonlight.

"Looks like you'll be a while," his dad said with a chuckle. He got out of the car and greeted Allie softly before turning back to Carter. "Thanks, son. I'll talk to you tomorrow."

Never taking his eyes from Allie's lovely face, Carter left his vehicle and walked slowly up the steps.

She kept the swing moving with her right foot until he stood before her and held out his hand. Stopping the motion, she curled her slender fingers around his.

In one swift movement he tugged her into his arms and held her tenderly, ever aware of the ring in his pocket. "Let's walk to the pond," he whispered in her ear.

She just nodded, and he led her down the steps and in the direction of the bench he had in mind.

Carter felt his heart would burst with love for this young woman beside him. At that moment, leaving her seemed like an impossible act. He wanted to lash out at the Japanese who started this whole mess with the attack on Pearl Harbor. Now half the world had been dragged into the merciless fighting, with men being killed by the thousands. He didn't want to go off to kill or be killed.

He just wanted to stay here, marry Allie, and raise a family with her.

When they reached the bench, she finally filled the silence. "How's Joey?"

"Doc says he has a concussion, but feels he'll be fine if he takes it easy for a few days. He was out for over three hours."

"Was your pop mad about the fire?"

She shrugged. "You know Pop. He's pretty easy going. He just said, 'Boys will be boys.'"

"If the howling I heard over by the barn was any indication, the parents of the boys involved weren't so gentle. Two of them were Reverend Joshua's imps, and you know his theory on sparing the rod and spoiling the child."

Carter reached out and ran his hand through her hair, twining the curling tresses through his fingers. "Did your mom or pop ever take a hand to you?" He couldn't bear the thought of anyone ever hurting her.

She shook her head. "Never. I guess the Reverend would think I was spoiled beyond redemption," she laughed lightly.

"You deserve to be spoiled. You're precious to me, and spoiling you would be my honor."

She snuggled against him and laid her head on his shoulder. "You're special to me too, Carter. I hate this stupid war. It doesn't seem fair that the government forces good men like you to go thousands of miles from home."

"Well, it's better that we go fight it far away, instead of here in our own country."

"That's true, Carter, and I am proud of you. I just don't want you to leave."

He fumbled in his pocket for the ring box and pulled back a little before turning to face her. "Allie, I love you. I love you so much, it's like a physical ache sometimes." He held up the tiny box and flipped it open. "When I get back, I want us to get married and spend the rest of our lives together. Will you wear my ring and wait for me to come home?"

The moon shone fully on her face, but Carter didn't see the joy there that he had pictured when he rehearsed the scene in his mind.

She took the box in her slender hand, looked briefly at the diamond as it sparkled in the moonlight; then she shook her head, closed the lid, and held it out to him. "It's lovely, Carter. I do care deeply for you, but I just can't take your ring right now."

Chapter Three

Allie's heart shattered when she saw the hope on Carter's face turn to bewilderment.

The grip of his hand tightened on hers around the box. "You can't mean that, Allie. I thought you loved me the way I love you."

"Carter, I do have very deep feelings for you, but I have plans for my life. I want to serve God in ways that you might not want to share, and God has to come first with me."

She watched as he stood, took the ring box into his own hand and sat on the bench beside her, obviously searching her face for answers.

"So what's this about? Why have we been going steady, if it wasn't heading anywhere? I thought we were looking ahead to marriage and raising a family together."

Silently praying for the right words to explain how she felt, Allie gazed up at the moon for a moment. When she looked back, he was sitting tensely, gripping the edge of the bench. His forehead appeared creased with anguish. "I think the Lord wants me to be a missionary, Carter—probably in a foreign country. It's something that only recently began to fill my soul, and if it's what God wants for me, then that's what I plan to do."

"A missionary? But you already work hard for the Lord. You teach Sunday school, and you're always helping needy families. Why would you have to go half way around the world to do what you can do here?"

She hesitated, praying silently again before answering. "Lately, I've felt smothered here. I want to move on to something more. The thought of staying here brings to mind walking across a bridge to nowhere." She laid her hand on his rigid arm. "I hope you understand, Carter. You know I've been at Moody Bible Institute the last two and a half years, and have only a few more months to go for my degree. After that, I hope to serve on a mission field, possibly in Mexico."

He jerked his arm from her hand, as if even her touch burned him. Standing, he shoved his hands into his pockets, a habit she recognized from when he was upset. She wished there was something she could do or say to make it easier, but she'd agonized over the matter for some time now, and knew she needed to go where she believed the Lord was leading.

"Let me get this straight. If you stayed here and had a life with me, it would be like crossing a bridge to nowhere. And if you go to some distant land, you would be crossing a bridge to somewhere exciting and doing something outstanding for God."

"You're speaking as though I think of you as an unexciting nobody, and that isn't true, Carter. If you shared my deep desire to serve the Lord in a foreign land and our love grew to a depth we would know was from God, I'd be proud and honored to be your wife and the mother of your children. I admire you so much, and I'll be praying daily that you'll come home safely, and maybe the Lord *will* bring us together. But at this time, I don't feel I can make that commitment to you."

Still clutching the ring box, he removed his hands from his pockets. "But I go to church with you every week, Allie. And I'd follow you to the deepest parts of Africa, if that was where you wanted to go.

"Please keep the ring. You don't have to wear it, but while I'm gone, I'd like to know you have it. And I want to be able to write to you and know you'll answer. I don't think I could bear to have you drift out of my life."

Again, he offered her the ring.

The desperation in his voice tore at her soul. *Lord, what should I say? How can I ease his pain, and my own?* She knew she was very close to loving Carter deeply in return. But her convictions were too strong to ignore.

She held out a hand to him imploringly. "Please sit here beside me." He sat slowly. The longing she saw in his eyes was almost her undoing. "I can't, in all good faith, take the ring right now. But I'll write to you at least several times a week."

He flopped back with a defeated sigh and gazed skyward. "So where does this leave us? Just friends? And what happens if you meet a nice Christian boy at your school, or on the mission field, who shares your dream of serving as a missionary? Will you forget what we've been to one another?"

She felt tears forming in her eyes, and she prayed he wouldn't notice.

"Those are all questions we need to leave in the Lord's hands. If he means for us to be together, he'll work it all out in his own time and way. We just need to trust him.

"As for this week, I hope you'll still want to spend time with me. I missed you so much when you were away in training, Carter. I won't miss you any less because of the decision I've made." And she could hold back the flood no longer. Leaning over onto his shoulder, she sobbed her heart out. She was thankful when he softened and held her close, and she could feel his tears mingling with hers.

The week passed all too quickly, and Allie was caught up in this new level of their relationship. It was like an ever-deepening friendship, and she was proud of Carter for not pressing her for anything more, though she had to admit she missed the occasional embraces they once shared. She could tell he was keeping a short leash on his emotions, and she admired him for respecting her wishes.

They spent time with Jesse and Annie and little Nathan, walking in the woods or making ice cream. Allie's heart warmed watching Carter cater to the baby. He carried him around, jiggling him and winning giggles and coos from the little guy. Jesse reported that Nathan had slept all night both days after they'd spent time outside, and the extra sleep was appreciated by both mom and dad.

Carter's parents invited the Prestons over for supper the evening before he was to leave, but when Mr. Benton opened the door, Allie hung back, feeling reticent.

"Good evening, Henry and Dorothy." He stretched his head around Allie's father's rotund frame. "Allie, are you feeling shy suddenly? It's not like you haven't been here a lot these past years. Come on in, folks. Marge is in the kitchen. Believe it or not, Joey's helping. He's been good as gold since the night of the fire."

"How's his head?" Mrs. Preston asked as they entered the house.

"He laid around a bit for the first few days and complained of a headache, but he perked up today. Doc was out this afternoon to check him over and was pleased with his recovery. In fact, there's Doc now. We invited him to join us tonight too."

Allie stayed quiet throughout the meal, and she was grateful the others kept the conversation going without her input. Carter touched her shoulder at one point and whispered, "You okay?" She merely nodded, and realized her withdrawal was due to a deep sadness over his leaving the next day. *Lord, have I misread you and made a big mistake?* But she didn't want to recant her words in the emotion of the moment, giving Carter false hope. She decided instead to continue waiting on the Lord.

Allie hugged him goodbye at the door. She spent a sleepless night, alternating between tossing, turning, and weeping.

Carter drove his car to the station with Allie in the front passenger seat and his parents in the back. The drive was made in near-silence. After removing his loaded duffel bag from the trunk, he handed his father the keys.

As the train tooted and chugged into the station, Carter set down his bag and drew Allie into a tight embrace, ending with a promising kiss. She held tight to him as tears ran down her face. "I'll miss you, Carter."

They heard a loud wolf whistle, and a male voice calling out in a Southern drawl, "Hey, Carter, go for it!" They turned toward the open window of the train and smiled at the freckle-faced, redheaded young man in uniform hanging out the opening as he waved.

"Hey, Sonny! I'll be right with you. Hope you saved me a seat." He kept his arm around Allie as he hugged each parent in turn, and then hefted his bag over his shoulder and entered the passenger car.

Allie stood waving and smiling through her tears until the train was out of sight.

Chapter Four

Sitting silently in the backseat of Carter's car, Allie tried to stem her flow of tears.

Mrs. Benton turned to pat Allie's leg and hand her a tissue. "Go ahead and cry, honey. We know how you feel."

Allie squeezed the hand and sobbed, wiping her face with the tissue.

When the Bentons stopped at her home, she thanked them, got out quickly and ran into the house. Thankful her parents weren't there, she flew up the stairs and threw herself onto her bed, weeping until a sleep of exhaustion overtook her.

Awakening in darkness, she felt for the quilt her mother had obviously pulled over her, and tugged it tightly up to her chin. The bedside clock showed 2:10am, and she wondered where Carter's train was at that moment, and whether he was thinking of her.

Overwhelmed by the ache in her heart, Allie doubted at the moment if she'd ever feel whole again without him. *Lord, was I wrong to refuse his ring? Is he the man you planned for me and I turned him away?*

She considered again her strong desire to go to the mission field. The picture of Mexico was deeply implanted in her heart, and nowhere could she see Carter in it. He'd said he would go to deepest Africa with her, if that was what she wanted, but he would be doing it for her, not the Lord. *But Lord, I know you can bring about a change in his heart. So for now, I'll just concentrate on finishing Bible College and serving you, and see where you lead in all of this.*

Feeling a sense of peace, she drifted to a more relaxed sleep until she awakened to the sun shining in her window and the aroma of bacon drifting up the stairs.

Stretching, and then sitting up, it hit her once more—Carter was gone and she may never see him or hear from him again. Dropping to her knees beside the bed, she prayed for protection for him and strength for her to get through the day.

❦

"Good morning," her mother greeted when Allie walked into the kitchen. "Did you sleep much last night?"

"A little." Allie took plates and juice glasses from the cupboard and placed them on the kitchen table. After pouring juice and getting out silverware, she went to stare out the kitchen window toward the pond where Carter had offered her the diamond a week ago. Tears stung her eyes once more. Wiping them quickly, she turned to her mother. "What can I do to help?"

"You can make toast, honey, and add lots of butter the way your daddy likes it." She patted Allie's shoulder in passing. "You'll be back to college in a few days. That'll help take your mind off things."

Allie's dad came from the barn with a large bucket of frothy, warm milk from the cow and set it in the sink.

"Wash up, Henry. I just put the eggs in to fry, and the bacon's done."

Throughout the meal, Allie barely spoke or ate, though her parents tried to draw her into conversation. "Do you mind if I take a walk?" she asked her mother when a desperate need for fresh air overcame her.

Mrs. Preston patted her hand. "Go, dear. Walking and talking to the Lord might comfort you."

Outside, she ran to the bench by the pond. Sitting, she pictured Carter kneeling awkwardly and holding out the ring to her. Then she envisioned his distraught eyes as she refused to accept his gift of love. Face in hands, Allie bent over and wept for a long while.

When something furry rubbed her leg, she jumped up and saw Bitsy—the grown runt of the last litter Maizie had produced—running away. "Bitsy, I'm sorry, girl. Please come back."

The small yellow tabby stopped and glanced at her in an offended manner. Allie coaxed again, and the little lady raced to be swooped up in a close hug. "I'm going to miss you, Bitsy. I wish I could take you to school with me."

The cat meowed and snuggled closer while Allie sauntered sadly toward the inviting woods at the edge of the field.

Chapter Five

***

*M*aking his way through the passenger cars full of boisterous servicemen, Carter felt sorry for the occasional civilian passenger he noted. Hopefully, Sonny had saved him a seat. Both were assigned to Communications, and had become good buddies during basic training.

Entering the next car Carter spied his friend standing by a seat, obviously watching for him.

"Hey country boy! Back here!"

Responding to his friend's contagious grin, Carter hefted his duffel bag up into the tight space overhead before enclosing his buddy's lean frame in a bear hug. "Thanks for saving me a seat, Sonny."

"Believe me, it wasn't easy. Fortunately, I was seated with a civilian who got off at your stop.

"Hey, your girlfriend's a little beauty. Did you give her a diamond like you planned?"

Carter shook his head. "I'll tell you about it later.

"How'd things go with your Betsy?"

Sonny's face clouded over. "Not so great. She's working in a factory that makes parts for planes, and I get the feeling she has her eye on one of the bosses. She promised to write to me, so we'll see what happens."

Knowing that Sonny sang in a band in Nashville, Tennessee, Carter nodded toward the small instrument case standing at his friend's feet. "I see you managed to bring your ukulele."

Sonny grinned. "Yeah. I wish it could have been my guitar, but it takes too much space; the uke's better than nothing."

"It was great in New Jersey when you played and we all sang."

After they shared food their mothers had packed, things quieted down in the packed train. Soon a soldier started playing a soulful melody on a harmonica.

Carter nudged Sonny. "Hey, get out your uke."

He didn't have to be asked twice. The small instrument was soon in Sonny's hands, the twangy sounds joining with the harmonica strains. The other musician looked back and saluted, then swung into a more lively tune, "Peg O' My Heart."

Before long, the others were singing, clapping and stomping feet, with the musical revelry not settling down until almost midnight.

Sleep didn't come easy for Carter. Realizing Sonny was still awake, he quietly told him about Allie's refusal of his ring, and the reason she gave for doing it. "I just couldn't believe she said staying where we are and raising a family felt like a bridge to nowhere. She believes the Lord is calling her to a foreign mission field. Doesn't that seem odd to you?"

Lying back against his seat, Sonny rolled his head toward Carter and looked at him with half-closed eyes. "I come from an area of Southern Baptists and shouting Methodists. They're all big on serving God in different ways. My mama used to drag all six of us kids to church down the road where the preacher did a lot of yelling, and the people would shout 'Amen' as loud as could be. At first it scared me a little, then I kind of got a kick out of it.

"My brothers and sisters and I would go home and play church outside. My oldest brother would preach at the top of his lungs and the rest of us would clap our hands and shout 'Amen! Hallelujah! Praise God!'

"Mama would come out and tell us we were bein' disrespectful to the Lord.

"Daddy never went to church with us, and when Mama died of pneumonia at an early age, he didn't take us either."

"I thought you said your mother packed you that food?"

"That was my step-mama. Daddy married her soon after, and she was always good to us kids. She didn't have any children and treated us like her own. She didn't go to church either, but I never forgot the enthusiasm of the people there. Some of them went off to foreign mission fields.

"So I guess it all boils down to your individual relationship with God."

After mulling Sonny's words over in his mind, Carter reminisced about the evening with Allie by the pond. He felt he would love her forever, and his heart would be a long time healing if he lost her to someone else.

Lorena Estep

When they finally arrived in Seattle, Carter and Sonny found transportation to Fort Lawton. They'd forged friendships with two other soldiers who were assigned to their unit, and the four traveled together by bus to the installation. Randy Billings was short, barrel-chested and hailed from Nebraska. His buddy, Arnold Nevins, was from Utah. Arnold was tall and lean, just over six feet, and said, "Just call me Arnie."

The four were early arrivals. After checking in, they had the choice of cots in the barracks and grabbed four together before heading out to look the area over.

Arnie walked ahead of the others with a long-legged stride. "Not a bad looking post, what do you think, fellas? I wouldn't mind staying here awhile."

Randy looked overhead at the blue sky. "We might have just hit it lucky today. I hear it rains almost half the year out here."

"Enjoy it while you can," Carter said. "I don't think we'll be here long."

Arnie stopped and looked back. "You hear something we didn't?"

"Just that they ship the troops through here pretty fast. They need men all over the Pacific."

The four walked quietly for a spell until Arnie stopped and looked back. "Then let's enjoy it while we can, gents!" and he took off running, the others following closely behind.

Breathing hard, they stopped at the view overlooking Puget Sound. It was a beautiful day. A few wildflowers dotted the tall grasses, swaying in the ocean breeze. They breathed in the salty tang of the Sound, and enjoyed the bright sunshine.

"When you look at that scene, it's not easy to ponder the havoc and bloodshed going on in other places in the Pacific." Sonny, usually a joker, sounded more somber than Carter had heard him in a while.

Carter touched his shoulder. "I'm hungry. Why don't we check out the food at the canteen?"

The now-solemn group headed back, noting that more soldiers had arrived and were making their way into the barracks. Not feeling up to getting acquainted with the new soldiers just yet, the four made their way over to the club for the enlisted men.

After reporting for role call and calisthenics the next morning, the group ate breakfast and caught a bus into Seattle. The weather was on the gloomy side, but at least it wasn't raining. They did a little sightseeing, then had lunch and went to a matinee. "Casablanca" was playing, starring Humphrey Bogart and Ingrid Bergman.

"Think we'll find any romance in this war?" Arnie asked in a grave tone as they walked to the bus after the movie.

"That only happens in the movies," Randy grumbled. "Not that I don't still have high hopes!" This time he grinned.

Sonny clapped a hand on Carter's shoulder. "Well, Carter's and my 'romantic hopes' are back home, so I don't imagine we'll be looking too hard; what do you think, pal?"

"My hopes there were all but blown up before I left. So I don't want to be disappointed by hoping too hard for change at home, but I still don't plan to look for any kind of romance when we get where we're going."

"My guess is you'll be getting some mail before long saying she changed her mind."

Carter only shrugged and kept walking.

Back at the camp they ate in the mess hall before returning to the barracks to flop on their cots. Most of the bunks had been taken, and a rowdy card game was going on at the end of the room. Smoke filled the air, and Randy and Arnie soon stood to leave. "We're going over to the club. You guys want to come along?" Arnie asked.

Sonny looked over at Carter. "You wanna go?"

Carter was undecided. He'd like to write a letter to Allie, but he thought he should wait until he got one from her first. He'd already written a couple to his parents. Maybe he'd write one to her tomorrow after church. For now he needed to get out of the noisy, smoke-filled room. "Yeah, let's go."

They entered the club that was also smoke-filled, but they found a table by an open door so it wasn't as bad. Carter ordered a Coke from the waitress, and the other three asked for beer. A band was playing and an attractive blond was singing "Dancing In the Dark" in a rather sultry voice. Some of the soldiers were dancing. Obviously, women from the area must come by to keep the men from being too lonely.

Someone tapped him on the shoulder and he looked up. An attractive young woman with dark, curly hair stood there. "You wanna dance, soldier?"

He felt his face flush, and saw the other three grinning. "Um, I'm not very good at dancing."

She grabbed his hand to pull him up. "Oh, come on. No one here cares how you dance; just so you don't step on my feet."

Her smile was rather beguiling, and he didn't want to hurt her feelings, so he got up and followed her to a spot on the dance floor. Thankfully, it was a slow one and he could just move around in one spot a little. "I'm sure any one of my friends would be a better partner for you."

She stood on her tiptoes and whispered, "Yeah, but you're the only one not having beer."

"You're not a drinker?"

"No alcohol of any kind for me, and I've learned to stay away from men who do. They can be a handful if they have too much to drink."

When they walked back to the table, his friends were already up dancing, so he and the girl, Nancy, spent most of the evening chatting. When she was ready to leave, he went with her to her car. "Thanks for a relaxing evening. You helped lift my spirits."

"I enjoyed your company too. When are you shipping out?"

"We haven't gotten our orders yet, but I imagine it will be soon."

"Yeah, they seem to move them through here rather quickly. Well, hopefully I'll see you again before you leave. If not, I have your address, and I'll be writing to you. Stay safe." She stood on her toes and kissed his cheek.

He opened her door and waved goodbye as she drove away.

Carter and Sonny went to the protestant Chapel on the Hill the next morning. The minister's message was about having courage and faith in God to face whatever was ahead for them. Carter couldn't begin to imagine what they might be facing, but he couldn't help but be thankful for the people back home who were praying for him!

Chapter Six

Settled back at Moody several days later, Allie sat in the library between classes writing her second letter to Carter.

"Care if I join you?" A familiar male voice asked.

Looking up, Allie smiled at her friend from several classes they'd shared over the past two and a half years. "Have a seat, Daniel. It's good to see you back healthy and sun-tanned. How were things back home?"

His smile faded. "Mom's not doing well. Her heart is going downhill fast, and there's not much more they can do to help her. She moved in with my sister and her family while I'm at school. Since Dad's death she doesn't seem to have much will to get any stronger."

Allie reached across the table to grip his hand. "I'm so sorry, Dan. I know how hard that must be for you."

He put his other hand over her small one and smiled briefly. "Thanks, Alice. But how was your break? Was Carter surprised by his going away party?"

She pulled her hand from between his. "Yes, at least I think he was. The evening ended rather badly though."

"Why? What happened?"

"Some of the older boys sneaked out to the barn to smoke, and the hay caught fire."

"Oh, no! Did the barn burn down?"

"Thankfully, no. Carter saw the smoke and ran to it while I called for the other men. They were able to douse it before it got out of control. But Carter's brother Joey had tried to put it out when the others ran. He fell and hit his head and had a concussion. But he's doing okay now."

"Thank goodness for that. So how are you holding up with Carter off to war?"

Glancing down at the letter, she twirled the pen in her fingers. "Something else happened that night." Hesitating, she looked up at him again. "Carter offered me a diamond, and I refused it."

"Why? I know you really care about him."

She doodled on the tablet beside the letter. "I don't feel he wants to serve God in the same way I do. I told him I thought we should wait and pray about it."

Daniel leaned back in his chair. "How did he take that?"

Breathing in deeply, she exhaled before answering. "Not well. The pain in his eyes will stay with me for a long time. But I said I'd write to him and keep in touch. So that's what I'm doing now." She smoothed her hand across the letter.

"Poor Carter. I know how much he cares for you. The couple times I met him when he stopped by, I was impressed with the loving way he treated you."

She sighed. "I realize what a gem he is, and I feel guilty for hurting him; but for now I'm not convinced he's the one God wants me to share my life with."

He took her hand again. "I know what a special woman you are, Allie, and I admire your determination to follow God's leading instead of what your heart might want. I'll be praying for you." He stood to go and released her hand.

"I'll be praying for you and your mother too, Daniel."

"Thanks, Allie." He stood a moment longer. "It's hard to believe we'll be graduating in a couple more months. If I could find a good job then, I'd gladly take my mother to live with me. Do you have any plans for after graduation?"

She twirled her pencil as she thought. "I'm not sure; I'm considering signing up for the mission trip to Mexico in January."

He nodded. "I've considered that too, but my mother has to be my first responsibility. I can't expect my sister to take all the burden on her shoulders. But hey, I need to go study and let you get back to your letter to Carter."

When he walked away, Allie thought what a good and caring man he was. Some woman would be fortunate to have him for a husband someday.

Chapter Seven

Carter stood hopefully at the mail call area. He rushed up when his name was called and—hallelujah!—six letters. Quickly checking the return addresses, he noted ones from his mom, dad, Joey, Jesse, and two from Allie! Excited, he tucked them into his pocket and took off running in the direction of the Puget Sound overlook.

Finding a dry, comfortable spot to lean against a tree, he held Allie's letters up to his face and sniffed the light scent of lavender that she always wore. Wanting to tear hers open first to devour every word, he forced himself to put them in his pocket to save for last.

Everything appeared to be going well at home, though he suspected they wouldn't tell him much if anything was wrong.

Jesse and Annie's baby was in the hospital with pneumonia, but they had faith in God and Doc Wilson to pull him through.

Carter bowed his head and breathed a silent prayer for Nathan, Jesse and Annie, also for his own family, and most of all for Allie. He also prayed her love for him would grow ever deeper, and she would wait for him to get home and change her mind about marrying him.

Slowly he pulled her letters from his pocket and opened the one first with the earliest date. She had written it before going back to Moody. Missing him was in every line, though she tried to add cheerful notes throughout. He held it close to his nose and deeply breathed in the scent of lavender. When he closed his eyes, it was almost like she was sitting beside him.

Finally, he opened the last one. She was back at Moody in the library, writing to him between classes. She said Daniel had stopped to see how she was holding up with Carter gone. He also said his mother was quite ill. "He's had a rough life," she added, "and he said to tell you 'hi' and he's praying for you." The tone of this letter was more impersonal than the first one, and somehow, the mention of Daniel caused a tingle of fear to run up his spine.

Taking out her first letter again, he leaned back against the tree and reveled in each word, trying to regain the sense of closeness he'd felt before.

"So here you are," a feminine voice intruded into his thoughts.

Irritated at the intrusion, Carter looked up at Nancy standing above him. Though she looked fetching in a pink and white striped dress, he still resented her presence. Folding Allie's letter and gathering up the other ones, he scrambled to his feet and shoved the mail into his shirt pocket.

She smiled, displaying straight, white teeth. "Looks like someone had a good mail day. Good news, I hope."

"Seems to be, though they might not say if it were bad. My friend Jesse said his baby has pneumonia, so I'm sure they're concerned. So how'd you track me down?"

"Sonny said he saw you head this way with a handful of letters. He looked happy, and said he got a letter from his girl. How about you? Did you get one from a special girl back home?"

"Not as special as I'd like it to be, but we're at least still good friends." He'd have to strangle Sonny for telling her where he was.

She slipped her hand under his elbow and over his arm. "If it's to be, it will, and if it's not, it won't," she stated philosophically.

Her words further irritated Carter as they walked slowly back toward the barracks. "That's a good theory, but it doesn't account for all the heartache when it doesn't work out."

"I've had a few heartaches in my life." She glanced down towards the ground where Carter caught glimpses of her white slippers showing through the grass.

She paused and looked back up at him. "One way or another we get on with life."

After finishing the walk in silence, they entered the club and joined Sonny, Arnie and Randy, the latter two looking well into their cups already.

"Where you been, Carter? But I see Nancy found you."

"I went for a walk to read my letters. Nancy said you had one from Betsy."

Sonny's freckled face lit up. "Yeah, and she says she misses me a lot."

Carter squeezed his shoulder. "Good for you. All my news was good too."

He turned to Nancy. "What can I get you?"

"Hamburger and a Coke sounds good."

He looked at the others. "Can I get anyone else anything?"

"Beer!" Randy and Arnie chorused together.

"Looks like you two have had enough already."

The three women from the night before came in just then and joined the men, so Carter walked over to the counter and ordered two burgers, Cokes, and an order of fries to share with Nancy. A niggling of depression hovered over him when he thought of Allie's second letter, and he'd rather go back to his barrack and write to her. Hopefully, Daniel meant no more to Allie than Nancy meant to him.

"So, did you hear the news, Carter?" Sonny asked when he returned to the table. "We ship out early Tuesday morning."

The hovering depression formed into a huge rock that slammed to the pit of Carter's stomach. "Where are we headed?"

"Didn't say. They just posted the orders on the bulletin board to be at the ship by 0500 Tuesday."

Right then Carter wished he were a drinking man. It didn't appear that Arnie and Randy were feeling any pain about heading out to war. When the band tuned up and started to play "My Prayer," Carter didn't object when Nancy tugged on his hand to get him to dance. They remained on the dance floor most of the evening. Nancy snuggled close with her head on his shoulder during the slow ones, and he pretended it was Allie.

Chapter Eight

After roll call and breakfast on Monday, the men were gathered for specific orders for Tuesday. Several hours were spent in drills and movies shown of actual war scenes taking place in the Pacific, which didn't encourage the soldiers one iota.

"As you can see, men, war in reality is nothing like the maneuvers you've been practicing. It's life or death out there, so be on your guard at every turn," Sergeant Hummer told the men in a loud voice. "And watch your buddy's back too. You're a team out there, so try to work together as much as possible. Any questions?"

In front, a small man with dark hair raised his hand.

"Yes, soldier?"

"Sir, can we know where we're going?"

"At this point, even I don't know. When I know anything else, you'll know. Any more questions?" No one else spoke.

"Then you're dismissed." They slowly drifted away in various directions.

Carter felt frozen in place, alternating between wanting to lay down somewhere and bawl like a baby, or go AWOL and jump a train to return to Allie and take her off to a mission field where they'd never be found. He felt a hand on his shoulder.

"You okay, buddy?"

He turned to Sonny. "You don't even want to know the ideas I've been contemplating."

"I gotcha. If any of them contain suicide, I'd wait, if I were you. When the right time comes, one of the enemy will take care of it for you and you'll be considered a hero. Come on, let's go partake of what might be our last good meal."

A Bridge to Somewhere

❦

None of the women showed up that night at the club and the men were in the barracks early, playing cards or writing letters. Sonny got out his ukulele and joined the harmonica tunes with Johnny, the guy who'd played with him on the train.

Carter finished his letters home and to Allie, and then laid back, arm over his face, a deep desolation sweeping over him. *Lord, how will this end for each of us? It all feels so senseless and useless. Will I ever end up with her? Will I even survive whatever's ahead for us? Will I live to serve you in some way? Or if I even do return, will it be as half a man, badly crippled, or worse?*

Suddenly a hand touched his. He moved his arm back and opened his eyes.

"You okay, soldier?" It was the small man on the cot the other side of him, the one who'd asked the sergeant where they were going. He'd apparently just come in that day and Carter hadn't met him yet.

Carter sat up on the edge of the bed, facing the man. "I guess I'm about as okay as anyone else. How about you?"

The man held up a Bible. "I get my strength and courage from here. Do you know the Lord?"

"We've been introduced. In fact I was just laying there talking to him. I always went to church with my girl back home. She's going to a Bible college and wants to be a missionary."

"So are you close friends with the Lord? Or is he just an acquaintance you turn to in times of trouble?"

Carter hesitated. "I remember asking him to be my Savior when I was twelve, but I'm not sure I grew much closer to him after that."

"Do you have a Bible with you?"

"Yeah, my girlfriend got me a nice small one that's waterproof."

The man nodded his head. "That's good. Just be sure to read it. There's a lot of comfort in that book. By the way, I'm Shakespeare. I've heard your friends call you Carter." He held out a hand.

Carter grasped it in both of his. "Shakespeare? As in William?" He grinned and sat back further on his cot.

The man laughed. "I'm Rodney James Gruber, born in Alabama. Lived there all my life until this war started. I felt this was where the Lord wanted me."

Carter felt drawn to this man and his southern drawl. "So how did you come to be called Shakespeare?"

"I started writing poetry, songs and stories when I was seven, so my parents and older brother and sister began calling me that, and soon it stuck until that was the only name I knew, except in school."

"Well, Shakespeare, it's good to meet you. You have anything you've written that I could read?"

"Sure do." He pulled out a folder and notebook from within a watertight pouch. "Take your pick."

Carter chose a piece entitled, *While I'm Away.* "Did you write this for your girlfriend?"

Shakespeare shook his head. "No, for my wife." His eyes lit up with his smile. "She's the love of my life. We got married six months ago. When I joined up it broke both our hearts, but we felt it's where God wanted me. She's working with the Red Cross making bandages and boxes of rations to send out to the men."

He took out the notebook and leaned back against his pillow. "I'm gonna write her a letter now, but feel free to read whatever you'd like."

Carter leafed through the stack of prose, deeply impressed with the man's writing skills. Each one held such meaning. When he found some that were written to music, he called Sonny over and introduced him to Shakespeare.

"Have you met Shakespeare yet, Sonny?"

Sonny grinned. "Not in the flesh, but I've read some of his writings."

"Well, this is another Shakespeare from Alabama, and he's also a writer. Shakespeare, this is Sonny Hawkins from Nashville, Tennessee."

Shakespeare sat up to shake Sonny's outstretched hand. "You play a mean ukulele, Sonny from Tennessee. You sing like a pro, too. Are you in a band back home?"

Sonny sank down at the foot of Carter's bed. "Yeah, we were doin' pretty good until we all decided to join up."

"Well, read some of these songs he wrote, Sonny. You might like to give 'em a try." Carter handed a few pages of music over to him.

Sonny picked up one entitled "Joining the Battle" and hummed some of the notes. "Sounds like a pretty lively tune, Shakespeare. You write the words and notes?"

"Yeah, I did. I majored in music and poetry in college and play a guitar in our church band—and the piano if no one else is available. In this song about what we're facing, I figure any battle's going to be action-filled, so the song should be too."

Sonny began singing the lines and Shakespeare joined in.

> *Across the ocean a battle rages,*
> *Many men dying for freedom to gain.*
> *Letters are written on bloodied pages,*
> *Showing the suff'ring of soldiers in pain.*
>
> *Help us, O Lord, to be strong and so brave,*
> *Watch over each one till vic'try is won.*
> *For those who are lost to an early grave,*
> *May their soul be yours and join with your Son.*

When the song had ended, a hush fell throughout the room. Then Shakespeare bowed his head and prayed aloud: "Precious Lord and Savior, may we feel your presence always with us. Not one of us knows what lies ahead, but help us remember that you know, care, and love us. Watch over us, please. I praise you, loving Father. Amen."

Chapter Nine

The four men and Shakespeare were among the first to board the ship the next morning and were pointed to the stairs down to the quarters where they would sleep.

In the first room there were canvas bunks hung three high by chains lining the walls from end to end. A wide passageway went through the center where two men could pass without turning sideways. They stopped by the available bunks closest to the door.

"You want bottom or next to bottom?" Sonny asked Carter.

"You and Shakespeare choose. I'll take the one that's left."

Shakespeare tossed his duffel bag onto the third cot. "I'll go above you, Carter. You grab the second one."

Randy and Arnie chose the two bottom hammocks across from them. After stowing their bags in the allotted spaces, all five laid back to get the feel of the beds they would claim for the length of the trip.

"A little claustrophobic, isn't it?" Arnie mentioned.

"Enjoy them while you can," Sonny said. "They might be the best we get."

"Thanks for those encouraging words," Randy told him.

Lying there until the bunks were filled and the confusion had died down, Carter stared up at the lump Shakespeare made in the cot above him. He thought of the poem "While I'm Away" and wanted to ask if he could send a copy of it in a letter to Allie.

Just then the bell rang for the men to gather on deck for roll call, and they took turns scrambling out of the small spaces, careful to avoid feet and legs from the men above.

The duties of the GIs on board were light, since the overall ship maintenance was the responsibility of the sailors assigned to it. The soldiers rotated cleaning the heads, showers and floors in their quarters, and each kept his bunk area and belongings neat. They played cards, passed around books and magazines that some had been wise enough to tuck into their bags, and when all those were perused from cover to cover, they traded with the sailors.

"Hey, Shakespeare, what about this line?" Sonny asked. They were working on some new songs in a secluded corner of the deck, while Carter sat nearby copying the poem, *While I'm Away*, to send Allie in a letter.

He'd read it so often the words were etched in his heart:

While I'm away, my love, my life,
My endless love calls out to you.
We'll both be facing diff'rent strife,
So let's try not to become blue.

Focus on our Savior and Lord,
We belong to Him forever,
Tied to Him by a blood red cord,
That no one can ever sever.

My soul is also tied to you;
Whether in life or in my death,
That love will be forever true;
I'll call to you with my last breath.

Carter laid down his pen and gazed off across the endless expanse of the ocean. He knew his soul was forever tied to Allie, but was hers forever tied to him? He was certain her name would be the last word he'd breathe, if he lay dying. If he had been closer to the Lord as she was, would it have made a difference with her accepting his ring and promising to marry him when he returned?

At this point it was useless to wonder "what if."

Lord, help me grow closer to you each day, seeking that peace and joy that both Allie and Shakespeare seem to have.

"Hey, Carter, you sleepin' over there?" Sonny nudged him with his foot. "Wake up and see what you think of this new song we put together."

Carter moved over closer and leaned back against the wall. Sonny strummed on his ukulele as he and Shakespeare began to sing. Soon Johnny showed up with his harmonica, and one of the sailors came with a guitar. Before long the area in front of them was filled with soldiers and sailors all joining in. They went from one song to another until the sun began to set over the ocean.

Shakespeare borrowed the sailor's guitar, and he and Sonny played and sang softly. Carter lay on a tarp drifting in and out of sleep, dreaming of Allie.

Each day aboard ship they exercised to keep them physically toned, and then practiced the combat moves they'd been taught in basic training. The days and nights grew warmer as they sailed into a more tropical climate. Some of the men slept on their blankets on the deck at night.

Finally the day arrived when they were called together on deck and told a little of what the next weeks would hold. They would soon sail into Honolulu Harbor on Oahu in the Hawaiian Islands. They would be there several weeks for intensive training in invasion landings, jungle combat and soldier survival. At that point, they would board another ship to take them to their assignment. That destination would be revealed once they were on their way.

They'd have three days leave after their arrival in Oahu before the intensive training began. They were to be stationed at Schofield Barracks, which was about twenty miles from Honolulu, and be taken there by bus. Buses would run from the base to other destinations throughout the day.

"Enjoy your short leave and see as much of the island as you can," Sergeant Hummer said. "Just stay out of trouble, or you'll see more than you'd hoped for! And that's an order."

Chapter Ten

Reveille moved the men out of their cots early the next morning with very few moans or groans from the soldiers, as all were anxious to set foot on the island they were going to enjoy for the next few days. Up on deck they saw that they were already anchored, so hurried for roll call to get the day started.

Carter, Sonny, Shakespeare, Randy, Arnie, and Johnny Stiver from West Virginia, who had linked up with their group, clambered onto the waiting bus to get to Schofield and settled so their leave could begin.

"Hey, would you look at those pineapple fields!" Randy exclaimed. "Guess we'll get some good food while we're here anyway."

The vegetation and terrain were different than most of them had seen. Before long they were turning into Schofield, with the driver pointing out some of the destruction the base had endured even this far from Pearl Harbor.

At the barracks, the six men were able to claim bunks together and store their belongings. Sergeant Hummer told them they could get breakfast at the mess hall before catching a bus into town.

"Sounds good to me. I'm starved," Sonny said.

Arnie headed for the bulletin board. "Wait. There's a bus leaving in five minutes, and the next one doesn't come for an hour. Why don't we get breakfast in Honolulu?"

"I'm with you," Randy said, and Johnny agreed.

"I think I'll eat here and grab the next bus. What about you two?" Carter asked Sonny and Shakespeare.

"Works for me," Sonny said, and Shakespeare agreed.

Sonny squeezed Johnny's shoulder. "You keep these two out of trouble."

"Just in case I can't, you guys better come lookin' for us when you're in town."

They all laughed in parting.

❦

"That mess hall food wasn't so bad," Sonny declared later as they sat waiting for the next bus.

"There might be days in the not-so-distant future when we won't know where our next meal's coming from, so anything we get now's gotta taste OK," Carter added.

"Just trust in the Lord, friend. He'll take care of us," Shakespeare reassured him. "And, I believe that's our bus coming."

With a little creative bus hopping in Honolulu, they were able to get from one site to another. Pearl Harbor was their first stop. Standing silent and sober in the harbor, they viewed some of the ravages still visible from the fateful day that had thrown many countries into this savage war.

Carter thought of the lives that were ended that day, and of the sailors who still lay in the sunken tomb of the ship U.S.S. Arizona.

"Let's pray for the men and women who are out there still fighting this war, so many giving their lives, that others can be free." With those words, Shakespeare dropped to his knees and prayed aloud, hands held up to heaven.

Carter and Sonny also went to their knees, one on either side of him, one hand on his shoulder and the other one raised to the skies.

"Father, we come to you in prayer for every man and woman serving some way in this war. Protect them, Lord, and may their hearts turn to you for comfort and peace. Comfort each husband, wife, child, brother or sister who has lost a loved one in this senseless killing of other humans. Help us as believers to reach out to others with love. We praise you, Father, and ask your blessings in the name of your Son, Jesus. Amen."

After seeing more of the city, they ended up on Waikiki Beach, walking barefoot, trousers rolled up. Diamond Head volcano loomed far in the distance.

Ahead lounged a group of soldiers and women on a large blanket, one man talking loudly.

"Looks like someone's in his cups," Sonny said.

"And he's someone we know. Let's join them." Carter said, grinning.

The three jogged up to the group with Sonny in the lead. "Well, what do we have here? Looks like a party. Mind if we join you men and your lady friends?"

"Welcome, soldiers." Randy slurred his words. "Ladies, these are the three friends we were telling you about. Sit down, boys, and I'll introduce you to some fine nurses."

He had his arm around a robust young woman with light brown hair. "This here's Jenny. She's a nurse right now at the hospital at Hickam Field." He turned to a dark-haired Hawaiian girl on his other side. "And this is Kalohi. She's also a nurse at Hickam Hospital with Jenny. The other three women—Catherine with the blond hair, Sandra the redhead, and Emma the brunette are nurses in a medical building at Schofield Army Barracks."

Sandra, the redhead who had green eyes, pulled out another blanket to spread over the sand, and Sonny moved over to help her. "Thanks, soldier. I see we have something in common, but you have more freckles than I do."

He grinned and smoothed out the blanket. "Yeah, I've been called 'Carrot-top' most of my life, but I prefer 'Sonny.' How about you?"

She laughed. "I've bloodied a few fellas' noses growing up for calling me that, so I'd suggest you stick to 'Sandra.' " She flopped down onto the blanket. "Come on you all. Have a seat," and she patted a spot beside her.

Sonny sat down cross-legged in the space she indicated, and Shakespeare and Carter joined them.

On the other blanket Johnny moved closer to Catherine, the blonde, putting an arm around her. "I've just claimed Blondie here, if she doesn't object."

Looking into his eyes, she reached over and took his hand. "It's fine by me."

Arnie moved over to attach himself to Kalohi, though she was about half his height. She waved at the newcomers and said "Aloha."

Arnie glanced around at the group and nodded to Emma. "So, Emma, maybe you and Carter could get acquainted, since Shakespeare there is married."

"Shakespeare? Are you related to the late writer?"

Randy guffawed. "Nah, that's not his real name, but he writes all the time, so he's just called 'Shakespeare.' Even writes some nice songs and sings with Sonny over there. Sonny plays a ukulele and Johnny here plays a harmonica."

"Interesting," Emma said. "So do you sing or play, Carter?"

"Me? I just tag along."

"He's kinda backward, especially with women," Arnie told her.

Shakespeare stood up. "If you'll excuse me, folks, I'm going to walk up the beach and find a quiet spot to do some of that writing. Not that I don't like the company, but I need to get a letter off to my wife so I can mail it while we're in town."

When he left, Carter felt ill-at-ease sitting there with Sonny and Sandra, while Emma sat over on the other blanket as the odd-girl-out. What should he do? He'd like to leave, but that wouldn't be very gentlemanly either. Finally he stood and looked straight at her. "Emma, would you like to take a walk with me along the beach?"

She first appeared startled—and then relieved—getting up gracefully and smoothing down her skirt before walking over to him. When they were far enough away from the others, she glanced over at him. "Thank you so much. I thought I couldn't stay there another minute, but didn't know how to make an exit."

"I felt the same way and didn't want to let you there with the rest paired off. So Emma, what's your last name, and where are you from?"

"My name's Emma Tanneyhill, and I come from Minnesota."

"Emma Tanneyhill. What a lovely name."

"And your last name, Carter?"

"Carter Benton from Illinois. I worked at the Ford plant from graduation until I signed up to be a soldier. How did you come to be here in Hawaii?"

"I was a nurse in a large hospital back home. When the war started, I felt my service would be needed more nearest the war zones."

"So, are you stationed here, or is this just a stop between assignments for you?"

"Right now Sandra, Catherine, and I are stationed in the medical center at Schofield, along with three other nurses from the states. It's not a large facility since there was only a doctor and a couple interns stationed there before the war. If there was a serious health problem, the soldier would be taken to a hospital in one of the cities. We came over soon after the December 7th attack. It was really a mess then, and hasn't gotten much better. They keep bringing sick and wounded here from some of the other islands, since there are now a few good doctors and a surgeon available.

"Do you know where you're headed from here?"

"Apparently it's a deep, dark secret that we'll be told when we're almost there."

"I hope it's not Guadalcanal. Right now it's mostly Marines trying to conquer the island and take over the airstrip. But conditions there are so bad, that we've had a lot brought in from there not only wounded, but also suffering from dysentery. The stories they tell are hair-raising. We've had to make room in the building for more beds."

He looked down at her with a half-smile. "Thanks for the warning. I'll start praying for anywhere but Guadalcanal."

She stopped and gazed at him questioningly. "Are you a praying man, Carter?"

"Oh, yes. And even more since this war began. How about you?"

"I cling to the Lord for strength and courage to go on. I had planned to go to a mission field as a nurse, and may still do it when this mess of a war is finally over."

"You, too? I have a friend back home who's in her last year of Moody Bible Institute and plans to go to Mexico as a missionary when she's through."

Emma nodded her head and began to walk again. "Good for her. It takes a lot of strength and courage for a woman to take on that ministry alone."

Walking on silently, Carter dwelt on Allie again and how much he missed her.

He saw Shakespeare walking towards them. "You'll like Shakespeare," he told her. "He's a dedicated Christian, and seems able to let everything in the Lord's hands."

"Hey, buddy. How'd the writing go?"

Shakespeare held up a notebook. "Came up with a new song Sonny should like. I'm about ready to head back to base. How about you?"

"Yeah, it's been a long day. Let's tell the others and catch the next bus back."

"I'll tag along with you two, if you don't mind," Emma said. "I'd also be interested in reading some of what you write, Shakespeare. I love music and poetry."

"Be my guest." He looked around. "Isn't this where we left the others earlier?"

"Yeah, and there's a note by the picnic table." Carter went to retrieve it. "Says, 'Went to the bar across the way for a little nightlife. Either join us, or we'll see you back at Schofield.' I dread thinking of the condition they'll be in when they get there tonight!"

The ride back was a silent one. Emma read some of Shakespeare's writings, Shakespeare's pen was flying across the paper, and Carter stared out the bus window thinking of Allie.

It was past the supper hour at the mess hall, so the three went to the club and ordered hamburgers, fries and Cokes.

"I'm off to the barracks," Shakespeare said when finished. "See you later Carter." He nodded at Emma. "Nice to meet you, Emma."

"I'd like to read more poetry and songs later, if you don't mind, Shakespeare."

He smiled. "Hey, most writers are happy to share their inspiration with others. Good night now." He waved and turned away.

Both watched until he walked out the door. Emma was the first to speak. "He's amazing, isn't he?"

"Sure is. I'll feel much safer with him, a strong praying man, watching our backs."

Hours later, Carter and Emma were still talking when the other four men, Sandra, and Catherine, arrived from the last bus back to camp and joined them at their table.

"Where'd you two get to?" Sonny asked, apparently the most sober of the group.

"A long walk on the beach, then caught the next bus back with Shakespeare."

Sonny glanced around. "Where'd he go?"

"The barracks, to finish a letter to his wife."

"Figures." Sonny pulled out a seat for Sandra.

"Actually, we were about to leave too." Carter stood as he spoke.

"Hey, the night's young, folks. 'Eat, drink and be merry, for tomorrow we may very well die,'" Randy said in a slurred voice.

"Not exactly tomorrow," Carter said. "And on a happier note, look at the lovely nurses we'll have to take care of us—if we get wounded and sent back here."

"Gotta point, pal. Gotta point." Johnny said, turning to Catherine. "Would you take care of me, sweetheart?"

She hesitated a moment. "Of course, Johnny. Just come back in one piece."

Carter pulled out Emma's chair for her to stand. "Hope you're this happy in the morning, fellas. Just don't come back noisy and wake Shakespeare and me up."

Sandra also stood. "I'm going back with Emma, Sonny. It's been a long day."

He followed suit. "I'll take my leave too. See you tomorrow, pals. And it was nice to meet you ladies today. You made a good day even better."

They walked the girls to their dormitory and bid them good night, but Sandra suggested that the four of them take a bus up to the North Shore Beach the next morning. "We both have the day off," she said, "and Emma and I could bring a picnic." She turned to Emma. "What do you think about that idea, Emma?"

Emma paused a second before agreeing. "Sounds like a plan to me," and the men quickly consented.

Later, Carter lay in the dark going over his afternoon and evening with Emma. She was so easy to talk to and never appeared to be flirting with him, so he looked forward to going to the beach tomorrow. His last thought, of course, was of Allie.

The next morning after breakfast, Carter and Sonny met Emma and Sandra at the bus stop and rode up to the North Shore. All wore swimsuits under their clothes.

Monstrous waves were crashing loudly against the beach. Finding a spot under a tree on the shore, the group soon had blankets and picnic items organized and situated.

"Last one in is a waddling walrus," Emma challenged, racing to the water with Sandra right behind her.

"No fair," Sonny yelled. "Your skirts come off easier than our shorts."

Shorts and shirt already tossed onto the blanket, Carter took off after the girls.

Sonny, thinking he was out of his shorts, started to run and tripped over them, falling flat in the sand onto his stomach. Carter passed Sandra and dived into a wave at the same time Emma ran in up to her knees.

Surfacing, Carter looked back at Sonny brushing off his abdomen and pulling one leg out of his twisted shorts. "I spy a waddling walrus coming toward us, ladies." The three turned and laughed at Sonny's antics.

"Yeah, sure, laugh," he said. "Some friends you are. I fell flat on my stomach, and not one of you came back to help me up."

Sandra went to him and gave him a hug, patting his red tummy. "Aw, poor baby. I'm so sorry."

"Well, you'd better be." He pushed her to the side and ran to dive into a wave. Coming up, he yelled, "Now who's the waddling walrus? Your feet aren't even wet yet, so don't tell me you were in."

She looked down at her feet, along with Emma and Carter. "You sneak!" Wading into the salt water, she pushed him backwards into an enormous wave as it pounded in.

He swallowed a huge gulp of the salty brine and came up spitting and coughing, only to be drawn under by a second wave that followed immediately after the first. He was starting to get in over his head, literally, as he couldn't get his feet under him before being pounded by another wave. The next two started to drag him out with the undertow!

Chapter Eleven

Carter jumped through an incoming wave and dived into the deeper water, swimming as fast as the current allowed. When he reached Sonny, his friend appeared lifeless. "Come on, Sonny, this can't be your ending, you have too much to do yet!" He flung him over his shoulder and started for shore, surprised to find Emma right beside him.

A large wave broke over them, and Carter stumbled with his burden.

Emma moved quickly to help hold him upright. "Let's carry him between us, Carter." They struggled to get him positioned in the frothing surf before the next wave crested.

He was apparently unconscious, but breathing shallowly. They pushed through the turbulent waters, finally making it to the shore. Sandra ran toward them with a large towel she laid on the sand, where they carefully placed him face down.

Sandra cleared his mouth of any seaweed, and Carter began pumping his back and arms, head turned to the side. Soon he coughed, and water gushed from his mouth along with most of his breakfast. He crawled to his knees, holding his stomach with one arm.

"Oh-h. I'm so sick. I think I'm dying!"

The three knelt around him. "Fortunately, you're still alive, Sonny," Sandra told him. "Thanks to Carter and Emma."

"I'll thank you both later. Right now I just want to lay down and die."

"Come up and lay on the blanket," Sandra urged. "The spasms will soon pass."

Between the three friends, they managed to get him to the blanket, where he curled into a ball and moaned.

"I'll stay with him," Sandra told them. "After all, I'm the one who pushed him backwards. You two go swim or take a walk."

"Are you sure?" Emma asked.

"Yes, go."

They headed up the beach, both stumbling from exhaustion and the deep sand.

Carter shook his head. "What a harrowing experience that was! How did it happen so quickly? I know Sandra shoved him jokingly, but he came up okay after that."

"I'm wondering if the one wave threw him to the bottom and he hit his head, knocking him out."

"I was thinking the same thing. He wasn't in there long enough to take in the amount of water to become unconscious that swiftly."

"When we go back, I'll check his head for swelling," Emma said. "Could we just sit for awhile? I'm still shaking a bit."

"Right here looks good to me." He took her hand and pulled her down beside him on the dry sand where they sat with hands around bended knees and staring out over the pounding surf that could so speedily become an enemy.

"Maybe we should go back and check on Sonny," Carter said a short time later.

Emma nodded and stood to brush off sand. When they got back to the others, both were sound asleep and Sonny was covered with a towel.

Sandra opened her eyes and whispered, "The spasms finally eased, and he laid flat on his stomach, shivering; so I covered him up and he fell asleep."

"We wondered if he hit his head and was knocked out," Emma said.

"I checked for lumps and swelling. He has a good-sized goose egg, so I'm sure that's what happened. He may have a concussion."

"I hope it's not a fractured skull," Emma said. "We'll check him over good when he wakes up."

"My brother Joey fell in a barn the night of my farewell party and had a concussion. He was much better in a couple days. Let's hope that's all Sonny has."

"You could talk to my face instead of my back, if someone would roll me over."

"Sonny, buddy, you're talking!" Carter moved quickly to his side and rolled him over as gently as possible. "Man, we thought you were a goner out there."

Sonny put an arm over his eyes. "All I remember is Sandra shoving me backwards into a wave, coming up and being knocked down by another big one. The next thing I knew, I was laying on the beach puking. Right now my stomach's empty, and my head's pounding."

"I'll get you a wet cloth and aspirin for your head," Emma offered.

"How about food first? As you recall, there can't be much left in there. My bellybutton is rubbing my backbone about now."

"Can you sit up, if I help?" Carter asked, and slid an arm beneath his friend's shoulders. Sonny was soon sitting with barely a moan.

The women opened the picnic basket, buttered him a roll, and opened a bottle of Coke for him. "Better keep it light until you know it will stay down," Sandra told him.

He nibbled at the roll cautiously, sipping his soda between bites. When that stayed down, he took two aspirin. "You three go swim now," he told them. "I'll rest for a while. When you're ready to eat I'll try some more food."

"If you're sure," Sandra said, a concerned look on her face.

He waved his hand toward them. "Go, go. Enjoy."

The three reluctantly headed toward the water, not as carefree and rowdy as they had been earlier. Sonny later joined them, wading to his knees in the surf, and the group soon decided it was time to enjoy their picnic lunch.

What a beautiful place, Carter thought, munching on a sandwich while staring out to sea. *I'd love to bring Allie somewhere like this for a honeymoon. But will it ever come to marriage and a honeymoon for us?* And heartache ripped through him like a dark wave, stronger even than the night she refused his ring.

When he was finished eating, Carter longed to walk the beach alone, but didn't want to be rude to Emma; he turned to her. "Would you like to walk the beach with me?"

She stood and brushed the sand from her legs. "Sounds good, Carter."

"What about you two?" He asked Sandra and Sonny.

"I think we'll just drowse here in the shade. I'm sure Sonny can use the rest," Sandra answered. "What do you think, Sonny?"

"I agree with her. You two go and enjoy a walk by the sea. I'll lay here and yell taunts at the ocean since it didn't manage to take me down this time."

"You need to be thanking God for that, friend." Carter nudged

Sonny's foot and grinned. "Relax as much as you want today. Day after tomorrow, we'll be getting trained so hard we'll be dreaming of being able to just laze around."

❦

Emma strode along beside Carter, staring out to sea. What a beautiful day! Walking beside the water and watching the waves roll in made it difficult to believe that a war was raging out in the Pacific with men—and women—dying by the moment.

She glanced up at Carter, who appeared to be miles away, most likely back home with that girl he'd mentioned. Would he survive the war wherever he was sent? He was a handsome man, and reminded her of the doctor she'd left behind in the states. He was unable to join up due to a partial paralysis of his left leg from polio as a child. He had been so angry when she enlisted, that he said their relationship was over; she had nothing to go back to.

"So, Carter, tell me about the girl back in the states who wants to be a missionary."

He turned toward her with a blank look for a moment. "Oh, Allie. It's still painful to talk about her. We dated for two years, and the night of my farewell party, I offered her a diamond and asked her to wait for me, but she refused it. Said she really cared deeply for me, but didn't feel that I was ready to serve my life with her as a missionary."

Emma stopped and placed her hand on his arm. "I'm so sorry, Carter. Was she right? Do you feel you would want to serve the Lord on a mission field? Or would you prefer going back to your job at the Ford plant and have a comfortable home and family like you were raised?"

He placed his right hand over hers and looked across the water again. "I told her I loved her enough to follow her even to the far corners of Africa, if that was where she wanted to go. But I don't think she really believed me."

"I'm sure you meant it, Carter, but she most likely wanted to hear that you would follow the Lord wherever He wanted you to go, instead of that you would follow her."

When he turned his blue eyes back to her, her heart did a flip-flop, and she hurriedly suppressed the feelings. It certainly wouldn't help to care for someone who may very well not survive the war, and especially a man who obviously had deep feelings for a girl back home. But there was something about Carter that touched her in a way that the doctor in Minnesota hadn't.

"You know, Emma, you're probably right. Now I see she most likely would have rather heard me say I'd follow the Lord where He wanted me to go, instead of her. That gives me something new to dwell on and pray about. I'll write to her tonight and apologize for putting her before the Lord, and maybe she'll see I'm thinking more deeply about spiritual things."

Emma took a deep breath and removed her hand from his arm, hoping her words wouldn't mess up whatever plans the Lord had for both Carter and Allie.

Chapter Twelve

Allie was seated beside Daniel in their class on the book of Hebrews when he was called from the room by a college administrative aid. He returned for the books on his desk and glanced at her with an ashen face before leaving. Allie knew it must have something to do with his mother, and she immediately prayed silently for Daniel and for her.

After class, she picked up a thick letter from Carter and took it to her room to read before supper in the cafeteria.

Dear Allie,

How are things going for you at school? I hope well. You wrote that Daniel's mother has been ill. I hope she's doing better. I know he's close to her.

Our time here in Hawaii is a welcome retreat before we get shipped off to our next destination, which still remains a secret from our unit.

Sonny and I, along with a couple others, had a picnic at the North Shore Beach today. The waves there were rather wicked. Sonny got knocked down and almost drowned. I swam out and brought him in unconscious, with the help of one of the others. He seems okay now.

Tomorrow is our last day to do our own thing, and then it will be back to the hard work of training. I hear that it will be even more intensive in order to get us ready to fight.

You would like the other man Sonny and I have befriended. He's from Alabama, and a very good Christian man. He got married six months before leaving for the Army. His name is Rodney James Gruber, but everyone calls him Shakespeare, because he writes poems, songs and stories every chance he gets. Sometimes he reads them to us, or he, Sonny and a couple others will sing and play a few instruments.

I'm enclosing a poem he wrote for his wife, but it also shows how I feel for you. It's titled "While I'm Away."

*While I'm away, my love, my life,
My endless love calls out to you.
We'll both be facing diff'rent strife,
So let's try to keep our love true.*

*Focus on our Savior and Lord,
We belong to Him forever,
Tied to Him by a blood red cord
That no one can ever sever.*

*My soul is also tied to you,
Whether in life or in my death,
That love will be forever true;
I'll call to you with my last breath.*

I've been thinking about some of the things we talked about my last week at home. When I said I'd follow you to darkest Africa, if that was where you wanted to go, I now realize I should have said if that was where God wanted me to go. I realize your life is all about serving him, and if we would marry, of course you would want me to put him first. So I'm working on that, Allie. Shakespeare has been a good influence on me regarding serving God. So please don't give up on me. I would like to spend my life serving God with you.

While walking on a beach and gazing out over the ocean, all I could picture was you and me walking here hand-in-hand on our honeymoon.

*All my love,
Carter*

Allie's vision was blurred from the tears that continued to fall as she read Carter's letter, and especially the poem. *Lord, is Carter really drawing closer to you, or is he saying what he thinks I want to hear?*

Just then there was a knock at her door. When she opened it to Daniel, he was also in tears.

"It's my mother. She passed away in her sleep at my sister's home, so I gotta go home to help make funeral arrangements. I'm just so sad and I don't know what to do with myself."

"Oh, Daniel, I'm so sorry." She moved to hug him, and was surprised when he clutched her tightly to him. Pulling away gently, she asked, "What can I do to help?"

"Would you come with me? You're my closest friend, and I could really use your support right now."

His request took her by surprise, but how could she refuse him? "How soon are you leaving?"

"The taxi should be here in half an hour. I'll buy your train ticket, if you'll come."

She decided quickly. "I'll pack a few things and meet you out front in half an hour. I need to clear the days off at the attendance desk too."

Soon Allie and Daniel were seated together in a nearly full passenger car that held a lot of military men—and a few women—in uniform. Looking around, she wished she could glance up to see Carter's face among them. She would rush up and throw her arms around him. *What am I doing here with Daniel, Lord, when all I can think about is Carter? I've never even met Daniel's family. What will they think when he arrives with a woman by his side?*

"You look deep in thought, Allie. Are you regretting coming with me? I know it was a lot to ask of you."

She jerked as if he had read her mind. "I was realizing that I don't know any of your family. I don't want them to jump to the wrong conclusion when I arrive with you."

He put his hand on her arm. "No, no, Allie. Don't worry about that happening. I've talked to them a lot about you as a friend, and I've also said what a good man Carter is. So they'll not put any additional significance on you coming with me to my mother's funeral."

Feeling more assured, Allie sat back and took pen and paper out of her satchel and began a letter to Carter.

Chapter Thirteen

Carter had asked Emma if she could get the next day off to go into Honolulu with him, though he felt rather guilty after he offered the invitation. When she showed up early the next morning ready to go, he felt both glad for her company, and remorse for spending time with a woman other than Allie. He consoled himself that Allie had been the one to leave their relationship before he left home.

"So what's the plan, soldier?" she asked with a smile when they were on the bus.

"You've been here longer than I have, you tell me."

She looked thoughtful. "Well, do you like museums, movies, nice restaurants?"

He smiled. "All of the above. You come up with the ideas, and I'll come up with the cash. How's that sound?"

"Sounds like a deal to me."

They toured a museum in the morning, lunched at a quiet restaurant, and munched on popcorn through a double feature movie in the afternoon. A relaxing dinner was enjoyed before returning to the base.

"What a great time, Emma. Remembering a day enjoying the finer things in life should help me get through a lot of what's ahead.

"Should we stop in the canteen to see if any of the group are there?"

"Let's do. I'm not quite ready to end the day yet, and I'm still thirsty after all that popcorn we gorged on this afternoon."

They spied their friends at a table in the far end of the room and joined them.

"Well, look who just dragged in!" Randy shouted in his usual rowdy voice when drinking. "Where have you two been all day?"

"Living it up in Honolulu, where else?" Carter answered as he pulled out a chair for Emma. "You want a Coke?" he asked her.

"Please."

Carter returned with the two drinks and heard the ribbing Emma was getting from the men and the other nurses. "Okay, if you want to pick on someone, pick on me. I'm the one who invited her to go and show me the sights in the big city."

"Hey, enjoy what's left of our lives while you can, buddy," Arnie said, appearing to be in a solemn drunken state.

Carter and Emma left shortly after, with Sonny and Sandra trailing behind. Carter hugged Emma at the door, and raised his eyebrows when he saw Sonny kiss Sandra rather passionately.

"What about the girl back home?" he asked as they walked to the barracks.

Sonny looked him in the eyes. "What are you? The pot calling the kettle black?"

"That hug tonight is the closest we've gotten."

"And you might be glad for it when you're dug into a foxhole with bullets whistling over your head."

Carter lay in the dark thinking of Sonny's words, and guilt washed over him when he thought how he would feel if he knew Allie was spending time with another man.

The soldiers were taken by truck the next morning to begin the rigorous jungle training. They were taught how to "dig in" to make foxholes, which wasn't so difficult in the sand. Survival techniques were stressed over and over: primarily how to defend themselves against the enemy in the jungle.

"There the enemy can have many faces," Drill Sergeant Hummer shouted. "The most dangerous will be the two-legged ones with a death wish. They'll each be taught to fight like they're avenging the death of their father. With them, no rules apply. You have to out-think them and out-maneuver them, if you want to see the next day, or even the next breath. So don't forget to check every tree and bush you walk by.

"Depending where you end up, you may even need to beware of crocodiles waiting in rivers, mammoth spiders—I'm talking the size of your fist—armies of biting white ants with a sting like fire, or sharp-edged grass that grows higher than your head. I'm sure some of you he-men are thinking 'I'm not afraid of any spiders or ants.' Believe me when I say the day will come when you run from bugs of many descriptions.

And the rats! You haven't seen a rat until you meet up with some of the ones you'll see in the jungle. And let's not even think about the range of poisonous snakes you might encounter. Some of the places you go could harbor huge pythons in the bushes. Just watch your step, and keep alert for the enemies that will be all around you.

"The heat will be terrible, sapping your energy. Then will come the torrential downpours, turning everything to a steaming sauna or a muddy swamp. Dysentery and malaria run rampant. These alone may take the lives of some of you standing here today.

"I don't say these things to cause you fear, but to instill in you a deep-seated caution that may save your lives in any of these circumstances. Once you land at your destination, the war games will be over. Once you leave your ship and set foot on shore, it will be the real life-or-death thing."

The men left the first session in total silence, partly due to exhaustion from the maneuvers of the day, but moreso because each man was pondering the solemn and frightening words the sergeant had just spoken.

"Ya think that stuff's all true?" Sonny finally asked Carter in a subdued tone when they were almost to the truck that would transport them back to the barracks.

Carter pondered before answering. "It could all be bunk to make us expect the worst, and then be relieved when the reality we experience won't be quite as bad as what we expected. Or, he could very well be giving it to us straight, to prepare us just a little for the worst nightmares of our lives."

"Yeah. Something tells me the second thing you said is more like it."

It was a very somber group that climbed up into the back of that truck to ride back to the installation.

Chapter Fourteen

When Carter returned from training later in the week, a thick letter awaited him from Allie. He hurriedly ate in the mess hall before going to a large tree where he sat in the shade to devour every word.

Dear Carter,

Thank you for your letter and the poem written by Shakespeare. It made me cry. I'm glad you have a friend like him to encourage you along the way.

Daniel received bad news this morning. His mother passed away. He asked me if I would go home with him to help him through it all, so we're on a train right now, headed for his sister's home in Indiana.

There are a lot of servicemen in our car, and I find myself searching among them for your face.

Carter stopped at that point feeling something akin to a lead ball settle in the pit of his stomach as he pictured his Allie riding on a train with Daniel to meet and spend time with him and his family. *Is that different than you spending time with Emma the past week and a half?* Somehow it felt different. He knew he was committed to Allie, but was she committed to him in her heart?

He read on.

It was awkward when we arrived at the home of Daniel's sister, Eileen, and her husband, Arthur. They have two darling children—Thomas, aged seven and Doris, aged five. I shared Doris' bed last night, and she snuggled up to me the entire night.

I'm adding to my letter as I watch over the children today while the adults are making the arrangements at the funeral home. They just arrived back, so I'll finish later.

Things got hectic, and I spent all day keeping the children occupied and helping to find places to store the food that continues to pour in from neighbors and friends. At least Eileen and I don't have to spend time with meal preparation. I've also taken over the chore of doing dishes, though I'm not complaining. I'm glad I can be of some help.

A viewing was held tonight, and I saw Daniel's mother for the first time. She was even lovely in death, and age fifty-nine was much too young for her to die. Daniel stood continually staring down at her as she lay in her casket. I saw him rubbing the inside of her arm, which he said was the only place that still felt soft. I wish I could comfort him, but feel at a loss as to what I can do. When I tell him that, he says being here for him is doing enough, so I'm glad I came.

How are things going in Hawaii since the intensive training is going full speed ahead? I find myself thinking back to the fun we had together before the danger of the war entered our lives, and wish we could flip back the pages to those days again. However, life doesn't work that way. We can only go forward and trust the Lord to lead us through the dark valleys as well as over the sunny mountaintops.

Well, it's time for me to crawl into bed and snuggle up to Doris for the night. She's been sound asleep the past hour while I've finished writing.

My thoughts and prayers are always with you, Carter. Stay close to God and trust Him to guide you through each day.

Your Friend Always,
Allie

Carter leaned back against the tree and wanted to weep endlessly. Somehow, he felt Allie slipping away from him, and little by little gravitating towards Daniel. He closed his eyes and prayed silently. *Please Lord, don't let me lose Allie. Help me become the Christian you want me to be; help me walk the same path with her for you, and wherever you would want to send us.*

❦

Emma finished her shift at the hospital and went out into the fresh air. She hesitated when she saw Carter sitting against a tree with his eyes closed and a letter lying open beside him. Should she join him, or did he need privacy right then? His face appeared rather drawn, so she walked over and stooped to lay a hand on his shoulder. "You okay, soldier?"

Carter jumped and his eyes flew open.

"Sorry, Carter. I didn't mean to scare you. I wasn't sure whether to join you or not, but you look so sad."

"Hi, Emma. I have to say I'm a little down right now after reading Allie's letter. Would you read it through and see what impression you get from it?"

She sat in the grass beside him. "If you're sure you want me to. Somehow it feels like invading your privacy."

"No, I've already shared a lot with you concerning Allie, and I'd appreciate an unbiased opinion."

She took the pages Carter handed her and looked more deeply into his electric blue eyes. While reading, Emma felt Carter's eyes observing her every expression as she scanned the pages. Drawing close to the end, she felt he had reason to be concerned about Daniel. He was definitely closing in on Allie, and would do it even more now that his mother was gone.

When finished, she folded it slowly and handed it back to him. How could she offer her opinion without causing him to lose all hope?

Carter grasped her hand that held the letter. "So? What do you think? Am I going to lose out to this man?"

She placed her other hand over top of the one holding hers. "Carter . . . you need to realize it's a possibility. He's there with her. He's attending a Bible Institute and most likely would go to Mexico—or wherever—if he felt that was where God wanted him.

"What's the chance of him getting drafted?"

"Allie once told me that he couldn't join because of a rheumatic heart condition from his youth—so no—he won't be drafted."

"All you can do, Carter, is pray for God's will in both of your lives, and trust him to do what's best in serving him. Do you want me to pray now?"

A Bridge to Somewhere

He gripped the letter in his hands and leaned back against the tree again. "Please do, Emma."

"Precious Lord, you know what a turmoil the world appears to be in right now, and you know how Carter's heart aches for Allie's love. Help him draw closer to you, trusting in your plan for his and Allie's lives. Amen."

"Thank you, Emma. Have you eaten yet?"

"No, I was on my way to the canteen; I'm not up to mess hall food right now."

"How about a large juicy burger and some fries? My treat."

"Sounds good, friend, but let me treat. You spent a lot on our day in Honolulu."

"Hey, wherever I end up, I doubt if there will be any place close by to spend my money."

Sitting beside Carter in the canteen, Emma knew she would miss him a lot when he was gone. It was totally unthinkable to imagine him dying somewhere far from here and being buried in foreign soil. So she silently breathed a prayer of her own for his safety, and also—if the Lord willed—that she might be back in his life again at the end of the war, for she knew she was already developing feelings for him.

❦

Carter waited a day or so before writing again to Allie. As low as her letter had taken him, he wanted what he said to be uplifting instead, not making her feel guilty for not loving him as he did her.

He was so thankful for his friends, especially for Shakespeare, Sonny and Emma.

They were the three he could share his thoughts and feelings with. Shakespeare and Emma both usually answered with something about the Lord, which helped, but they made him realize they both walked closer to God than he did. He longed to experience the same closeness to the Lord, but wasn't quite sure how to make that happen.

Realizing his unit would soon be moving out—and who knew where they would end up, or if any of them would even survive—he sat again under his favorite tree and determinedly wrote a cheerful letter to Allie. Who knew—it could be the last one he'd ever write and she'd ever get.

Chapter Fifteen

*A*llie was glad to be back in her dorm room at Moody. It had been a trying few days. Daniel's sister and her husband had been kind and friendly, but in her heart, she felt they were picturing her and Daniel as a couple. She herself kept longing to feel Carter's arms around her and wondered constantly where and how he was.

Disappointed no letter had awaited her from Carter, Allie poured more of her time into her studies. She would graduate in December and decided to make plans to go to Mexico in January with a group of other graduates. There they would help out in one of the missions. That experience should put her on a path toward what God wanted for her.

Daniel continued to seek her out, talking about his mother and the good life he'd had growing up in a good Christian home. His father had died when Daniel was twelve and his sister fourteen. His mother had a good job teaching at the same school as his father, so financially they had suffered very little hardship.

Feeling lonely and missing Carter, she welcomed the time with Daniel. The few girlfriends she had at the institute were recently graduated, or had dropped out of school and found jobs due to the war.

Finally a letter arrived from Carter. She escaped to her room to read it in privacy.

My Dear Allie,

I was so sorry to hear about Daniel's mother dying. I know how close they were. Please offer him my sympathy. It was kind of you to go with him to help the family and offer comfort through their time of need.

Our training here has been extremely tiring, sometimes verging on brutal, though our sergeant assures us it will seem mild compared to what we will encounter on the battlefield. At the end of each day, we drag ourselves to a shower and clean clothes, and over to the mess hall for supper. The group I mentioned before—Randy, Johnny, Arnie, Sonny and I usually go to the canteen for an hour or so in the evening to unwind. Once in awhile Shakespeare will go, but usually he heads back to the barracks and writes songs, poems and letters to his wife, and then studies his Bible. I've been doing that some myself before lights out, thanks to the Bible you gave me before I left.

Rumor has it that we will be shipping out soon, though a certain date hasn't yet been given, or the destination. Apparently, we're only told where we're going when we're out on a ship and almost to our station. So it could be a while before you get my letters, or I get yours. I see by the calendar that you will shortly be graduating. What are your plans after that?

Many factories are hiring women now to take the place of men who have gone into the service, so that would be a possibility for a job. Of course, I realize that isn't what you've been training for at the Bible Institute, but it does help out in making needed war supplies.

Sonny and I have also been getting more training in communications. Possibly we won't be doing as much fighting, but we've been warned there will still be danger all around.

I had planned to make this a cheerful letter, but as I read over it, some of it sounds rather formidable. But then, what good is there about war, except for the end where freedom is gained for those who have been living under tyranny.

Have you talked to my parents any time you've been home? I get letters from them and Joey.

Tell your parents I said "hi". Your mother has written me some too. I've gotten several letters from Jesse. He says the baby is strong and healthy now and sleeps all night, much to his and Annie's delight.

Take care, sweetheart. I miss you a lot, and pray that when this war is over, you and I might still have a chance together. I believe I'll be more than willing to go wherever the Lord sends me.

All my love,
Carter

When Allie finished his letter, she lay on her bed and held it close to her chest before reading it over twice more. His handwriting had always been neat, and she traced over the letters with her index finger.

Noting it was time for dinner, she made her way to the cafeteria. Filling her tray, she glanced around the room and saw Daniel at a table by a window motioning her over. She had tucked Carter's letter into a pocket and looked forward to rereading it over her dinner, but instead headed for Daniel's table disappointedly.

He stood and pulled out the other chair for her. "You have a happy glow about you this evening, Allie. Did you get some good news?"

She opened her napkin and spread it across her lap. "I received a letter from Carter. He said they should be leaving for their destination soon. That isn't really good news, but it was great to hear from him."

"That's nice. I see you got the meatloaf. It's delicious this time. Last week it wasn't very tasty."

She looked over at him, annoyed that he often made disparaging remarks about the cafeteria food. "I thought it was rather good last week. That's why I got it again."

"Oh well, we each have our own tastes." He settled into eating quietly for the rest of the meal.

It was fine with Allie, since she preferred to eat quietly and think of Carter.

When they had returned their trays and dishes, Daniel finally spoke. "Would you like to play checkers in the game room before going upstairs?"

"I think I'll pass tonight, Daniel. I want to get off a quick letter to Carter so he might get it before leaving Hawaii."

"Oh. Fine. Give him my regards, and I'll see you at breakfast."

Puzzled, she watched him walk away, thinking he was acting a little jealous, but hoping she was imagining things.

Chapter Sixteen

Several days later, Sergeant Hummer gave them the word. "We'll be shipping out on Thursday at 0800. Be sure you're packed the night before and, after the morning mess, have your bag and belongings waiting at the bus-loading area. Any questions, except about where we're headed? That information will only be given out when we near our destination. Anything else?" No one raised a hand, and they were dismissed.

"Well, I guess our turn has come, fellas," Sonny lamented, as he, Carter and Shakespeare walked to the Barracks.

"Yeah, and all the news we hear isn't very encouraging when we see injured men being brought here and some shipped out soon after in boxes." Chills radiated up Carter's body thinking about the horrors that awaited them.

Shakespeare finally spoke up. "When we know the Lord, we can trust him to either see us through it all safely, or take us to heaven to be with him for all eternity. It's a win-win situation, the way I see it."

Sonny stopped. "Wait!" The other two turned to face him.

"I'm not sure I know the Lord like you and Carter do, Shakespeare. And if there really is a hell, what if I end up there?"

"The Bible states the way to heaven plainly, Sonny. John 3:16 says *For God so loved the world that he gave his only begotten son, that whosoever believes in him should not perish, but have everlasting life.* We have to recognize that we are sinners and that we need a Savior. Then confess our sins to Jesus and ask Him to forgive us and dwell within our hearts as our Savior. It's that simple."

Sonny looked thoughtful. "I'll mull that over in my mind, and talk to you more about it again."

The five men met later in the canteen, and the three nurses joined them shortly after. "How did all of you manage to get time off together?"

Randy asked.

"Our sergeant rearranged our schedules with the other nurses so we can spend tonight and tomorrow evening with all of you, since you're scheduled to leave on Thursday," Sandra said as she sat beside Sonny.

Carter stood to pull out a chair for Emma and returned the smile she gave to him.

"Where's Shakespeare?" she asked.

"Writing a long letter to Marietta. He plans to have at least five to mail out before we leave. He said he might stop over later."

"Would you like a Coke and something to eat?"

"Why don't we share a large order of fries? I'm not very hungry this evening."

He squeezed her hand. "One order of fries and two Cokes coming up."

※

Emma turned to watch Carter walk to the counter. She felt her heart would shatter into a thousand pieces just thinking of him going off to some distant shore to be shot at—and possibly die—and she'd never see him again. He was such a kind, gentle man, and she couldn't believe she had come to care for him so deeply in such a short time.

When they'd finished their fries and drinks, she suggested they go outside for a walk. The other men were getting rowdy from drinking, except for Sonny, and she no longer felt comfortable in the atmosphere.

"See you later. We're going out for some fresh air," Carter told the others.

Emma ignored the remarks from the men and walked out in front of Carter. Taking a deep breath of fresh air, she said, "This sure beats the smoke-filled environment in there, doesn't it?"

"Sure does."

Emma stumbled and Carter grabbed her arm, and then took her hand. A thrill pierced through her, and she wanted to hold on to him and keep him close by forever. "Don't you ever smoke, Carter?"

"I took a few puffs once from a cigarette a friend handed me, but it tasted awful and I started to choke. I threw it away and never touched one again. My parents were always religious and didn't believe in smoking.

I told you about the boys smoking in Allie's barn the night of my going away party, with the barn catching fire. My brother Joey stayed behind to try to put it out when they all ran away. Joey fell and was knocked unconscious. I hope they all learned a lesson from that night."

"Tell me more about your life growing up. Do you have a lot of relatives?"

"Not really. An aunt on my mother's side and an uncle on my dad's side, each with one child. But we have a lot of friends and neighbors around, and church members. Tell me more about you? Have you always lived in Minnesota?"

"The Land of a Thousand Lakes! Yes, I was born and raised there, and loved everything about it. We have a house on one of the lakes, and my parents and younger sister and brother still live there. My brother, Kevin will graduate from high school next June, and my sister, Netta will graduate two years later. I miss my home and family, but I feel this is where the Lord wants me to be right now as a nurse."

They walked and talked until Carter was due back at the barracks. Emma felt she could have gone on all night, knowing tomorrow would be the last day she had any time with him.

Back at the medical center, she turned toward him and he took both of her hands into his. "Emma, I can never thank you enough for making my time here special, helping to keep my mind off what lies ahead. Will you write to me?"

"Of course I will, Carter. Every day, if I can."

"I can't promise I'll answer every day, but I'll write every chance I get."

He pulled her close for a long hug, and how she wished he would kiss her. After releasing her, he touched his lips to her forehead and quickly turned to walk away.

"Good night, Carter," she whispered. "I'll see you in my dreams."

Chapter Seventeen

The Drill Sergeant was easier on the men the next day and dismissed them early. Carter was happy to see Emma waiting for him when the truck returned to the base. "Give me a few minutes to shower and change and I'll be right with you."

"Take your time, Carter. I packed us a picnic. I thought we could take a walk and find a nice spot with a view."

"Sounds great to me. See you in ten minutes."

Carter grabbed a change of clothes and ran to the showers to beat the crowd. He was back out with Emma in ten minutes as promised. He carried the picnic basket and took her hand as they walked. Finding a spot under some trees, Emma opened the basket and laid out a thick blanket for their spread.

"Wow! Where did you come up with this feast?"

She grinned. "I have my ways." She took out fried chicken, potato salad and rolls, with iced tea and, last but not least, cupcakes for dessert.

They lounged while they ate and talked more about their lives and childhoods. Carter felt they would never run out of things to talk about. He pushed back the sadness that threatened to engulf him when he thought what tomorrow would bring, and was surprised at how it hurt to think he might never see Emma again. The times he'd spent with her would give him a lot of good memories to dwell on wherever he was.

He'd received mail today from his family, Jesse, and Allie, and had put it all in his duffel bag unopened so he would have something to read on the ship tomorrow.

He and Emma spent the rest of their time together outdoors, and this time when he walked her back to the medical center to tell her goodbye, he held her close and kissed her lips softly. "I'm going to miss you, Emma. You've made my time here special. Take care, and if the Lord's willing, maybe we'll see one another again when the war's over."

He was surprised at the tears streaming down her cheeks when she handed him a letter.

"I wrote you a long letter, Carter. One you can read while you're away, and I'll keep writing while you're gone."

"Thank you, Emma. You can't know how uplifting your friendship here on post has meant to me. I even hate to say goodbye, so I'll just say 'farewell until we meet again.' "

She grabbed his hand. "Carter. I'm glad you said 'farewell until we meet again.' Right now I don't want to hear the word 'goodbye.' "

Then she turned and walked in the door.

It was a quiet unit that waited for the bus the next morning. Boarding the bus, the six men—Carter, Sonny, Shakespeare, Randy, Johnny and Arnie—grabbed seats together. Even Randy had nothing to joke about.

When the bus pulled up to the dock closest to the ship that would take them to their next destination, Carter was relieved to note that it didn't look rusty or unseaworthy.

"Hey, it's not a topnotch cruise ship, but at least it's not a tugboat!" Randy exclaimed, staring out the window, and the others chuckled.

Aboard ship, the men were pointed down to the quarters where they would sleep. The six friends managed to get bunks close together again. After roll call on deck, the GIs hung over the sides, watching the island of Oahu slowly disappear into the distance.

Following daily exercise and more training regarding the use and cleaning of their weapons, the men grouped to play cards, read or sing. As usual, Shakespeare continued to write and entertain sometimes by reading his writings to the soldiers and sailors who wanted to hang around to listen.

Music was often heard over the loudspeakers. Sometimes they'd listen to the infamous "Tokyo Rose," who would play songs like "HOME SWEET HOME" to try making the men even more homesick. The men were told to ignore her and not listen to anything she said when she spouted anti-American propaganda, but sometimes they tuned in anyway.

Carter spent a lot of time writing to his family, Allie, Emma and Jesse.

He would be able to leave the letters with the ship to be mailed when it docked at a city. He found writing to Allie much more difficult than writing to Emma, for with Allie he felt he had to weigh each word he penned. He had saved her letter until last when he was able to read on the ship, but was disappointed in what she wrote:

Dear Carter,

I keep wondering where you are right now and what is happening. I pray for you daily. I stopped by to see your folks and Joey the last time I was home. They're doing well, but I can tell they think of you constantly. Daniel is doing better after dealing with the death of his mother. I've tried to be a comfort to him whenever I can. We're both studying much harder now, and in another month or so we'll be facing our final tests. When we have our degrees it will be time for each of us to decide what direction we want to take in serving our Lord and Savior.

Those words were like bayonet wounds to his heart and stomach. He quickly read over the rest of the letter searching for something more encouraging about her feelings for him, but all he got were the closing words, *"My prayers and love are with you."*

He was tempted to mention Emma in his letters to Allie, but so far he felt that would be childish and just cause bad feelings when he was trying to build her love.

Emma in turn wrote about how much she had enjoyed the time they'd spent together, and spoke in detail of all the walks they had taken, the day at the beach, and especially the day they had in Honolulu. Her words lifted him up and warmed his heart.

Carter lay back against a heavy net and relaxed as he listened to Sonny and Shakespeare singing a new song they had co-written. If only this part of the trip could go on indefinitely until the war was over. But who knew how long it would last, and who, if any, of them would still be alive when it was over?

Carter later stood staring out over the water, running thoughts of Allie and Daniel through his mind, when someone tapped him on the shoulder.

"A penny for your thoughts, soldier."

Carter turned to see Shakespeare who was grinning ear-to-ear.

A Bridge to Somewhere

"What's got you so happy, buddy?"

"I had great news from Marietta, but took time to enjoy it myself awhile before sharing. But now I want to tell someone, so I chose you, my special friend."

"Well tell me, don't keep me in suspense."

"I'm going to be a father! Marietta was four months pregnant when she wrote the letter, so she'd be about five months now. Do you think this war might be over in time for me to be home for the baby's birth?"

"It's something we can certainly pray for, buddy. Congratulations!" He gave Shakespeare a hardy hug. "Let's go back and tell the others and we can celebrate."

The GIs and sailors cheered for Shakespeare, and told him to write a song they could all sing to celebrate.

So he sat down and penned a quick verse:

Good news arrived from home today,
a child of mine is on the way!
Let's clap and sing a joyful tune,
hoping the war will end real soon.

We'll fight for our country to win,
and soon be home to see our kin.
Cheer and shout and pray to our God,
'return us safe to our home sod,

seeing wife and babes, mom and dad,
will make our hearts happy and glad.'"

All the men cheered, and Sonny made up a tune to fit the words. Soon they were singing and their hearts momentarily lifted at the revelry.

The next morning at role call, the men were given the news they'd dreaded. "Tomorrow, men, we'll be anchoring off the beach of Guadalcanal and you'll be taken in groups by landing barges."

Chapter Eighteen

*A*llie was working hard on her studies, trying to prepare for the final exams coming up. Needing a break, she stood and stretched her back and gazed out the window at the trees blowing in the cold wind. She'd love to go outside for a walk and breathe in some fresh air. She rubbed her arms and shuddered at the frigid air sneaking around the edges of the window frame and reached for a warm sweater that lay on the bed. The thought of Mexico and the warmer climate sounded rather enticing.

Her thoughts drifted to Carter and where he might be at that moment; what might he be facing? She prayed for him again, but the place he had held in her life seemed so distant now, and she wondered if he would ever be the right mate for her. How long would she be willing to wait? *Should I wait, Lord? And if so, how long?*

Then there was Daniel. Now that his mother was gone, he was clinging more and more to her, and she had to admit he appeared to be the right man to spend her life with. He talked a lot about wanting to go to the mission field, and mentioned Mexico as a definite possibility. They had been friends for the past three years, but in some ways he felt like the brother she'd never had. Would a friendship be enough to take to a marriage? And would a brotherly love eventually turn into a passionate love? *Lord, please give me wisdom, and show me the direction you want for my life.*

Noting the time, she closed the book on her desk and headed down to the cafeteria, knowing Daniel would be patiently waiting for her. She saw his face light up when he noticed her coming toward him.

"Hello, Allie. How's the studying going?"

"It will never feel like enough, even when the test is over and I'm doubting half my answers. How about you?"

"I'm feeling rather good about it. I can help you with any problems, if you'd like to study together in the library." He handed her a tray and took one for himself.

"You know I have a problem studying with someone else. I do better alone." He already knew that, and it rather annoyed her that he kept asking in spite of knowing.

They found a table by a window. He set his tray down and then hers before pulling out her chair for her and, after sitting, asking a blessing over the food.

"Have you made a decision yet about signing up for the mission trip to Mexico after graduation? It would be a good chance to see how you like it before making a longer commitment."

Allie took a bite of her fish and shook her head before answering. "I go back and forth. What about you? Do you plan to go?"

He sliced open his baked potato, slathered butter over it, and looked up at her. "I guess I've been waiting to see what a certain young woman decides to do. I'd rather go with a friend in the group, than with comparative strangers."

His waiting for her to make a decision first was rather aggravating to her too. She laid her fork down. "Daniel, that decision should be between you and the Lord, and have nothing to do with me and what I decide."

He reached across the table and took her hand in his. "Allie, you must know by now that I have strong feelings for you. With Carter out of the picture, I'd hoped you would soon care for me and, hopefully, we could go to the mission field as a couple."

Allie jerked her hand from his. "What makes you so sure Carter is out of the picture?"

She regretted the sharp words when she noted the pain crossing his face. "Daniel, I'm sorry. I didn't say that to belittle your feelings, but I cared a lot for Carter, and he for me; those kind of emotions don't just go away over night."

"I realize that, Allie, but how long do you plan to wait for him to come home a changed man who wants to serve the Lord in the same way you do?"

"I keep asking the Lord what He wants for me, but it all feels so confusing, like He's not even listening. Am I to just step out and make the decision on my own? If so, I'm not sure what I would decide. I'm also sorry if that's not the answer you want to hear right now."

He stood and picked up his tray. "I'm not hungry any more. I'm going to my room and pray. I'll make a decision tonight regarding the trip to Mexico, but I won't tell you my decision until you make yours. We'll see where we stand then. Good night, Allie. Sleep well."

She looked down at her food and found her appetite had fled as well. One thing she was sure of—she definitely wouldn't sleep well that night.

Chapter Nineteen

*E*mma wrote a letter to Carter every day, hoping that wherever he ended up, the mail would one day catch up to him and give him encouragement.

She wondered how Allie could have walked away from a man like him. She was sure Daniel couldn't begin to compare with Carter. *Lord, will Carter and I ever meet up again?*

She realized Christmas was only weeks away. She would go into Honolulu tomorrow—her day off—and find some useful gifts to send to Carter. It would make her feel closer just shopping for him.

It was amazing how someone you knew so briefly could make such an impression on your heart and mind.

And now Tony, better known as Dr. Anthony Delasko, was writing her again, begging her forgiveness for his anger when she joined the service as a nurse. He wrote:

> *I still think we make a great combination—me a surgeon and you my nurse. But I know the war won't go on forever, and I have a deep fear that you might meet someone and never come back to Minnesota. Please don't forget me, my darling Emma, and write to me often.*

All my love,
Tony

She had mixed feelings about his attempt to rekindle their love, but she knew she no longer had the strong feelings for him that she once had. For her there was no future in the relationship.

She took a bus up to the North Shore with Sandra the next day. Sandra went sunbathing, but Emma was restless and needed to walk. The loud crashing of the huge waves suited her mood well. *Why, Lord? Why do there have to be endless wars—country fighting country and men fighting men? Why can't the world bask in continual peace and love, or at a minimum acceptance of the ways of others?*

She knew all about the fact that God had created man and woman with a free will and they had disobeyed Him and sinned by eating fruit from the one tree He had forbidden. That act of disobedience brought sin into the life of each person born into the world, except for Jesus who came as God-man and lived a sinless life. He later gave His life as the only pure sacrifice for the sin of mankind to all who would accept the free gift of salvation.

But sometimes she wondered if Adam and Eve hadn't sinned, would life on earth have continued in a perfect manner? Or how long might it have taken for someone else to come along and sin, introducing evil into the world anyway? Would it have been Cain instead, who murdered his brother Abel due to jealousy? It appeared mankind couldn't put all the blame on Adam and Eve. Of course Lucifer—who wanted to become like God—had a huge hand in tricking Eve into taking the fruit first and giving it to Adam. It was all so confusing to think about.

How Emma longed for the day when believers would live forever with Jesus in a world of total peace and love. Meanwhile, as a human on earth, she couldn't help but yearn for a time in the future when she and Carter might end up together, serving the Lord wherever He wanted to send them. However, in her heart, she knew that dream was about as far-fetched as man one day flying to the moon.

Chapter Twenty

Carter and his close buddies stood on the deck with their unit, guns and belongings at the ready to be transferred along with them to the smaller craft that could make it to the shoreline of Guadalcanal. *Why, Lord, after all our praying, do we have to end up on Guadalcanal, one of the worst areas for combat and disease?* And in his heart he felt that God might be answering, *Why not you? I promised to always be with you and not to forsake you.*

He felt a hand on his shoulder. "You okay, buddy?" It was Shakespeare, always calm and caring about others.

He smiled shakily at his friend. "I imagine I'm not any worse off than anyone else on this ship. How about you?"

"My God is right beside me. That's all I need to know. I'm concerned about Ryan, though. I've heard him crying in the night. Have you seen him this morning?"

Carter shook his head. "I know what you mean about concern for him. He seems so small and young, it makes you want to protect him as much as possible."

Shakespeare looked around again. "I think our group is gathered next to get into the barge. I wish Ryan were with us."

Carter picked up his rifle and bag and felt a tug on his sleeve. He turned around to look down at Ryan's frightened face staring up at him. "I think I'm in with you and Shakespeare, Carter. I hope I don't drop my rifle in the water when I'm climbing over."

Carter's fear dissipated with the desire to help calm the small man. "How about I go down before you, Ryan, and Shakespeare will come after you. That way we can lend you a hand if you get into trouble."

"Thank you both. I'm sorry I'm such a baby."

Shakespeare moved behind him. "Every man here is shaking in his shoes, Ryan, so don't feel bad. We'll be watching your back, along with God. Just keep praying."

Soon Sergeant Hummer barked out, "Next in line, move up fast and over the side!"

Carter hurriedly went to the side of the ship and—with rifle on one shoulder and duffel bag on the other—he climbed over and down the rope ladder. Glancing up, he saw Ryan having trouble getting over with his belongings. Shakespeare was quickly there to adjust them so Ryan could move over the side before the sergeant could notice.

Carter was soon in the barge and took Ryan's bag as he stepped on. They both moved over to make room for Shakespeare and the few others who would fill the landing craft that would take them to the beach.

From the distance, the shore looked like the ones he'd walked on in Hawaii, but the sounds of gunfire and explosives coming from the jungle beyond told him they were definitely not here for a walk on the beach. The real war was just beginning for him and his group. In his heart he prayed fervently for protection for him and his unit, along with all the men who were already there fighting for their lives.

The soldiers were given orders to shoulder their gear and disembark into the thigh-deep water a short distance from the beach. Carter and Shakespeare helped Ryan as much as they could while struggling with their own gear and trying to keep it out of the water. As each man hit the beach they hurriedly headed for the high grass and trees at the edge of the sand while glancing in every direction for signs of the enemy. Carter was thankful the gunfire and explosives sounded much away.

They were greeted by a Marine in a jeep who waved them to follow him through the jungle path. Carter glanced back at the long line of soldiers trailing behind as far as he could see. Hopefully everyone had made it safely off the ship and across the beach with Sergeant Hummer bringing up the tail end.

A mile or so later a volley of shots scattered all around them, and everyone hit the ground as they had been taught, bringing up their rifles and cocking them. Carter peered in all directions trying to spot the enemy. The Marine stopped the Jeep and fired up into a tree. A Japanese soldier fell face down about ten feet away.

"Don't go near him," the Marine warned. "He might not be dead." After leaping to the ground, he scurried in a crouched position to the man, rolled him over and felt for the pulse at his neck. He shook his head and sprang back into the vehicle while Carter heard other shots ringing out back along the line.

"I got one," someone shouted, and another man yelled, "I've been hit!"

Carter wondered which soldier it was, and prayed he wasn't badly injured. The battle went on for an hour or more. Carter fired at another man in a tree who fell to the ground. It sickened him to think his bullet might have been the one to end the life, though several shots from others had been fired at the same time.

Ryan crawled up close to him. "Are we going to die already?" he whispered.

"Only the good Lord knows, Ryan, so just keep talking to him."

When the shooting hit a lull, the Marine stood and motioned for them to follow him. The jeep chugged to life, ending the silence as the men grappled mentally with their first encounter of the realities of war and death.

It was a silent troop that trudged seemingly endless miles until canvas tents and a few roughly constructed buildings were sighted ahead. Shirtless men in shorts came running to greet the soldiers with cheers.

"We're so glad to see you fellas!" A tall, thin man shouted. He rushed up to Carter. "Where you from, soldier?"

Carter, still in shock, answered tiredly. "Illinois. Where you from?"

The man kept smiling and slapped him on the back. "Right next door to you, buddy. I'm from Indiana." He moved on to Shakespeare, and the other Marines infiltrated through the new men shaking hands and exchanging news and greetings.

A large heavy-set man came up to Ryan and lifted him up over his head. "Ain't you a little fella! You sure you're old enough to be enlisted?" He laughed and set a red-faced Ryan back down while the others in the area laughed.

"Don't you pay no attention to him, young man," another Marine said. He likes to tease, but he's a good one to watch your back."

Soon Sergeant Hummer made his way through the crowd giving orders to his men. "Let's get the tents up and gear stowed, men. Those in charge of chow can get things set up for mess."

The Marine colonel in charge came over. "Thanks for the new provisions you brought, Sergeant. The rations here have been getting rather slim. Half of these men will be leaving in a few days—the ones who've been here from the start. They've fought hard, and we've lost quite a few. You'll likely run across the cemetery where the dead who couldn't be transported home have been buried."

The Sergeant called over Carter and Sonny who had been waiting for their orders. "These are my radio men: Carter Benton and Sonny Hawkins. If you could have someone show them where to set up the extra equipment they brought along, your radioman can be relieved after he catches them up on his setup."

The Colonel pointed them to the building where they would find the man in charge. "Carl Dorman's his name. Drop off your radio equipment and introduce yourselves, then take the time to set up your tent and stow your belongings before you take over."

Carter and Sonny headed for the wooden building the Colonel had pointed out. "What do you think of our new digs?" Sonny asked.

Carter glanced all around. "You mean the steamy terrain, or the building where we'll spend a lot of our time on the radio and forwarding messages? At least we might be a little safer when we're inside unless a bomb is dropped on us."

"I doubt anyone's safe anywhere around here. Did you see how many men are wounded in sickbay, or skeletal from malaria or diarrhea, and waiting either to be transferred to a hospital or die?"

Carter stared straight ahead. "Yeah, I tried not to look too close; I can't help but wonder which ones from our group will be joining them."

They heard the static from the radio first before entering the open door. "You must be Carl Dorman," Carter said.

"In person," the man at the desk responded. He had a round face and short curly light brown hair. "I'm sure glad to see you gents!" He stood and came around to shake their hands, standing about the same height as Sonny. "You can put your equipment over on that table while you get your tent up and your other belongings stowed away. Then I'll show you the ropes before I take a break. You boys seen any fighting yet?"

Sonny shook his head. "Nah, just the little action coming here from the boats. We're fresh from the states by way of Hawaii. How long have you been here?"

"Too long by any time frame. I started out in France, which was a darn sight better than this hole. Then our Marine Corp was the first group sent here to try to get rid of the Japs and take over the airfield. Fortunately for you guys, this job's a little safer than hacking your way through the jungle and watching for enemies in the trees. Though I have to say, I've brought down a few of my own when I've been off duty. Don't ever feel safe enough to stop looking at every bush and up every tree, and always keep a weapon of some kind on you."

"Thanks for your advice," Carter said. "We'll be back shortly so you can have your break."

Both men were silent as they sought a space to put their tent. They set up close to Shakespeare and Ryan on one side, and Arnie, Johnny and Randy on the other. Carter prayed they would all survive their time on the island.

Chapter Twenty-One

*A*llie was glad her finals and graduation were over. Her parents had come for the ceremony, and she was signed up for the mission trip to Mexico the middle of January.

Daniel had signed up for it too and was coming to her home to spend the holidays. She wasn't sure how she felt about it. Her parents had met him several times before at her college, and again at the graduation ceremony.

"Are you having Christmas with your sister and her family?" Her mother had asked him.

"No, they're going to spend two weeks with Arthur's family over the holidays. I'll be staying at my apartment."

Her mother had looked over at Allie before extending the invitation. "Why don't you spend the holidays with us? What do you think, Allie?"

At that point, what could she have said? "Why yes, Daniel. We wouldn't want to think of you spending the holidays alone."

He was scheduled to arrive two days before Christmas. In the meantime Allie was making cookies and candy to send off to Carter, along with a few small gifts.

Allie picked Daniel up at the train station. So many soldiers and civilians were getting off or loading; she stood on tiptoe trying to locate him among the crowd.

"Allie!" she heard him call from the top step of the train doorway, suitcase in hand. She waved at him—suddenly glad he was there. It would help keep her mind from Carter, wondering where he was. She knew she would be remembering how good their Christmas together last year had been, in spite of the attack on Pearl Harbor on December 7th. Soon after the New Year, he and some of his friends had planned to enlist in the Army, and before long he was off for long periods of training with few home visits between.

Daniel made his way through the horde, smiling the whole way, and hugged her close after setting down his luggage. "So great to see you, Allie. I've been counting the days and hours until the holiday season."

"Good to see you too, Dan. Did your sister and family get safely to Arthur's parents' home?"

They called from there right before I left and wished us both a Merry Christmas. We exchanged gifts the day before, and they sent one along for you, too."

"How nice of them! Now I wish I had thought to send them something, and especially for Thomas and Doris."

"No, no. They appreciated all the help you gave when you went to Mother's funeral with me."

They got to Allie's parents' Ford coupe and he stored his suitcase in the trunk before opening her door on the driver's side.

"Mom will have lunch ready when we get home, and then we'll be sent off to the woods with a saw to find the perfect tree. 'Hopefully perfect' tree," she added with a laugh when he was seated.

He smiled over at her. "Even some spindly little pine would satisfy me. Just being with you is all I need to make it beautiful."

She started the car to hide her flushed face, suddenly feeling a jolt of guilt as she pictured Carter's pain the night she refused his ring. Was he still alive and well? She knew how hurt he would be if he knew Daniel was spending the holidays with her and her family. She only hoped no one would write and tell him after seeing her and Dan together at church.

After lunch they traipsed through the ten inches of snow to the woods, Daniel carrying the saw and humming a Christmas carol. Allie glanced up at him. He was a nice-looking man, taller than Carter, though Carter was more muscular. She resented the way her mother had fawned over Daniel, and wondered if she preferred him instead of Carter—though it was her own choice between Daniel and Carter that would matter in the end.

Not far into the woods, Allie spotted the "perfect" tree she had eyed up the week before when she had taken a walk. "What do you think of that one, Dan?" She pointed over to it. "Is that near-perfect, or what?"

He glanced at the one she meant. "Not as perfect as the lady beside me, but it should make a great Christmas tree, I'd say."

She ran over to it and shook off some of the snow. "Well, I think it will do quite nicely. Let's cut it down and drag it home."

Her father got the tree set up in a bucket and the lights on before supper. A fire in the fireplace gave the room a cozy feel. Then Allie's heart grew sad wondering where and how Carter would be spending his Christmas.

Chapter Twenty-Two

"Mail call!" Carter heard from the doorway of the switchboard building, named the Guadalcanal Telephone and Telegraph. Some of the earlier Marines had jokingly hung a smaller sign over the door that said: USO CLUB. He'd have to pick up his mail later, since he was in charge of the switchboard. Sonny, Carl, and another Marine named Sammy were out hacking their way through high grasses and thick jungle vines trying to locate hiding places of the enemy. Sammy had sent through a message on the field telephone earlier giving a location for some of the men to check out.

Standing shirtless in the steaming heat, Carter didn't know which was worse— staying in the little building trying to get any messages through to the right places and people, or being out on patrol gathering intelligence on the Japanese to forward back. On patrol one had to be constantly on the lookout not only for the Japanese, but also for snakes, spiders, sharp grasses, and mosquitoes larger than any he'd ever seen before. And the downpours! They'd had several days of those that left six or more inches of water through their entire compound to constantly slosh through just in the last week.

Mail had been handed out to those hanging around the area after the lunch mess, and the fortunate ones who'd received mail or packages were reading and sharing any food items from home. Carter realized it was only a few days until Christmas, and his thoughts went to Allie and remembering the great Christmas and New Years they'd celebrated together last year.

He saw Bernie, the "mailman," coming toward him with an armload of packages, letters and a huge smile. "Looks like you got the most mail today, Carter. Lots of cards and letters and three boxes of stuff to keep you from being too homesick on Christmas day."

"Wow, thanks, Bernie. If there's anything good to eat in those boxes,

I'll be sure you get a share."

"I'll hold you to it, buddy. I'll bring the mail over for the other three who are out in the field."

Carter started looking through the cards and letters to see who sent them, but was soon interrupted by static and a message coming over the switchboard. He took the message and passed it on to one of the units. The past week or so had been a jungle nightmare of fierce fighting on the ridges and steep slopes of Mount Austen where supplies had to be man-packed and casualties evacuated back the same way. Carter had picked up a lot of the information from men straggling back for a short rest and new supplies, and also from the infrequent messages received on the switchboard.

The radiomen weren't in on much of the heavy fighting, but there was still danger anywhere you walked. Carter tried not to think of the enemies he'd taken down himself. He hadn't seen Johnny, Arnie or Randy since the hard battle had started in the Mount Austen area, and he prayed constantly for their protection.

Shakespeare and Ryan had been back from a shorter maneuver with a patrol two days ago, but were gone again. Carter was glad Shakespeare had taken Ryan under his wing and prayed they would both stay safe. While they were there Shakespeare had entertained as always with his poems, stories, and songs. The few soldiers and marines in the area joined in on the singing. Who would still be here at Christmas?

That thought took Carter back to his cards and letters, saving Emma's and Allie's for last. A lot of the cards came from folks in his church back home. How he wished he could spend Christmas Eve there for the special service; but most of all he wished he could be having Christmas with Allie and her parents, and his own parents and Joey.

All the wishes in the world couldn't change anything for him right then, so he pulled his mind back to the present. He went next to the letters from his parents and Jesse. Jesse was still considering joining up, but if he were there now Carter would beg him not to do it. He had a wife and a son who needed him right where he was.

He read Emma's card and letters next, and as usual was uplifted by her encouraging words. He leaned back in his chair and remembered their last evening together, holding her close and finally kissing her the one and only time. Would he ever see her again? In so many ways she was much more mature than Allie had been, and easier to talk to. But Allie was his first love, and he so hoped they'd be together as his last and only love.

He opened the two letters and card from her, but the words felt distant and unfeeling. At least she had written in the Christmas card that she kept thinking of the great time they'd had together last year, and wished that he could be there now. Did those words ring real and true? Was there still caring in them, or was he just feeling around in the dark for something that was no longer there?

Christmas Eve dawned amidst yet another drenching downpour. Sonny ran from the mess tent to the switchboard hut wearing a waterproof jacket and carrying two cups of coffee. "Merry Christmas Eve, friend. If only this rain were snow, then we could dig out a huge fortress a lot easier than using sand, rocks and brush."

"Come in and get dry. Just don't stand in the right hand corner. It's dripping again."

"I brought you some coffee made from the container of grounds my stepmom sent me. I thought you might finally open one of your boxes and share something good to go with it."

"I was just planning to open the one my mother sent. We've already eaten and shared around the cookies and candy from my church. I'm saving the ones from Emma and Allie for tomorrow morning."

"Whoa, look at all this!" Carter had ripped open the large box from his home address and pulled out more coffee and his mother's famous fruitcake. The women from the church bought some from her each year, and hers was said to be the best in the county. He cut off a hunk for Sonny and one for himself. "Isn't that the best fruitcake you've ever tasted?" he asked after Sonny had taken a huge bite to see for himself.

"That is so good! For someone who never liked fruitcake before in my life, it's the best thing I've eaten in a long time." Sonny gazed down into the box. "Any chance she has another one stashed away in there?"

Carter laughed. "No more fruitcake, but lots of great cookies and homemade candy. But we'd better share some around with the others still here. Hopefully, Johnny, Arnie, Randy, Shakespeare and Ryan will be back by morning."

Lorena Estep

Shots and grenades still blasted in the distance, but at least there hadn't been much shooting in their general vicinity the last few days. Shakespeare and Ryan dragged in towards evening with their patrol.

Carter went over to greet them since Sonny was in charge of the switchboard. "How are things going out there?"

"The Japanese appear to be well dug in, and the general's trying to come up with a plan to flush them out. We're to rest a bit here until morning, and then go back out with several days supplies and join one of the units to make a stronger push to find where they're hiding."

"How are you holding up, Ryan?"

He grinned. "Growing stronger every day, and getting some shooting in with the others."

Shakespeare put a hand on his shoulder. "And he's doing right well out there in the field. He now watches my back more than I watch his."

"Way to go, soldier," Carter said. "Show them what a tough American looks like.

"But, first, come on over and have some good coffee my mother sent along with great cookies."

"Sounds like Christmas to me," Shakespeare said and smiled with his usual good humor.

Shakespeare prayed for the gathered group before they ate a Christmas Eve meal of canned meat with beans and rice. After the meal he led them in more singing, with the men's requests for Christmas carols like "Silent Night, Holy Night" bringing home thoughts of family and friends back in the states.

The melancholy mood of homesick soldiers and marines could be sensed throughout the evening. The battle noise in the distance wasn't the Christmas background they wished for, but all knew they had a dangerous job to do, whether it was Christmas or not.

Some wonderful baked goods had come for Shakespeare and some of the others, so the men shared treats, sang a few more Christmas songs and Shakespeare closed in prayer before they crawled into their tents for a very short 'long winter's nap,' reminding each of Christmases past.

Chapter Twenty-Three

*I*t was the day after New Years, and Allie had gotten up early after a rather sleepless night. She put on heavy clothes and trudged through the new snow that had fallen overnight. She was very confused, and needed to talk to God where she felt closest to Him, out in nature.

Daniel had proposed to her by the fire last evening after her parents had gone to bed. She certainly hadn't expected it so soon, though she knew he cared for her. He wanted them to get married before going on the mission trip to Mexico. He said the missionaries in charge there now were looking for another couple to join them for at least a year, and if they were married, it would give them time to be sure it was where the Lord wanted them.

So Lord, what do you want for me, and for Daniel? Is he the one I should marry? I still miss Carter a lot, and know I don't care as deeply for Daniel, but will the feelings come later? He's a good man, and I know he loves you and wants to serve you. I need to make a decision, Lord. I guess I want you to spell out the answer in the sky, or something. She looked up at the sun shining through fluffy white clouds. There were no words written there, but was the sun her answer?

She brushed snow off a fallen log and sat down. Maybe the fact that they both planned to go to Mexico should tell her something. Her mother kept throwing out broad hints about what a nice man Daniel was, though her father was rather distant towards him. She sensed he felt she had sent Carter away with a big letdown when he was going off to fight a war for their nation. "Help me, Lord," she spoke softly.

"Allie," she heard Daniel call out, and saw him following her footprints toward her. Her heart sank, not ready to talk to him yet, but she stood up. "Over here, Dan."

He soon joined her, but stopped a short distance away with hands in his pockets. "Did you come up with any answers, Allie?"

"That's why I came out here this morning to talk with the Lord. It's all so soon since I broke the relationship off with Carter. Marriage is a forever thing, and I don't want to make a mistake."

"We've known each other the last several years, and though you were hooked on Carter, I've always had deep feelings for you. I think your mother would approve. She told me she feels much safer knowing I'd be along on the trip to Mexico."

"My parents will trust whatever decision I make, Daniel. Right now let's just go in. I'm sure Mom has breakfast going."

"Yes, she was frying sausage when I came out, and I passed your dad leaving the barn with a large bucket of milk." He removed his hands from his pockets and reached out one to her.

Allie hesitated a moment before placing a hand in his and moving toward the house.

He stopped her and looked into her eyes as though searching there for an answer. "If you're so unsure, Allie, we can put it off until after the shorter trip with the group."

"It was just so sudden. Give me a little more time."

"Whatever time you need. I think I should go home this afternoon to give you space to talk to the Lord and make your decision. If you decide to marry me before we leave, we could have a small wedding in your church. I like the folks I met there at the services."

"Allie and Daniel, breakfast is ready," Allie's mother called from the kitchen door.

"Coming, Mom." She turned from Dan and they moved toward the house.

"I'll drive you to the train station after lunch and let you know soon what I decide," she said before entering the kitchen.

They played some games of checkers between breakfast and lunch. He packed while she did the lunch dishes, and they were soon on their way to the train station.

It was a quiet ride. Allie could sense his disappointment, but it took her back to the night she refused Carter's ring and how his pain had ripped through her. It still hurt her deeply. Would she ever forget her first love?

She glanced over at Dan as he stared out the side window. He was handsome even in his sadness. Would he make a good father? She thought back to their time at his brother's home when they were there for his mother's funeral. She didn't remember him interacting much with Thomas and Doris.

Carter, on the other hand, loved being around the little ones at church, and he carried Jesse's son Nathan around much of the time they were together, making him giggle over so many things. She saw great father potential in him.

But would he ever come back from the war? And if so, would he want to serve the Lord?

After pulling into a parking space at the station, she got out and opened the trunk. Dan set his suitcase down and took Allie into his arms. "Thank you so much for sharing the holidays with me. It meant a lot with Mother being gone. I'll miss you every minute until I see you again, Allie." He leaned over and kissed her lips gently.

It was only the second time he'd kissed her, the first being New Years Eve. It was much different from Carter's embrace, less passionate. If she married Dan, would she always be comparing him to Carter? It was something she would have to consider seriously before making her decision.

Stepping back, she said, "I'll call soon. We'll make whatever plans we need to based on my decision."

He nodded. "You know the answer I'll be praying for. Take care, Allie. Thanks again for everything." He hugged her, picked up his suitcase and walked away.

Supper was ready when Allie returned home in a somber mood. Her father asked the blessing, and she put small amounts on her plate, eating slowly.

"If you're sad over Daniel leaving, Allie, you'll see him soon for the mission trip to Mexico," her mother said.

Allie put down her fork and folded her hands in her lap. "It's more than that. Dan asked me to marry him on New Years, and I'm so confused as to whether my feelings for him are strong enough for marriage. I still care for Carter, but I felt he didn't want to serve the Lord the way I was being led to serve, and Dan does. He and I have been friends all through school, even before I had cared deeply for Carter. I'm just not sure I want to accept his ring and marry him before we leave for Mexico."

Her mother looked shocked. "You mean like marry him in the next ten days before you go away?"

Allie nodded. "Yes, that's what he wants. The mission is looking for a couple to stay on for at least a year, and he feels it would be a chance for us to see if it's really where we want to serve."

"But Allie, we know how much you cared for Carter, and he's only been gone a couple of months. It's hard for me to believe you could switch those strong feelings so quickly," her father said.

"But Daniel's a good man too, Henry. He and Allie have known each other for some time. Maybe she cared more for him than she realized. Carter's been gone a lot over the past year for training," her mother defended.

"Well, Allie, it's a decision only you can make," her father added. "Your mother and I love you, and will stand by whatever you decide."

"Yes, dear," even if we have to plan a wedding in a week." Her mother reached over and hugged her.

When Allie got up the next morning, she had made her decision after a night of tossing and turning. When she and her parents were seated at breakfast she made her announcement. "Mom and Dad, I've decided to marry Daniel."

She waited for a response.

Are you sure that's what you want, Allie?" her father asked, laying down his fork.

She nodded. "Yes. I prayed and thought most of the night. I care a lot for him, and we both appear to have the same desires in serving the Lord."

Her mother reached for her hand. "Honey, then we're here for you. Let's finish breakfast and start making plans. There's a lot to do!"

Allie grinned. "First I'd better call Daniel and let him know. Maybe he's changed his mind by now."

Her mother smiled. "We doubt that, dear, after seeing how much he cares for you.

The wedding was put together in ten days time. Allie wore the white dress she'd bought for her graduation, and her mother got her a white hat with a short veil. The service was held in the church sanctuary on a Saturday afternoon with a reception following in the church hall. The Prestons supplied the refreshments and the cake.

Most of the church members attended except for the Bentons, which made Allie feel sad. She had grown close to them while dating Carter, but she understood they probably felt betrayed by her actions. Most of the guests who came gave gifts of money. Daniel's brother and sister-in-law stood for them and drove them to Daniel's apartment afterward where they spent the next few days as a short honeymoon.

Daniel stored his belongings in Arthur's garage and gave up the lease on the apartment; the next day they took the train to meet the mission group. It had all happened so fast!

Through it all, Allie continually pushed thoughts of Carter out of her mind, knowing any chance for them to be together was now gone forever.

Chapter Twenty-Four

*T*oward the end of January the combined Army Marine Division were preparing for a final push to move the Japanese from Guadalcanal. Carter and Sonny had just returned from making a scouting mission and had found more Japanese hidden in another area. They reported the information to the leader of the patrol Shakespeare and Ryan were with. That evening they ate a meal with their friends who would be leaving early in the morning to root out the reported enemy.

Mail Call was soon after, and Carter was thrilled with his handful of letters. The folks at home would never know how important reaching out was to the morale of the men risking their lives every day for their country. He felt blessed.

He opened the one from his mother first and all his good feelings were blown apart:

Dear Carter,

I'm afraid we have bad news for you, Dear. Yesterday Alice Preston married her friend Daniel Martin from Moody Bible Institute, and they're leaving for a mission trip to Mexico. We were so disappointed on your behalf that we didn't go to the wedding, though everyone in church was invited. I'm so sorry to have to tell you this, but I didn't want you to hear it from someone else.

Carter stopped reading, dropped the letter along with the rest of his mail and ran off into the jungle.

"Carter!" Sonny called out, and stooped to pick up the opened letter and the mail. He read the letter quickly, handed it to Shakespeare and ran after Carter.

Shakespeare glanced over it and soon followed. He came upon the two men by a small stream where Carter was sitting on a log, shoulders shaking and sobs coming from his throat. Sonny had an arm around him, trying to give him comfort. Shakespeare sat on the other side of Carter and began to pray. "Our Lord God, we live on earth as mortal men, trying to make sense of the pain we so often have to endure, often a result of others' actions. Carter has loved this woman deeply and had great hopes of being with her when this war is over. Now she has gone to another. Please ease his pain in some way, and let him feel your presence and love. Help us remember that our final hope of unending joy as believers is looking forward to spending eternity in your presence when our time on earth is done. Amen." He put an arm around Carter and sat silently along with Sonny.

Soon the three men stood and headed back to camp where Carter burned the unfinished letter from his mother and the unopened one from Allie. He was sure she had written an apology for her decision, but he had no desire to read it. If any of the other letters mentioned it, he burned them too. He felt a hardness growing inside him, and knew he could now face the enemy with no fear of dying or killing. His reason for living had been Allie, and now that reason was no more.

The four letters from Emma consoled him somewhat, but he felt he would never be whole again.

Several days later Carter and Sonny went back into the area where they'd seen Japanese troops to see how the patrol was making out. As they drew closer, the sounds of battle grew louder. Rifles at the ready, they stealthily moved forward, concerned for Ryan and Shakespeare. Bullets whipped over their heads, breaking limbs in the trees behind them. They hit the ground, crawling toward some of their men ahead.

Arnie crept up to their side, blood showing through a tear in his shirt. "You seen Johnny or Randy back at the camp?" he asked.

"Not recently," Sonny said. "What happened to your arm?"

"A bullet grazed me; nothin' serious. Johnny was hit in the right shoulder, and I think the bone was broken. It just kind of hung there. Randy was trying to help him get back to camp for the medics to check him out. I passed Shakespeare and Ryan a few minutes ago down yonder." He nodded to the right.

"Thanks," Carter said. "Watch your arm doesn't get infected in this humidity." We're going to check on the others to send back a report."

"I'll watch yer backs. Just keep low."

The gunfire was slowing down, which they hoped was a good sign. They began to see more dead Japanese and checked each one for signs of life.

Two Marines and a soldier from their own division were lying face down, and when Sonny felt for pulses, he shook his head at Carter. They would report to the medics when they got back.

Up ahead they spotted Shakespeare and Ryan in a foxhole and crawled towards them. Shakespeare stood and fired towards a tree across a ravine. Another shot rang out and Shakespeare crumpled over.

"No!" Carter yelled and ran past him firing continuous rounds from his automatic rifle. He saw several of the enemy falling down into the ravine before he felt searing pain in his left side and then his right leg. He kept moving until he was out of ammunition and was tackled to the ground by Sonny.

"Carter, stop! You're wounded, and so is Shakespeare. We have to get both of you back to the medics before you bleed to death."

Carter looked up at him with glassy eyes. "Take Shakespeare back, but just let me die."

"Don't say that! You have to fight to make it. Think of your parents and brother."

Carter struggled to get up, but his leg wouldn't cooperate. Sonny put an arm under his right shoulder and drug him over toward Shakespeare and Ryan. Ryan had taken some heavy bandages from his pack and attempted to stop the bleeding in Shakespeare's chest.

Arnie soon ran to them in a crouch and took bandages from his pack for Carter's side and leg. "If you can deal with carrying Shakespeare, Sonny, I'll help Carter along. Ryan, how about you grab the equipment."

The men managed to escape the worst of the fighting without anyone else getting hit, and get the injured back to camp and to the medic tent.

"Work on Shakespeare first, please. He got hit the hardest," Carter said, slurring his words.

"Bill is checking him out. I've got to work on your side. It's torn up some, so it's gonna hurt a bit."

"Already feels like it's on fire, so go to it." Seconds later he heard and felt no more.

Carter woke in the middle of the night with pain and chills racking his body and groaned aloud.

A medic was soon by his side. "You need something, soldier?"

"I'm hot and freezing all at the same time."

"Your face and forehead feel like their burning up. We're low on medical supplies, so right now, I can only give you some aspirin and water."

"How's Shakespeare doing?"

"Not so well. We've been notified that a plane will be landing on Henderson Field tomorrow to take five of you out to a hospital. We've immobilized your leg as best we can for you to make the trip. Try to get a little sleep until then."

"Do you know where they're taking us?"

"No, sir, I don't. Sorry, but any hospital should be a lot better than here."

Carter dozed off and on throughout the night, gritting his teeth against the pain in his side and leg, and praying for Shakespeare to make it so he could get home to see his wife, and be there for the birth of their baby. *At this point,* Carter thought, *I would definitely give my life for Shakespeare to live, if the Lord worked that way. But the Lord seems to have His own plans and we're supposed to trust that whatever they are, they'll work out for our best in the long run.*

The last time he had slept he'd dreamed first of Allie in a wedding dress, and then of Emma on the beach with him in Hawaii. He didn't believe they'd be fortunate enough to be taken back to the medical unit at Schofield, but guessed the Lord would have them taken where he felt they should be.

Chapter Twenty-Five

"Sandra did you get the latest report that we'll be getting in five wounded from Guadalcanal?" Emma asked.

"Yes, I heard that. We're to get beds ready in the same room so the men can be near each other. You don't think any of our guys are with them, do you?"

"We won't know until they arrive, but I have an inner fear that at least one might be. I keep praying that whoever they are, it won't be fatal. Let's take the time to find the best spot for them and make up the beds."

Emma and Sandra found a room with eight beds and only three occupied. They checked the three men, refilled their water, and straightened the blankets before making up the remaining five beds with fresh bedding.

One of the Army doctors stepped into the room. "Here are the names of the men they're bringing in. The plane just landed, so they'll be here shortly. They'll all need immediate attention, but we'll take the worst injuries first." He handed the list to Emma.

She glanced over the names quickly, and when she saw Carter's information, her face paled.

"What is it, Emma?"

"It's Carter, wounded in his left side and right leg. Oh no! And Shakespeare too! He was hit in the chest and is in critical condition."

Sandra looked at the list in Emma's hand. "Sonny's name isn't here. I'm assuming that means he's still okay."

Emma nodded. "Two of the names I don't recognize, but Johnny's on the list with a broken arm."

"I'll let Catherine know about him," Sandra said.

Soon they heard the ambulance coming in and ran to show them where to put the men. They brought Shakespeare in first, pale and unconscious.

"This man needs immediate surgery if he's to make it through the day and night," the medic said.

"Follow me," Sandra told them.

Emma returned to the ambulance to see if the other soldier was Carter. It was, and she crawled in beside him. "Oh, Carter, I've been praying for your safety and longing to see you, but not this way."

His eyes were closed, and he mumbled deliriously. She felt his forehead, and he was burning with fever. He apparently had infection.

He opened glassy eyes at her touch. "Allie, is that you?"

She wanted to weep at his words, but what did she expect? Of course he would still be in love with Allie, and think she was with him in his physical state. Most likely he barely remembered the times he'd spent with Emma in Hawaii, even with the letters she'd written to him.

"Where am I?" He reached up to grip her hand.

"You're at the medical center in Schofield, Hawaii."

"Thank you, Lord." And he was out again.

The medics came out for him. "We need to take him in now, nurse, so we can go back for the other three men."

She led them inside to the bed she'd chosen in case he would be one of the wounded men coming in. When they moved him from the stretcher, he groaned in pain. The medics left, and she got a basin of cool water to sponge him. Blood seeped through the bandages around his waist. Her heart ached for this man she cared for so much, and who was in love with another woman instead.

The ambulance soon returned with the other three men. Johnny dragged in on his own, and she got him clean white hospital clothing to put on. She was glad when Catherine showed up and took over with getting Johnny settled in.

Emma talked to the other two as she got them situated one at a time, trying to keep her eyes from constantly roaming to Carter, praying for him and Shakespeare.

Hours later, Sandra came in. "They're bringing Shakespeare in shortly, and then plan to take Carter to surgery next. How's he doing?"

"He's feverish and pretty much delirious. I've been sponging him off and on, and getting him to take sips of water. What about Shakespeare?"

Sandra shook her head. "It's not good. There was some damage to his heart and lungs, and the doctor did what he could with the equipment we have, but he didn't give much hope.

"Do you want to assist with Carter's surgery? If you do, I'll work in here with Catherine, and watch over Shakespeare while you're gone."

"If you don't mind. I'd rather know firsthand just what Carter's injuries are."

Two medics brought Shakespeare in just then, and they moved him as carefully as possible to the bed beside Carter. All Emma could think about was the day she, Carter, and Shakespeare walked together on Waikiki Beach and talked about the writing that Shakespeare was doing. Now his wife was expecting their first child, and would he even live to see the baby born?

Emma walked beside Carter's gurney as he was wheeled into the operating room. She prayed as she handed surgical instruments to the doctor and tried not to cringe with each cut he made into Carter's flesh. This had to be the hardest surgery she'd assisted with in the years since she'd started her nursing career. There was a lot of torn flesh and infection in his side wound, but finally the doctor finished with that area and moved to Carter's leg.

There was shattered bone in the femur. "Well, I think this young man will walk with a limp the rest of his life," the doctor said. "I'll do the best I can with what we have to work with."

Emma felt tears streaming down her face and tried to wipe them with the shoulders of her uniform.

The doctor paused and looked over at her. "Do you know this man, Emma?"

She nodded.

"If he's special to you, you should have had another nurse helping me instead."

"I needed to know the extent of his injuries."

"When he's healed enough, he'll be getting a discharge, I can tell you that. I'm afraid the man I worked on before him won't be so fortunate. Did you know him?"

She nodded again. "Yes, and he's special too. He was married six months before joining up, and he had a letter recently saying that his wife is expecting a baby."

The doctor shook his head. "How sad. I wish I could perform miracles for these men that are moved through here in bad shape. At least this man will walk again, even if it is with a limp." He returned to working on Carter's leg with renewed energy.

With Carter back in bed, his leg strapped securely to forms and wrapped, Emma worked back and forth between him and Shakespeare, praying constantly for both of them. *Please Lord, heal Shakespeare so he can return to his wife and baby. And heal Carter's side and leg that he will be able to walk without pain and a limp.*

Both men were still in a deep sleep—Carter breathing deeply, but Shakespeare inhaling shallowly and erratically, and gurgling on the exhale.

Emma brought in an army cot and placed it between the two men so she could hear the slightest sound of a problem in the night. When the night nurses came on duty, Sandra brought Emma food, knowing she wouldn't want to leave her patients for any length of time.

Chapter Twenty-Six

*E*mma woke each time Carter groaned or Shakespeare gasped in the night. When the first light of day showed through the window above her cot, she hurriedly went to the restroom to wash and run a comb through her hair, wanting to be ready to work with the men as soon as possible.

The two night nurses checked the other six patients and waved at Emma before leaving the room. Sandra and Catherine came in bringing her a sandwich and hot coffee.

"Thanks so much. I sure need the caffeine to help me stay awake."

"Was it a rough night?" Sandra asked.

"They both slept, but I woke up each time one of them made any sound."

Sandra moved over to check out Shakespeare's breathing and heart rate. "No change either way. He must have a strong constitution."

"He certainly has a deep trust in his maker, I know that for sure."

"Well, I see Catherine's getting Johnny washed up and ready for breakfast. I'd better get busy helping with the other men too."

"As soon as I finish my sandwich, I'll help out, if these two aren't awake yet." Emma hurriedly ate, then helped with two of the others before she heard Carter's voice.

"Where am I?"

Moving quickly to his side, she took his hand. "You're at Schofield, Carter. I'm Emma. Do you remember me?"

He looked up at her and squinted his eyes. "How could I forget a lovely woman like you? Are you sure I'm not in heaven?"

She heard the other two women chuckle, and smiled. "No, you made it through being wounded, getting an infection, having surgery, and are now tucked safely in a hospital bed."

He sat up halfway, moaned, and laid back again. "Guess I'm not quite ready for that yet. Wait a minute. What about Shakespeare? He was hit before I was. When he fell, I remember running past him and emptying my ammunition at the ones who got him. Is he okay?"

She nodded over to the bed beside him. "He was brought in with you, and the first one the doctor worked on."

He turned to look over to the bed. "Why isn't he awake? And why is he making those strange noises each time he breathes." His voice became anxious and louder. "Where's the doctor? Why can't they do more to help him breathe better?"

Emma touched his shoulder gently and tried to help him relax. "The doctor will be in shortly to check him over again, Carter. Try to stay calm to help keep your friend calm."

He rolled his head back onto the pillow and put a hand over his face. "He can't die, Emma. He has a wife back in Alabama due to have a baby soon. She'll need him to be there for both of them. 'Dear Lord, if one of us has to go, let it be me, not Shakespeare. He has so much to offer to others for you.' " And he began to weep.

Emma grasped his other hand tightly. "Carter, you have a lot to offer for the Lord too. It's God's choice which ones he takes to heaven and which ones he leaves behind, not yours."

He pushed her hand away. "But I have no reason to live anymore, and Shakespeare does."

"Hey, buddy." The words came in gasps from Shakespeare. "I…believe…God…has…already…chosen."

Carter sat up straight. "You're awake! Thank the Lord! We gotta get you home to your wife again."

Emma gasped when she saw blood ooze through the bandage on Carter's side, but knew he would fight her off if she tried to get him to lie back down. Sandra and Catherine came to stand by her. "I'm going for the doctor," Catherine said, and rushed out.

"I'm…counting…on you…going…for me…Carter. Take all…my writings…to Marietta."

Just then the doctor came into the room with Catherine right behind him. "What's going on in here, men? Being upset won't help either one of you heal." He went to Carter first. "Soldier, lay back down. Your side is bleeding and I need to check it and get it re-bandaged."

"But doctor, he's the one who needs help. He has a wife at home who's due to have a baby soon." But he went back onto his pillow and closed his eyes while the doctor cut off the bandage.

"If you don't take it easy for several days to let the wounds heal, you might be here a lot longer than you want."

Carter opened his eyes. "What's wrong with my friend? Will he make it? He has a lot of reasons to live, and I don't."

The doctor finished the new bandage before speaking. "I can only do my part to help each soldier who comes through here, with the tools I have. Your friend Shakespeare's in God's hands now. I suggest you pray for your friend, and talk softly to him so he stays calm."

While the doctor checked on Shakespeare again, Carter prayed hard. He couldn't believe God would take someone like Shakespeare to heaven now when he had such talent and love for the Lord. Look how many he had encouraged each step of the way from the day they met at Fort Lawton until two days ago when they were wounded. *I would gladly give my life for his, Lord, if you only worked that way. Please heal him, take me instead.*

When the doctor stepped away from Shakespeare, Carter saw him shake his head at the nurses. Carter knew he wasn't giving much hope, but he refused to believe it, he needed something to hold onto.

Chapter Twenty-Seven

Allie and Daniel had been settled in their room at the Mexico Mission for a month. They had also signed up to stay on with the missionary couple, David and Joyce White from Ohio, who had been in charge of the mission for ten years. The remainder of the group who had come with them had gone home that morning.

Allie didn't want to regret the decision to stay since being a missionary had been uppermost in her mind through most of her last year of school. The problem was, every decision she'd made in the past couple months had felt like the wrong ones, from the moment she walked down the aisle of her church to marry Daniel. Her heart kept telling her it should be Carter standing up there waiting for her. But she had gone ahead, despite her misgivings, and made her vow before God to stay with Daniel for better or worse, richer or poorer, until death do them part. And she meant to keep those vows forever.

She hadn't known Daniel as well as she had thought in the time they'd been friends at Moody Bible College. He was certainly more particular and precise about everything he did than she realized. If she placed one piece of clothing on the bed or dresser, he either gave her a look and hung it on the hangers along the wall, or she'd have to rush to do it herself before he did.

His eating was another pet peeve that bothered her. He'd never said he didn't like Mexican food, so when he looked disgruntled about eating it, she'd asked him what kind of food he had expected to eat in Mexico. "Half the people who work here aren't Mexican, so I assumed the food selections would be more varied," he'd said.

Then she'd remembered his many complaints about the food they had eaten in the cafeteria at college, and realized the hints had been there all along; she just hadn't paid enough attention.

At least they would be moving to a larger room with a closet since the others had gone, and they'd be next door to the shower and washroom. She thought how the others had appreciated his concise sense of organization and reminded herself to appreciate his good points instead of dwelling on the traits that bothered her.

"I've cleaned our new room really well, Allie, so we can move our belongings over now," Daniel said when he walked in.

She decided to begin appreciating him right then, and walked over to give him a hug. "Thank you, Dan. I had planned to clean it shortly. You're always several steps ahead of me." She stood on tiptoe and kissed his cheek.

He smiled and pulled her close, kissing her lips. "It was worth it to have this response. Let's get everything moved now so we'll be done before dinner. I discovered they're having roast pork and yams tonight, so that should be a step up in our menu."

She stepped back and walked quickly to the bottom dresser drawer that housed her folded clothing, trying not to focus on the food issues she'd just been bothered by, again.

"The other dresser is larger, Allie, so you'll have a little more room to place your folded items more neatly."

At those words, she grabbed a huge armful and paraded down the hall to the other room, tempted to just throw them all into her bottom drawer helter-skelter. She instead plopped them onto the bed and returned for another load, passing him in the hallway. He, of course, was carrying his slacks in front of him all neatly folded and ready to place into his middle drawer. His perfectly folded shirts would go into his top drawer with underwear and nightwear. The socks would come last and go into the middle drawer with the slacks and be perfectly mated and folded over by color. *Lord, here I go again, picking out his good traits that shouldn't be annoying to me. In fact, I should try to be more organized like him instead. Help me, Lord, to be a better wife.*

The dinner bell rang just as everything had been moved and in place exactly where each thing belonged. Allie looked around and had to admit that the places she had shared with Dan since their marriage had all been much neater than her room at the farm had been.

A Bridge to Somewhere

Two weeks later Allie realized she and Dan had fallen into a routine that kept them each busy in different jobs. She helped with the children in the orphanage, playing games and teaching some in each grade level. While the younger ones napped in the afternoon, she taught classes to the older girls and the homeless women who lived there in dorms. The women did chores like cleaning, laundry and cooking in exchange for a safe place to rest their heads.

Dan had found a joy in planting vegetable gardens, and even some flower seeds he'd decided to try. He was also good at keeping the old station wagon running, and it was always clean, of course. He worked mostly with David and the men who lived in another dorm and helped around the mission with outside work and the gardens. Dan and David both taught lessons to the older boys when chores were finished, and took turns speaking at the Sunday services and also Wednesday evenings. More folks came for those meetings from the surrounding towns.

Dan and Allie both enjoyed the weekly trips into one of the towns for supplies. He chose more of the foods that appealed to him, and since those who lived at the mission were satisfied with any food they were served, Dan was much happier with the meals.

Allie was beginning to feel more satisfied with her life as it was now, but often wondered where Carter was and if he was still alive. She received frequent letters from her parents, but they never mentioned anything about him, and she didn't want to ask when she wrote back.

Toward the end of March, she began to feel ill. She wondered if it had anything to do with something she had eaten, but didn't want to mention it to Dan since he always seemed to be so healthy and well. She also didn't want to mention it to Joyce who would likely try to get her to rest more, and Allie knew her help was much needed. Hopefully, whatever problem she was having, it would soon go away.

A week later she felt even worse and just wanted to sleep all day. Her appetite was gone, and in the mirror on the dresser her wan face looked back at her. She tried pinching her cheeks to bring color to them. Dan had been up early and gone to work outside after breakfast. Allie donned the first dress she saw hanging in the closet, brushed her hair, and headed out to the kitchen to try a piece of toasted bread and a cup of tea. She joined Joyce at a corner table.

"Allie, are you feeling all right? I've been noticing the last few days that you don't appear to be well."

"I don't know, Joyce. I've lost my appetite, and I've been feeling rather ill most of the time. I thought it may have been something I ate, but I can't think what. I didn't want to mention it to anyone, since I know everyone's help is so needed here."

Joyce reached across the table and put her hand over Allie's. "Dear, do you think you might be expecting?"

Allie was puzzled. "Expecting? Expecting what?"

Joyce chuckled. "A baby, dear. Could you be expecting a baby?"

Allie gasped and put her hand over her mouth. "Oh goodness! That never even crossed my mind, but you could be right. I remember some of the young women at church who were pregnant, and they complained about morning sickness and wanting to sleep a lot. How did you feel when you were expecting each of your children? I know they're adults now and back in the states, but do you remember anything about when you were carrying them?"

"That's something a woman never totally forgets. I didn't get morning sickness, but I felt run down and wanted to sleep a lot, just as you say. Why don't you get Daniel to take you into the hospital tomorrow when you go for supplies, and they can check you out."

Allie did her work in a daze all that day, forcing herself to have toast and tea for her meals. Could she really be pregnant? What would happen then? The baby would be due before their year at the mission was up, and she didn't want him or her to be born in another country. She'd much rather have the baby in her mother's home with Doc Wilson delivering it, just as her mother had done with her. *Oh Lord, I don't think I'm ready for this, and I'm sure it would mess up Daniel's carefully laid plans.*

Chapter Twenty-Eight

*E*mma wished the doctor would give Carter something to sedate him, but she also knew Carter would want to be awake as much as possible to watch and pray over Shakespeare. At least Shakespeare slept much of the time, if only sleep would bring about a healing miracle for him. She gave him liquids any time he woke up, and she knew he was fighting the good fight. But according to the doctor, there still wasn't much hope.

Carter lay with his eyes closed most of the day, but Emma knew by his tenseness that he wasn't asleep. He would turn his head to watch Shakespeare each time his friend mumbled. Emma took him a light lunch with coffee and put two extra pillows behind him so he could sit to eat. She would gladly have fed him, but knew he would refuse the help.

"Emma, you can take this tray now."

"You've left half of it, Carter. Are you sure you can't eat a little more?"

He shook his head. "If you could see all the men have to eat in the field, you'd feel guilty eating more too."

Johnny walked over from a window where he had been staring outside and sat on a chair beside Carter. "Hey, buddy. I'll finish that for you if you're done. I'll be going back to the unit as soon as the arm heals."

"Help yourself. I wish I were going back with you. I'd like to get even with the enemy who did my friend in."

Johnny took the tray from Carter's lap. "I'll do my best for both of you when I get there, and that's a promise." He quickly wolfed down what remained on Carter's plate.

Emma felt it wasn't too sanitary to be eating someone else's half-eaten food, but Carter was right. What a lot of soldiers had to eat to survive in the field would most likely be much worse, and these men probably shared food to survive all the time.

Shakespeare woke just then gasping for breath. "Carter," he whispered.

Emma ran to his side and lifted his back and head up a little.

Carter handed over one of his pillows. "Try putting this behind him, Emma. It might help his breathing."

Sandra rushed over to help.

"Better," Shakespeare whispered. "Need…talk to…Carter."

Sandra brought a wheelchair over between the two beds. "Let's see if we can help Carter get into this so he can be closer."

"I can stand on my good left leg if you two can lift my bandaged one over and put the leg rest up for it."

The two women managed to get him moved, though Emma was concerned that his left side would bleed again. "How's that?" she asked.

Carter nodded and reached out for Shakespeare's hand.

Shakespeare opened his eyes and smiled radiantly at his friend. "You're…one of…best friends…Carter. I know I…can trust…you to be…a good…friend to…Marietta."

Carter was shaking his head and Shakespeare squeezed his hand.

"Carter. I need…to know…she'll get…all my…writings. Can I…count…on you to…take them…to her?"

Carter leaned over, kissed the hand he held, and began to weep.

"Don't cry…for me…I'm going…to my…eternal home…now. Tell Marietta…I love her…and the baby…Goodbye, friend." And he breathed his last.

Emma and Sandra wept right along with Carter. Sandra left to bring back a doctor, and Emma sat on the edge of Carter's bed, putting her arms around his shoulders. "I'm so sorry, Carter. We all loved Shakespeare too, and prayed hard for a miracle cure for him."

Carter gently lay his friend's hand down on the side of his bed just as Sandra and the doctor came in.

"Let's get you back into your bed, soldier," the doctor said to Carter.

"Is there someone who could push me outside for awhile? Some fresh air would help me deal with this better."

"I understand. I'll take you out right now and get you set up. Emma can check on you shortly and bring you back in when you're ready."

※

The doctor pushed Carter outside and over under a tree. "Please don't try to get out of the chair. You'll do a lot more damage to your side and leg." The doctor squeezed Carter's shoulder. "Hang in there, soldier. This war's been a rough one." He hung his head as he walked inside to prepare Shakespeare's death certificate, like the weight of the world rested on his shoulders.

Carter sat staring up into the bright blue sky and then looked around at all the buildings in sight. How could the day seem like just any normal day when wars were being fought in countries all over the world, and only a few were mourning his friend who just died? He gazed up again into the azure blue heavens and wondered if Shakespeare's soul had passed up through the sky and clouds to see the face of Jesus, or if he first saw a light as some have said they did when they died before being brought back to life.

And now he had the duty of taking Shakespeare's writings back to his wife and giving her his last goodbye. Carter knew she would soon be notified in person by Army officers who would go to her home; at least he wouldn't be the one to have to break the news. *How would she deal with that? If she was as strong and as close to the Lord as Shakespeare was, maybe she would deal with it better than I'm dealing with it now,* he thought.

Lord, give Marietta the strength to get through the news and funeral, and then to have and raise their baby alone. And give me the strength to go back and encourage her to go on living without the presence of someone as caring and positive as Shakespeare to share her journey with.

Where do I go from here, Lord? My life feels like it has stalled on a dead end street, and I have no idea which way to turn.

"Hey, soldier, do you want some company?"

He turned and saw Emma walking toward him hesitantly, and he knew at that moment he would gladly welcome her quiet and encouraging presence.

Chapter Twenty-Nine

That evening in their room Allie finally found the nerve to tell Dan how she'd been feeling and what Joyce expected could be her problem.

His eyes widened at her words. "Allie, why haven't you told me you weren't feeling well? And do you really think you could be expecting a child this soon after our marriage? I just assumed that part of our lives would be way down the road for us."

Of course those weren't the words she had hoped to hear from him, though she had noticed he gave very little attention to the babies and small children in the orphanage. "And I'm sure it must upset you a lot if it's true and messes up the plans you've made for the next ten years of our lives." She knew the words were harsh, but she had to admit she rather enjoyed the shocked open-mouthed look he gave her.

"Why would you say such a thing? As the man of our family, of course I want to plan ahead for our future. And if a baby will be part of that future before I'd planned, then I would consider it God's will and revise my thinking."

"As your wife, don't I have a say in any of the plans for our future?"

"Well of course you do. You're the one who planned our wedding, and I thought we had mutually planned to come on the Mexican mission trip and stay on for another year. But if you're expecting, what will that do in regards to the rest of the year we decided to remain here? When would the baby be due?"

"That I'm certainly not sure of, or even if it's true yet. Anna suggested we go to the hospital tomorrow when we're in town and see what one of the doctors has to say."

He looked thoughtful and nodded his head. "That's a good idea. At least then we'll know how to plan from there." He moved over and hugged her close. "You know I love you, Allie. I'm sorry you haven't been feeling well. If it's not a baby, but something else, you should definitely be checked out to figure out what has been causing you problems for so long."

Allie was glad her illness was finally out in the open and after tomorrow they would know one way or another if she was pregnant. She felt more understood and cared for again, snuggling closer to her husband and hoping everything would be alright.

※

The next morning Dan drove to the hospital first. "We'll get the supplies later after we know what's going on with your illness." He reached over and squeezed her hand.

Allie nodded. "That's a good idea. Hopefully I'll feel better just knowing what I'm facing."

They walked into the reception area and Daniel went to talk to the woman in charge. Allie stayed close behind, concerned what she might learn here today.

"We're Allie and Daniel Martin. We've been serving at the mission outside of town. My wife hasn't been feeling well the past two weeks, and we'd like her to see a doctor if one's available."

"Why yes, I believe Doctor Ambrose doesn't have a patient due until 10:00. Let me check with him."

They waited while she phoned back to his office. "Thank you doctor. I'll send them right back." She gave them directions and they were soon in his office and greeted by a nurse.

"Mrs. Allie Martin?" Allie nodded her head. "Could you please fill out this form and write down the symptoms you've been having?"

Allie completed the form as quickly as possible—grateful it could be done in English, though thankful she had taken the Mexican language in her institute training as it helped with basic understanding and speech. When finished, she handed her information to the nurse and was told the doctor would be with her shortly. Waiting nervously, she wondered what the examination would involve.

After the ordeal was done, the doctor called Daniel into his office. "Have a seat, Mr. Martin. My conclusion is that you and your wife should be proud parents in approximately 7 months. Mrs. Martin, I know you haven't felt like eating much the past few weeks, but it's important that you try eating fruit, vegetables and protein to keep up strength for both yourself and the baby. You should also come in every two months so we can check the growth of the child and your physical health. Do either of you have any questions?"

Both just shook their heads, and Allie was amazed that Dan for once didn't have anything to say. She would definitely like to peek inside his brain to read his thoughts, for she felt he was even more dumb-founded than she was. Most likely, he was mentally rescheduling the order of the plans he'd made for their future.

Back in the station wagon he finally spoke. "So, we're going to be parents. How do you feel about that?"

She thought a few seconds. "I guess I'm in a bit of a shock. I hadn't thought of having a child any time soon. What are your feelings about this change of plans?"

"What can I say? It's obviously the Lord's will; so be it. We'll have to make bigger decisions about the immediate future soon, though. Hopefully your sickness won't last much longer, and as the doctor said, you'll need to eat as healthy as possible. Thankfully, we're able to get fruits and vegetables here, along with the meat that's often available."

They were both silent riding into town and while picking out food and supplies to take back to the mission. "I guess we have no choice but to tell David and Joyce now. At least this will give them more time if they need to find someone to take our place," Dan said before pulling into the parking space outside the kitchen.

Allie helped carry in the lighter items with the help of some of the men and women who came out. Joyce followed in behind Allie and looked at her questioningly.

"Can we go have tea, Joyce? Then I'll tell you all about it."

"Sure. You go sit and I'll get the tea and a couple slices of the banana bread some of the women made this morning."

Allie sat at a table in a corner and waited for her friend, who soon joined her. Suddenly she was starving! "That bread looks wonderful, and so does the tea." She sipped her tea and then broke off a piece of the banana bread, chewing it slowly and enjoying each morsel.

Joyce sat watching and waiting. "So, what's the verdict, unless it's none of my business?"

Allie reached over and took her hand. "Of course it's your business. You're the one who suggested I go to a doctor, and you were right. I'm going to have a baby. Neither Dan nor I know quite how we feel about it. The doctor said the due date will be around 7 months from now. Dan is mostly concerned with the affect it will have on our plans to finish out the whole year we agreed to stay."

"Yes, I realize Daniel's a man who likes to live his life by planning ahead. And it's sometimes harder for a man to realize he's going to be responsible for someone else soon in his family and his plans. Parenthood usually comes more naturally for the mother. As the baby grows, so does the maternal love. When the baby comes, Daniel will love him or her too. As far as plans go for staying the full year, we have time to discuss that and work it out. We just need to remember that we might make our plans, but God carries His out in His way and His time.

"So just take care of yourself, dear; watch the heavy lifting and eat healthy foods. Then let the rest up to our wondrous God."

Daniel ate beside her at supper. "I saw you talking to Joyce. What did she have to say about it all?"

"Basically that it's a natural happening, and in God's hands. She said they'll work something out with us later about the remainder of our term here."

"Yes, David said pretty much the same thing. So for now we'll just go on the way we have been—as long as you're feeling able—and see what the next month brings into our lives."

In Allie's mind, she bitterly thought he should be called 'Daniel, the great planner.' She pushed away all thoughts of how Carter might have reacted if she was married to him and he got the same news. She knew it would have been different, and more joyful; but this was her life now.

Chapter Thirty

"Hello, Emma. Please come talk to me. Right now my whole life feels like one big jumbled-up mess. Maybe you can help me make sense of it."

Emma was thankful he appeared ready—and even anxious—to talk. She picked up a chair and carried it under the tree, placing it beside his wheelchair. "I'm so sorry about Shakespeare. I know how you cherished his friendship." She placed a hand on his arm, and was encouraged when he reached over and squeezed it.

He gazed into her eyes. "You were so right about how horrible Guadalcanal was going to be. It was even worse than you can imagine. Sonny and I had it safer than the others, as we worked in the communications building most of the time. Times between, we had to go out into the field and search for enemy troops and report the information back to HQ. You would think we'd get used to seeing dead bodies, but they haunt me every time I close my eyes."

He was squeezing her fingers so tightly that Emma moved her other hand over his and gently loosened his hold.

"Sorry, I didn't mean to clutch your hand so hard." He surprised her by pulling her hand to his lips to kiss it.

"I'm here for you as long as you need to talk, Carter," and she touched his lips with her fingertips in return.

"I thought of you so much out there, Emma, and your letters encouraged me more than you'll ever know. How long do you think this war will go on? Did you hear any promising news?"

She shook her head. "Not yet. But at least you'll be going home as soon as you're able to travel, so you won't be enduring any more of what you've already been through."

He stared off into the distance. "I'd rather go back to Guadalcanal to take Shakespeare's place; I know all those men who will continue to suffer there. Sonny's still there too, as well Arnie, Randy, and Ryan. They need me."

"But you have something important to do for Shakespeare too, Carter. You know he's leaving behind his most treasured writings for you to take to the wife that he loved."

"I know, and for me, that's harder than going back to war."

"You'll most likely go home first to see your family until you're able to walk again. It might seem easier to see Shakespeare's wife when you're feeling better."

"Will I ever feel better again, Emma? First I lost Allie, and now Shakespeare."

"You're not sure you've lost Allie yet. Maybe that relationship will change after you're home." Though Emma hoped in her heart that it wouldn't, if she was honest with herself, so that she'd have her chance with him.

Carter kept shaking his head. "No, Allie's gone. I never wrote to you about it, but she married her friend Daniel from college, and they went to a mission in Mexico together. So that part of my life is over and done."

Emma felt guilty for her feelings when she saw how deeply his pain went over the loss of Allie. "Just don't draw away from the Lord, Carter. He has special plans for you, if you'll just follow where he leads."

He kissed her hand again. "You're such a good woman, Emma. The man who gets you one day better by worthy of the gift that you are."

Oh, Carter, how I wish it could be you, she thought.

"And now, I'm suddenly exhausted. If you can push me back into my room I think I'm ready to sleep. Shakespeare won't still be there, will he?"

"No. They took him out before I came out here, and I changed his bed. I also put his writing materials with your belongings. So, if you're ready, I'll take you in and get you something to drink."

Sandra helped Emma get Carter settled into his bed. When Emma brought him some juice, he took several sips before lying back onto the pillow and was soon sound asleep.

Seeing there was nothing else she could do there at the moment, she went back outside to the tree to sit and pray for Carter, Allie, and Shakespeare's wife. She finally wept the tears that had been pent up since Carter arrived at the hospital.

Chapter Thirty-One

Carter knew he was beginning to heal when he didn't need the pain pills as often, but he didn't look forward to the day he would be sent home. He loved his family, but he didn't want to have them, or friends and neighbors, fussing over him. It was more comfortable here with the attention of nurses when he needed medical help or someone who understood what he was going through emotionally. Emma, especially, seemed to know when he wanted to talk, or when he preferred to sit or lay in silence.

Then there was the overwhelming notion of his pending visit with Shakespeare's wife, to give her the belongings he'd left for her. Carter wondered if she'd had the baby yet, and how she was faring after all she'd been through. He didn't know what to say to her, and dreaded making the call and the appointment to see her when he got back home.

He enjoyed just sitting outside under the trees, looking up at the blue skies and watching the birds. He hoped to try walking on his leg soon, though the doctor kept telling him not to expect too much for quite some time. His side was pretty well healed—though still tender to the touch.

Glancing over to the door of the infirmary, he saw Emma coming out with two glasses he knew would contain iced tea for both of them. He was surprised at the excitement that flowed through him just seeing her lovely face and watching how gracefully she moved toward him. He couldn't contain the smile he felt crossing his face. *What would life be like married to her?* But then he remembered she also hoped to be a missionary when this war was over, and he wasn't sure he would ever be ready for serving the Lord in that way. Not after being in this war and seeing so many good men die.

She reached him with a smile of her own and handed him a glass. "Are you enjoying this glorious weather, soldier?"

"Sure am, my lady, and thanks so much for the cold drink. Can you visit awhile?"

"It's my afternoon break, so I have some time. What's been running through your mind while sitting out here?" She sat in the chair facing him.

He wondered what she would think if she could have read his mind when he wondered about life married to her. "Oh, just thinking that they would soon be sending me back to the states, and dwelling on where my life might go from there."

"You're a strong, intelligent man, Carter. Where would you like your life to go?"

He looked off into the distance. "I'm not sure. I don't particularly want to spend the rest of my life working in a factory. What about you? What do you plan to do when this war is over and you're back in Minnesota?"

"My parents have a home on a lake that I told you about. I'll most likely go there to spend some time recouping, and I'm not sure what will come after that. I've written my family about you, Carter, and they said you would be welcome to go there for some rest before or after you go home. They're quite a friendly group, and being by the lake is really relaxing and healing."

"Are you serious? I don't think I'd be comfortable going into the home of strangers and feeling at ease, though spending time by a lake does sounds inviting."

"Well, just consider it as an option. There might be some job choices in the area too, and a university where you could take classes."

"Taking classes is something I've been considering, though I'm not sure what I'd want to major in."

She stood to go and laid a hand on his arm, sending chills up through his shoulder. "The world's before you, Carter. You won't be sent back to war, so consider carefully what you want to do, and don't forget to pray about it."

He captured her hand in his. "Thank you so much, Emma, for all you've done for me; especially in the many ways you've encouraged me. And thank your family for their offer. I just might take them up on it."

Carter watched her walk across the lawn to the door, where she turned around and waved before entering. He raised his hand in response, wishing he were able to walk so they could go back to that beach where they'd walked before. Or just spend a day in Honolulu—watching a movie, eating in a nice restaurant, or touring a museum.

Why did nations and people have to fight one another? He remembered, though, that even in Bible times, there were wars and they seemed even more violent. *Why God? Why can't people love one another?*

Then his reflections turned to Allie. He had thought she loved him as much as he loved her. Then not long after he'd offered her a diamond—which she'd refused—she went off and married another man. *Would he ever be able to trust the love of another woman?*

He believed he had strong feelings for Emma. He felt she would make a good wife and mother. But it still came back to the same obstacles: *if they did one day get together, would she too want to go to a mission field—as Allie did—and if so, would he have the faith to serve the Lord in that way?*

Emma's heart ached with the love she felt for Carter, but she knew he still harbored feelings for Allie, even though she'd married another.

Lord, if only I could go back to the states when he goes and help encourage him to settle into a new life in whatever way you would lead him. I know he's angry about many things right now, and his faith in you is shaken. He'll likely be leaving soon, and I pray he'll draw ever closer to you and live the life you've planned for him. And guide me to whatever is best for me too.

"Emma, is Carter outside?" Dr. Sanford asked.

"Yes, I took him some iced tea and talked to him briefly."

"I need to examine his leg and side again. The Army is requesting that we send him back to the states as soon as he can travel. What is your opinion? I know you're his main nurse. Could he be flown out still in a wheelchair?"

Emma's heart flopped several times, and she wished she could lie. "He's gained back a lot of strength and gets himself from the bed to the chair and back without any help. So I guess he could make the trip."

The doctor nodded. "Would you bring him in and back to my office?"

"Of course, Dr. Sanford. I'll have him there shortly."

She felt as if her legs and heart grew heavier with each step across the lawn to Carter again. He was asleep when she got to him. "Carter," she touched his shoulder as she spoke.

He jumped and grabbed her arm with one hand and reached out his other hand, apparently searching for his rifle. She forgot the rule of carefully waking any men who were back from a war zone.

"Carter, I'm sorry. I shouldn't have touched you before calling your name."

"Emma! Thank goodness it's you. I was back on Guadalcanal again, seeing the carnage all around. I didn't mean to scare you. Is it time to go in?"

"Dr. Sanford wants to examine you now. It seems the Army is pushing to have you sent back to the states as soon as you can travel."

"I guess I've looked forward to this day, yet dreaded it too. Staying here has been like being stuck in the middle of a good dream where you can just float along, and most of your decisions are being made for you. Well, if I have to go back in a wheelchair, it gives me more time before I have to face Shakespeare's wife."

Emma didn't respond, afraid she would start to weep. She pushed him slowly to the door, up the ramp, and back to Dr. Sanford's office.

Carter took her hand. "I'll let you know what the good doctor decides to tell the officer in charge of my transfer."

Emma nodded and returned to make rounds for some of her other patients, her heart breaking more with each passing moment.

Chapter Thirty-Two

Carter thought Dr. Sanford was taking a long time in going over his injuries and vitals. "How's everything looking, Doc?"

"Well, I think we should keep you here another week, though your heart and lungs sound strong. It would be better to let that leg and side heal a little longer before getting you into an airplane. I'll send in the report and let the man in charge make the decision. Do you feel ready to go yet?"

"To be truthful, I wish I'd be able to go back to the war zone. I have a few scores I'd like to settle and some remaining friends I wish I could protect."

"I realize how you feel, but you would never know if you got revenge on the right ones; maybe the ones you would do away with have a wife and children at home too."

"That's true, that's something to think about. I guess the hatred has become ingrained in both sides. If the Japanese hadn't started the war, I'd have had nothing against any of them if I passed them on the street. Anyway, I'll make it back to the states one way or the other whenever the man in charge says it's time for me to go. I know my family and friends back home are waiting for the day I arrive."

"Well, I'll let you know the decision as soon as I know. Take care, soldier."

Carter's stay had been extended for the week the doctor suggested, but five of the days had already gone by. In two more days he'd be put on a plane and flown to Los Angeles, and from that point he'd finish the trip home by train. He was able to stand a little with his leg still in heavy bandages and a brace around it, and was trying to take a few steps each day. Dr. Sanford felt he should go back home in the wheelchair to prevent falling, and he agreed—there was no way he could walk any kind of distance at this stage of recovery. It made him sad to think he may never see Emma again; he now thought of her as his very best friend and would miss her greatly.

Emma was completing rounds of the soldiers in the ward when Dr. Sanford stopped her. "How would you like two weeks leave to the states and time with your family, Emma?"

"What do you mean?"

"Since Carter isn't ready to walk more than a couple steps yet, I requested someone be allowed travel with him to assist. I felt you would be the obvious choice." He smiled when he broke that news.

Emma could feel her facial expression changing from shocked to excited, and smiled broadly in return. "Do you really mean it? It would be great to see my family again, and I'd love to help Carter get started back to a normal life. When do we leave?"

"Day after tomorrow. I didn't want to tell him you might be going with him until I'd spoken with you about it. I'll let you give him the good news, and I'll put in the order for your two weeks in the states." He smiled again and walked away.

Emma silently thanked the Lord for such a great answer to her prayer and almost ran to Carter's room in her excitement. His bed was empty and the wheelchair gone, so he must have wheeled himself outside to sit under his favorite tree. She couldn't believe she was actually going to the states for two weeks—with Carter, no less! She felt like singing and dancing across the lawn to where he sat staring off into the distance. Slowing to a more sedate pace, Emma wondered how he would feel about her going with him.

"Hi, Carter."

He spun his chair around and grinned at her. "What! No iced tea?"

"Sorry. I was so excited about the news I just received that I never thought to bring out drinks for us."

"So how about sharing this good news with a friend."

"I hope you'll like hearing it. Dr. Sanford just asked me how I'd like to have two weeks back in the states. He feels you should have a companion to go back with you, and asked if I'd like to be the one. Of course I immediately said 'Yes!' "

His mouth and eyes both flew open. "Are you kidding me?"

She laughed. "I certainly wouldn't kid about something like that. Would you want me along?"

He grabbed her hand and laughed. "Lady, I would love to have you along. It sounds like a bit of heaven, instead of the overwhelming event I've been dreading."

"I'm hoping you'll be willing to spend a few days on the lake in Minnesota with my family before we go on to your home."

"Well, count me in, if it's okay with your family."

"I'm sure it will be. I'm planning to put a call through to them this evening, and they'll be as excited as we are. You'll see that when you meet them. I have a few chores to finish before I'm off duty, and then I'll bring out our meal and drinks. See you then! We have a lot to discuss."

When Emma went back inside, Carter breathed a thank you prayer to the Lord. Maybe He did have a special plan for him. *Lord, give me strength to go on, and to have the courage to follow You wherever You lead me.*

The next two days seemed to drag for him now that he had something to look forward to, though he spent more time learning to walk with crutches.

He could sense Emma's excitement. She wore a constant smile that lifted the spirits of the other men in the room as she came and went. Johnny had left to go back to Guadalcanal a couple weeks ago, and Carter gave him letters to take back to the others. He hoped they were all in one piece and had enough to eat. He especially thought of Sonny and Ryan a lot, and hoped to see them both when the war was over.

Emma could barely hold back her elation as she prepared for the flight back to Los Angeles. She had a small bag with her belongings, along with gifts to take to her family, and something special to leave with Carter before she returned to Schofield.

Carter refused to go in a wheelchair and did well using the crutches getting into and out of the Jeep and onto the plane that would fly them to the states. The flight was long, and Emma was glad Carter slept much of the way while she read a Christian novel she picked up in Honolulu while shopping the day before.

The trip from Los Angeles to Minnesota would be more of a challenge because they were going by train and would have to make at least one transfer. *One thing at a time, Lord. Please give us both strength to get through each obstacle as it is presented.*

Chapter Thirty-Three

They finally arrived at the Los Angeles airport, and Carter managed to get off the plane and into the airport while Emma carried what they'd brought from Hawaii. She could tell Carter was tired, but he stubbornly kept moving along on the crutches.

"Hey, Emma!" She heard someone calling out. She looked up to see her brother Kevin, who ran over and hugged her, a huge smile on his face.

"Kevin! What are you doing here?"

"I came to pick you two up, Sis. You don't think I'd let you waste valuable time getting in and out of cabs and on and off trains, do you?" He didn't wait for an answer and turned to Carter. "And you must be Carter. You look exactly the way Emma described you. Welcome back to the states. Let me pick up your luggage and then I'll bring the car around so you don't have to walk any further with your crutches."

Emma grabbed her brother and gave him another big hug. "Kevin, what a blessing you are. Let's get Carter a place to sit and we'll wait for you."

Just then a porter brought over a wheelchair. "Here's some transportation for our soldier," he said. "Just leave it by the door where you load your baggage." He motioned to Kevin before continuing, "This young man and I had a good long conversation while he waited for your arrival, and I was watchin' out for you." He reached for Carter's hand and shook it. "Thank you, soldier for fighting for our country." Then he smiled as he walked away.

Carter was beginning to feel like a piece of luggage himself, being pushed around and every decision being made for him. He had to admit that Emma's brother was quite a live wire, but one that drew people in. "Well, Kevin. I guess that took care of that challenge. It's been rather hard for me to get used to feeling like a 'problem' ever since I was wounded. Though your sister here took great care of me and made me feel like I wasn't a huge pain to be around."

He smiled over at her, and she laughed and squeezed his hand before urging him to sit in the wheelchair. He had to admit it felt rather good to be looked after—especially as tired as he was feeling from the flight.

It took awhile to locate everything they had brought with them. Thankfully, Emma had hand-carried Shakespeare's belongings that would later go to his wife. When Kevin brought the car around, he was glad to see it was a 1938 Ford with a nice wide back seat. "Why don't you sit up front and get reacquainted with your brother, Emma. I'll just sprawl out back here and doze now and then."

"It's going to be a really long drive, Carter. We'll probably have to stop at a motel tonight." She turned to her brother. "It was thoughtful of you to come pick us up, Kevin. How long did it take you to drive from Minnesota?"

He flashed her a big grin as he pulled out. "I left early yesterday morning and drove on and off until this morning, just stopping now and then for gas and something to eat. I slept in the car for awhile in the parking lot, so I'm prepared to drive all night while you two get some sleep."

"Well, I'll at least trade off and on with you so you can get some sleep too. We don't want to put anyone in danger due to lack of rest. And that way, Carter can sleep as much as he wants while we make more progress getting home."

"I'm not asleep yet, folks, so remember I can hear anything you say," Carter reminded them with a smile, though he already felt his eyes beginning to droop.

Emma was concerned about how Carter was handling all the jostling that came with travel, especially after hearing him moan in his sleep. She was afraid to sleep very long herself after Kevin had run off the road, though he declared he hadn't been dozing. During the night the stops for food, gas and restroom were few and far between, and she was thankful when the sun finally peeked across the horizon. An hour later she was driving when they came to a diner with a gas station, so she pulled over, breathing a sigh of relief that she could get out of the car for a break.

"Hopefully we're somewhere that has a restroom," Carter mumbled from the back seat.

"You got it right, soldier. We can all use a longer rest," she said and opened the door to stand and stretch.

Kevin got out and came around to her side to help Carter sit up while Emma took the crutches from the floor and got them positioned for him. They helped him up the two steps into the diner and back to the restrooms.

"Sorry I can't help drive, folks," he said when they were seated at a booth with him in the seat across from Emma and Kevin. "Hopefully I'll be able to handle the peddles in my car when I get back home. Breakfast is on me, and I'll pay for the gas, so feel free to order whatever you want."

They all ate a hearty breakfast and were soon back on the road, Kevin refreshed and ready to drive again. "How long do you think it will take from here, Kevin?" Carter asked.

"We should be there in time for supper. How are you doing back there?"

"Probably better than you two, since I got to sleep through the night."

They had one more stop for lunch and gas before arriving at the family lake house late in the afternoon. Now that Carter was there, he could feel a reserve and nervousness sweeping over him—especially when four people came rushing down the steps of the deck. Emma jumped out to hug each one in turn—her mother first, then her father, her sister Netta, and another young man who hugged her last and swung her off her feet. Hopefully it was a cousin or uncle, he thought, as a surge of jealousy overcame him.

Then the group rushed over and opened the back car doors on both sides. Carter sat in confusion, wondering what he was expected to do at that point.

Emma leaned over and put a hand on his shoulder before turning to the others. "Folks, this is my friend, Carter Benton, from Illinois. Carter, lets get you out of there so you can meet my family."

Kevin took out the crutches and gave them to Emma before reaching a hand back in for Carter, helping him step out onto his good leg. Once situated, Carter forced a smile when Emma's father came up to him with a grin.

"Hi Carter. We're so happy to have the honor of sharing our home with you. I'm Emma's father, Dennis Tanneyhill." He shook the hand Carter held out to him, and turned to his wife. "This is the wonderful woman who shares her life with me, Irene Tanneyhill." She stepped over to Carter and held his hand in both of hers.

"We've heard so much about you, Carter, and we're so thankful for the part you played in helping to protect our country." She turned to the young woman who looked much like Emma. "This is our daughter Netta, and she's been watching out the window on and off all day for the arrival of the three of you. Why don't we go up on the deck for some refreshments, and supper will follow soon. Oh, and we didn't introduce Dr. Anthony Delasko. He's a surgeon in our hospital, and a good family friend."

The doctor moved over in front of Carter. "It's good to see you were able to get back to the states after being wounded, Carter. If you have any problems while you're here, I'll be glad to check you out and help in any way I can." He glanced over at Emma. "It's great to have Emma home for a bit, too."

Carter felt a pang deep inside when he saw the feelings the doctor obviously had for Emma, and he knew the man could offer her so much more than he himself could. *But one day at a time, Lord,* he reminded himself. *One day at a time.*

Chapter Thirty-Four

*S*ettled on the deck with an iced tea, Carter leaned back on a lounge chair—legs stretched out—and eyes gazing over the beauty of the lake. The sound of small waves rolling up over the beach was relaxing until it brought the memory of the larger ones on Guadalcanal crashing into his mind. He clutched an arm on the chair tightly.

"Are you okay, Carter?" Emma's father asked. "Are you in pain?"

He shook his head. "No, not physically. The waves coming in took me back to the day we landed on the beach at Guadalcanal. I thought of this small soldier named Ryan, who was panicking due to his fear of what we were facing. My friend Shakespeare and I were trying to help him out of the landing craft in thigh-deep water, while still carrying our equipment, and the water was up to his waist. But after that initial panic attack, he got through and was still okay when Shakespeare and I were flown back to Hawaii. I pray he's still alive."

"Emma wrote us about Shakespeare. I'm sorry you lost a good friend," Dennis spoke quietly.

Carter murmured, "Thank you," and was grateful that Emma came out of the house just then.

"Mom says dinner's ready, gentlemen." She smiled over at Carter and went to pick up his glass.

He moved his legs around to the side and she handed him the crutches. He tried to stand up deftly and caught himself when his good knee threatened to give way. Kevin ran up the deck steps from the beach, stepped in front of the others and held onto his elbow to stabilize him; the boy's presence helped him relax. During dinner he was glad when the others talked mostly to Emma and he didn't feel put on the spot. He enjoyed hearing stories of her childhood and nursing school, but when Anthony turned to funny tales of the times she had worked as his nurse, stabs of jealousy kept running through his heart.

He concentrated on the delicious fish they'd caught in their lake, and the baked potatoes were superb covered in butter and sour cream.

"Carter?"

He looked over at Emma's mother who had obviously asked him a question. "Sorry. I was so enjoying the home-cooked meal that I missed what you were saying."

She smiled. "I asked if you wanted to use the phone later to call your family."

"Thank you. That would be wonderful."

"If you give me their number when you're done eating, I'll see if I can get the call through while the girls do up the dishes."

He looked around and noted they had all finished eating and were waiting for him. "I'm afraid I'm rather a slow eater these days, but I'm already rather full if you don't mind me leaving the last few bites."

"Of course not. Why doesn't Kevin show you to the bathroom and you can wash up and put on something cooler than your uniform while I try putting your call through."

Carter was grateful that Kevin was so handy at getting his crutches and situating them at the perfect angle for him, and he even carried in his overnight bag so Carter could change to a short-sleeved shirt.

When he came back out Mrs. Tanneyhill called him over to the phone. "I have your mother on, Carter. She sounds like a lovely person. I told her you're doing well and looking forward to getting home. I said we'd like you to stay here a few days with us, if that's OK with you."

"Thank you." He took the phone. "Hi, Mom. How are things at home?"

"Hello, dear. Not much has changed here, except for worrying about you. How are your leg and side healing?"

"I think as well as can be expected. The Tanneyhills have a great home here on a lake. It's relaxing to sit and stare out over the water and watch the ducks. If it won't upset you, I'd like to stay here a couple days before heading to Illinois."

"Mrs. Tanneyhill said you're more than welcome, so I think it would be great for you to rest there a while before traveling again. We can't wait to meet Emma too, since she took such good care of you in the hospital and on the trip back. Will she be coming with you?"

"I don't know, Mom. She hasn't said, but I know she needs to go back to Hawaii in less than two weeks. Are Dad and Joey around?"

"I'm sorry, dear. Joey went to a friend's house after school, and your dad just left to pick him up. They'll both be sorry they missed talking to you. What is the number there? Maybe they can ring through to you tomorrow."

He noted the number printed on the front of the phone and repeated it to his mother. "It's great to hear your voice, Mom. I'll see all of you soon."

He moved to the kitchen where the three women were finishing cleaning the mess from supper. "Thank you, Mrs. Tanneyhill. It was great to hear her voice. I gave her the phone number here so Dad and Joey can try calling tomorrow."

"You're more than welcome, Carter. You just stay here as long as you'd like. I know it's getting late, and if you want to turn in for the night your room will be the one right beside the bathroom. Kevin will sleep on the daybed in the living room, so he'll be close if you need anything during the night. The rest of us will be upstairs."

Kevin came in from the deck just then. "Am I chasing you out of your bed, Kevin? I can sleep in the living room instead."

"No, I sleep in the living room much of the time anyway. I can open the outside door and hear all the night sounds through the screen door. If you're ready to turn in, I'll help you get situated."

Emma hung up a tea towel and came over. "You are looking tired, Carter. It should be good for you to get a long night's sleep, and we'll be better rested to do a few things tomorrow. I'm about ready for bed myself. Do you need anything besides your pain pills?"

"No, and the pills are in my bag. I'm looking forward to seeing more tomorrow, so I'll just say good night."

She walked over and hugged him. "Have a good night, Carter. If you need anything, just call Kevin. If there's a bigger problem, he'll come up and get me."

Carter watched her walk out onto the deck, and heard the murmur of the two men and her talking. He was soon in bed, but unable to sleep until he heard her go up the stairs and the doctor's car leaving. He had to wonder what her feelings were for Dr. Delasko.

Chapter Thirty-Five

*E*mma woke early and lay in bed with a smile on her face, thinking how great it was to know Carter was sleeping downstairs in her family home. *O Lord, how blissful it would be if he were actually part of the family as my husband. But, Lord, I know you are in charge of both our lives, and you know what is best for us—either together or apart.* At that point, she jumped out of bed and went to the window overlooking the lake. Kneeling as she always did in the mornings at home, she prayed in depth for each one in her life, and others she barely knew by name.

Her parents were already up and having coffee on the deck overlooking the water. After pouring herself a cup, she joined them. "What a beautiful morning!" she exclaimed. I've missed this place so much, though the ocean and scenery in Hawaii are breathtaking too, of course."

"Your father and I would like to visit there at some point, but I'm sure in the midst of a war wouldn't be the best time."

"Hopefully, the war won't go on forever, Mom. The beaches there are still lovely and peaceful, but there will be time to go when the world is not so dangerous again."

"Carter seems like a good and caring man," her father said, changing the subject.

"And very handsome, too," her mother leaned over and whispered.

Emma grinned. "I have to agree with both of you."

Kevin stepped out onto the deck. "I hear Carter moving around in the bedroom. Do you think he'll need any help getting over to the bathroom?"

"I wouldn't suggest it, Kevin. He's quite determined to be self-sufficient these days. If he gets in real trouble, he'll call for help."

Her mother stood. "If he's up and around, why don't we go in and start breakfast, Emma."

By the time the pancakes were ready, Carter made his way into the kitchen quite efficiently on his crutches, just as Emma had predicted. "Good morning, soldier. I presume your nose told your stomach that breakfast was ready."

He smiled. "Yep, I just followed my nose right in." He moved over to the screen door. "What a gorgeous day! The sun's shining across the water and the lake appears so calm."

"It's a great day to take the rowboat out," Kevin said as he stood on the deck drinking iced tea. "Too bad Netta and I have to go to school. You and Emma will have to enjoy it by yourselves, Carter." He grinned as he came in and sat down at the table.

"What are they going to enjoy?" Netta asked as she went into the kitchen to pour herself a glass of milk.

"A beautiful day on the lake in the rowboat."

Netta crinkled her forehead and teased, "Well, is Emma doing the rowing?"

Emma swatted her with a tea towel. "I'm certainly better than you, little sister."

Netta laughed and turned to Carter. "I wouldn't trust her, if I were you. I'd grab the oars before she gets a chance."

"I'm sure Carter would like to do the rowing anyway," Mr. Tanneyhill said when he came in from the deck. "I'd recommend it, Carter," he said in an undertone.

"Dad, remember the time I won the rowing race they had in town?"

He grinned. "You mean when you were fifteen and the other contestants were between ten and twelve years old?"

Carter put his crutches aside and hopped to a chair. "I'll trust you, Emma. You can row as much as you want. After being shot, how dangerous can someone's rowing be?"

That started everyone laughing as they sat down and—after prayer—each told a funny story about Emma and her rowing.

❦

Carter put his crutches on the bottom of the boat and looked up at Emma. "Are you sure you wouldn't rather row instead of me?" He grinned. "In spite of what your family said, I'd still trust you."

"No, you get into the middle seat by the oars. I'll sit at the back facing you after I push us out."

Carter managed to get to the middle without toppling the boat, and after Emma shoved it out far enough and got in, he rowed them out from the shoreline. Surprised he didn't feel more pain, he was able to move along at a nice steady, and the Tanneyhill home was soon out of sight. It felt good to do something, anything, physical again, to not feel like an invalid. He watched Emma trailing her fingers in the water as she lay back against some waterproof pillows behind her.

"How wonderful it is to be out on the lake again," she said. "One of my best friends used to live in the house closest to ours, and in the summer we would row into town and have lunch at the soda shop."

"Which one of you rowed?" he asked, smiling.

She splashed him with water. "Just for that, I'll row coming back and show you my family is wrong about me."

"You know what they say: 'seeing is believing,' " and he hit the water with an oar to get her wet.

"You're asking for war, friend, but I prefer to wait until we're on our way back—after we have lunch at the soda shop. I'm sure you don't want to go in there totally drenched."

"You're on, lady. We'll see who ends up back at the house sopping wet."

When they got to town, Emma got out and tied the craft to the dock, then Carter handed out his crutches and pulled himself up onto his good leg. He looked around at the small town with unique shops lining both sides of the gravel road. The store directly in front of them was named 'Lakefront Lunchroom,' so he figured it was the soda shop.

Once they were seated at a booth by a large window, an older woman came to take their order. "Well, as I live and breathe, if it isn't little Emma Tanneyhill, all grown up and back from Hawaii. How are you doing, honey?"

Emma smiled and stood to hug the woman. "Hilda, it's so great to see you. I'm just back for a short visit." She turned to Carter and sat back down. "This is Carter, a friend of mine from Illinois. I met him in Hawaii."

Hilda turned to shake Carter's hand. "Glad to meet you, Carter. Since you're here with crutches, I'm assuming you were wounded in battle. Welcome home, young man."

"Thank you, ma'am."

"What about your son, Andrew, Hilda? Didn't I hear that he was hurt in one of the battles, too?"

She nodded and tears came to her eyes. "Yes, in Germany. They flew him back home, but he's not doing so well. The doctors fear he's not going to make it."

"Oh, Hilda, I'm so sorry to hear that. How's his wife Audrey doing, and their little boy Andy?"

"Audrey is wearing herself out trying to take care of both of them. I go over several times a week to let her take Andy out to have a little fun. The poor little tyke curls up by his daddy's side to nap and doesn't want to leave him. It just breaks your heart." She wiped her eyes on a napkin. "But enough of the sad talk. What can I bring you two for lunch?"

They both ordered a hamburger, fries, and a milkshake, sitting quietly and dwelling too much on how the horrors of war were affecting folks all over the world.

Chapter Thirty-Six

*A*fter eating, Emma hugged Hilda again, and Carter shook the woman's hand, holding it in both of his to offer comfort. The couple walked up and down both sides of the street, going into a few of the shops that interested them the most. By the time they got back to the boat, Carter was glad Emma was insisting on rowing home. His arms were tired and aching after the strenuous exercise of rowing over. He pulled himself into the back seat first and held onto the dock while she untied the boat from the hooks and sat in the rowing seat.

"Well, soldier, here we go. Hopefully, I can disprove everything my family has to say about my handling of the oars." She grinned and rowed far enough away from the dock, using the right oar to turn the boat around in a spin. "Oops! I guess that wasn't the way to do it, was it?" and she laughed aloud.

He grabbed both sides of the craft and pretended to be frightened. "Now then, young lady, maybe we should change seats and let me take over."

She laughed again and began pulling hard on the oars to row back the way they had come. "Just kidding." She glanced at her watch. "I recall it took us forty-five minutes to get here. Bet I can get us back home in thirty."

She pulled even harder, and they were soon close to the middle of the lake. "Emma, we're not in that big of a hurry to get back to the house. Why don't we just slow down and relax as we go. It's not a race." He didn't want to admit it, but the thought of overturning that far from shore made him a bit edgy. He didn't think he could swim with a heavy cast on his leg.

"Nonsense. I made a bet, and I have to stick to it," Emma replied, and then continued to move at a rather fast pace.

He gripped tightly to the bottom of his seat. "I didn't agree to any bet,

Emma. You don't need to hold to anything."

She just smiled and kept rowing, so Carter remained silent and prayed.

Soon the sun dropped behind some dark clouds, and a minute later a loud clap of thunder reverberated through the air. They both jerked and looked up as huge beads of water began to drop on them.

"Uh, oh, we should have left half an hour sooner," she said.

"Why don't you let me take over, Emma?"

She stared across the water. "See how the waves are starting to roll across the surface? We could easily upset if we changed seats. I'll try moving over closer to the shore in case of trouble."

Thunder boomed again and lightening radiated across the sky. *Lord, I think we're sitting ducks!* And he was momentarily back on Guadalcanal with the noise and flashes of gunfire all around. He saw Shakespeare fall, and himself running toward the enemy firing as he ran, then the pain of the bullets hitting his side and leg, but he kept moving. *Lord, help us all!*

"Carter! Carter, are you okay?"

He opened his eyes to Emma's frightened face. "Carter, you weren't struck by lightning, were you?"

He shook his head to console her fear. "No, it's okay, Emma. I just wish I were doing the rowing right now, I'm having flashbacks to the Guadalcanal battles." He bellowed the words, but it was raining harder, and thunder was exploding overhead, sounding just like bombs in his mentally anguished state.

She gave a little shrug of her shoulders. "I can't hear you," she yelled and pulled harder toward shore just as lightening struck a tall tree on the beach.

Carter saw her eyes grow huge and her mouth open in a wide O-shape. He quickly turned his head and saw the tree moving. He called out "Lord, please help us!" as they watched the pine make its way toward them in slow motion. *Had he escaped death in the war just to have his life end here along with Emma?* For the first time after the horrors of Guadalcanal, he actually wanted to live his life for the Lord, and share the rest of it with this woman in front of him.

"Let's go over the side, Emma! It's our only chance!" He grabbed the crutches and moved quickly to her, tilting the boat onto its side, and dumping them both into the water.

Chapter Thirty-Seven

The water was cold as they hit the surface and went under. All Carter could think of was getting Emma away from where the tree was about to hit. He held tightly to the crutches, looking under water for her, and was surprised to see her close beside him. He pushed a crutch over to her and she clutched it in her right arm. Both of them shoved hard to get away from the overturned craft.

A loud crash reverberated around them, and the rowboat went under close behind them. Carter knew they needed to breathe soon and grabbed her hand in his, keeping the crutch on his left. They reached the surface together, gasping and taking deep breaths.

"Oh, Carter, I'm so sorry for bringing you out here today. Thank the Lord we're still alive. Can you make it to shore?"

"The Lord brought us this far. One way or another we'll make it the rest of the way in." Carter felt the weight of his wet clothes, heavy bandages and metal strapped to his leg. Thankfully his arms were still strong. They both pulled hard on their free arm to sidestroke toward the beach that was, thankfully, closer than he thought.

The falling tree had made waves that helped push them more quickly to the side, and they both lay face down on the sand as the water washed over them.

Emma was the first to roll over and sit up. "Are you OK, Carter?"

He raised his head and looked over at her. "My leg is so heavy; I don't know if I can get turned over."

She stood and tried to wring some of the water out of her pants and moved to his side, shoes squishing. "At least we didn't lose our shoes." Kneeling beside his injured leg, she tried to squeeze some of the water out gently. "Okay, if you're able, I'll try to lift this leg as you attempt to roll over. Ready?"

"Ready when you are."

She lifted above and below the knee to keep his leg straight. Carter pushed up with his arms and good leg to roll as she turned his leg over. He tried holding in a groan as he struggled to sit up. "Okay, nurse lady, what do we do now?"

"Pray, maybe, unless you have any other ideas. It's going to be a long walk home. I can't believe I got you into a situation like this, Carter. I was sent along to get you home safely, and now look what I've gotten you into!"

He laid back and laughed. "Believe me, Emma, this is mild compared to what went on, and is still going on in Guadalcanal. At least no one's bombing us or shooting at us."

"There is that to consider." Then she gasped. "Carter, look out there just beyond that wave! The boat is actually floating upright. The tree must have spun it over when it struck!" She took off her shoes and headed into the water.

He struggled up to a sitting position again. "Emma, what are you doing?" He grabbed a crutch and tried to stand.

"The boat isn't out that far. I'm sure I can reach it and pull it in. Rowing will be a lot faster than walking home. With your cast waterlogged, you just won't make it."

Carter felt so helpless. As a man, he was always the one to protect a woman, and now he was barely able to move. What would he do if she got into trouble out there? *Pray, Carter, pray,* went through his mind. He prayed as hard as he could while watching the woman he would give his life for, putting hers on the line for him.

❦

Emma swam quickly to the boat and grabbed the piece of rope tied to the prow. Using her right arm, she kicked and pulled backwards, with the boat amazingly following behind. *Please, Lord, forgive me for getting us into this mess, and please help me get Carter back safely without any further injury to his leg, or having him come down with pneumonia.* Soon she felt ground beneath her and stood to pull the boat to the edge of the sand.

Her arms were aching, but she knew she couldn't give up yet. Then Carter was beside her and pulled it back further.

A Bridge to Somewhere

"Great job, lady. I can't believe the oars are still locked in the tholepins! I was wondering what we would do for oars. God really does answer prayer, doesn't he? Now I know you're exhausted, so I'll row the rest of the way, and I'll not take 'no' for an answer. The only problem is, I'll need to get in first and you'll have to push it out a little and get in the front."

Emma was too tired to argue, and she knew Carter didn't enjoy feeling useless. So she just nodded and handed him both crutches so he could boost himself into the middle seat.

Thankfully, the storm had passed shortly after the tree had been struck, but the water was still rough. She watched the muscles in Carter's arms tighten each time he dipped the oars and pulled, moving the rowboat rather quickly through the choppy water. Soon she saw the small alcove and the large tree with the rope swing tied to a branch, and knew that home was just around the corner. She and her brother and sister had swung from it to splash into the water so many times growing up.

"There they are!" Emma heard Kevin yell as he tore off the deck and down to the beach to pull the rowboat up onto the sand. "What happened to you? We've been waiting for you to come back for supper. And why are you both soaked?"

Netta and their father were soon close behind. "Did both of you fall in, or did the boat overturn?" Mr. Tanneyhill asked in a distressed tone.

"Yes, to both, Dad. Right now Carter needs help getting out and into the house, and after supper we'll have to drive him to the hospital to have his leg checked and re-cast. We can tell you all about it over dinner."

Kevin lifted Emma out and then went back to help Carter. Carter stood on his good leg, trying to keep the injured one straight and put the crutches over the side. Mr. Tanneyhill moved to Kevin's side and they both lifted Carter while he leaned on the crutches, with Emma keeping his leg straight until he was over the side and on dry ground.

"Thank the Lord you two made it back safely; this is definitely a story we need to hear after you're both dry and warm again," Emma's father exclaimed.

Emma went upstairs to change into dry clothes and towel-dry her hair. Thankfully, Kevin was available to help Carter change, but she needed to check his leg. She didn't like the way it looked and planned to get him to the hospital right after supper. Maybe she could call Anthony instead to see if he could come to the house and re-wrap Carter's leg.

The meal was a lively one with each family member taking turns asking questions until they were finally satisfied they knew all the details involving the accident.

"Wow, what a story," Kevin exclaimed. "We should phone the reporter for the daily paper, and he can do a write-up for the next issue."

"Please, no! How will that make me look? I accompany a wounded soldier home and place him in another dangerous situation only a day later!"

"But it wasn't your fault that lightning struck a tree and fell on your boat. You both reacted heroically to survive the accident and get back home. I think it's a good idea," Emma's father said.

Carter sat back in his chair, grinning. "It might make national news, Emma. Your dad's right. You might come out looking like a real heroine."

Emma stood up and took her dishes to the sink. "Do whatever you want, Kevin. Right now I plan to phone Anthony to see if he can come over to fix Carter's leg. If not, we need to go to the hospital." She walked into the other room to make the call.

The reporter arrived first and wrote down everything they told him about the relaxing day that had turned into such a traumatic situation. By the time he finished and took some pictures of the two, Dr. Anthony Delasko was knocking at the door.

Chapter Thirty-Eight

*A*llie was feeling much better since the nausea had passed and she was into her second trimester, but now she was having a problem fitting into her skirts and blouses. They were waiting for a shipment of used clothing to come in from her church back home, and her mother had written that Annie was sending some of the clothes she'd worn when she was expecting Nathan.

Allie pulled her largest one-piece dress from her closet and was putting it on when Daniel returned from his morning shower. "Look at this Daniel! I'm getting so big that hardly any of my clothes fit now!"

He walked over behind her as she stood in front of the mirror and put his arms around her and one hand on her tummy. "You're beautiful, sweetheart, and it's exciting watching our baby growing as your waistline expands."

She turned and kissed him. "Daniel, that's so sweet. You're a good husband, and though I sometimes tease about your planning, it's comforting to know you'll always take care of me."

"Of course I'll always take care of you and our baby, dear. You're my life, don't you know that?" He kissed her lovingly and left for the work that needed done before breakfast.

When he left, she dwelt on how caring he'd become since knowing there was a baby on the way. When they shopped for groceries, he chose carefully what would be best for her and asked what most tempted her appetite. She knew her feelings for him were growing deeper, and she thought of Carter much less these days.

Her mother had written that he had been wounded, but thank God he's survived. She would have liked to send him a card, but felt it might be hurtful to Daniel, causing him to think she still cared for Carter.

That afternoon the clothing arrived from the church with all sizes for all ages. All who lived or worked there were excited and encouraged to look for something that would fit them.

The clothes from Annie to Allie were in a special package, so she took them back to their room and tried several on. Luckily, they all fit comfortably, so she wore her favorite one back to dinner.

"Well, look at you, young lady," Joyce said. "You must feel much more comfortable now."

Allie twirled around. "I almost feel thin again! I think I'll wear this tomorrow when Dan takes me in for my next check-up."

Daniel came up and grabbed her hand when she twirled again. "And who is this lovely young woman in a pretty blue outfit?"

She laughed. "Finally, I can breathe in something that fits—and there are four more outfits! I'll have to send Annie a special thank you note. "But let's eat, husband of mine. This mother-to-be is starving!"

He put an arm around her waist and they went to join some of the workers who were filling their plates.

They left early the next morning and drove to the hospital for Allie's appointment with Dr. Ambrose. She was in high spirits, and knew it was partially due to the new clothing, but also because she felt Daniel and she were growing closer.

As they drove along a road that hugged a mountain on the right and a steep drop-off on the left, she felt fear overwhelm her, especially when a bus full of passengers passed on their left. Daniel slowed and stayed as close to the right as possible to give the driver more room. She sighed in relief when the bus had passed and they were on a section that was wider, the drop-off not as steep.

When they reached the clinic, Dr. Ambrose checked Allie over and talked with her and Daniel afterward in his office. "Mrs. Martin, you and your baby are both doing well. Keep up the good work with eating, exercise and rest. You're halfway through your nine-months, and I expect all will go well the rest of the way."

He stood and shook their hands to congratulate them.

Daniel hugged her outside before helping her into the jeep. "Halfway there, sweetheart. Just think, in four and a half more months we'll be holding our son or daughter!"

They were both deep in thought when Allie looked up and saw they were on the same road that had scared her so badly earlier. Suddenly another bus was coming their way and the driver was glancing back over the seats and moving toward their side of the road. "Daniel, watch out!"

He blew the horn too late, and the bus clipped their vehicle, shoving them over the side of the drop-off. They both screamed as the jeep rolled several times, and then all was silent.

Chapter Thirty-Nine

*E*mma answered the door. "Thanks for coming out, Anthony. The family is in the living room. I checked Carter's leg, but it looked like the extra stress on it today might have caused a new problem."

"I'm glad you called, but I don't understand why you took him that far on the lake when the weather's been so unpredictable lately."

"I guess I forgot how fast a storm can brew around here. I just wanted him to enjoy something different than war and hospital life."

"I understand, Emma. I guess the best place for me to fix up his leg would be on the bed where he's sleeping." He put down his medical bag and followed her into the living room where he greeted each of the family, and turned to Carter.

"Well, soldier, I guess your first day back in the states didn't go so well after all."

"Hey, the first part was great, and the fact that we survived made the ending good too. I appreciate your coming to take care of my leg for me. I wasn't looking forward to another hospital visit."

"If you can make it back to your bed, I'll check the leg over to be sure there aren't any new damages, and put on a fresh set of casting bandages."

Emma watched as Carter took the crutches and stood, but noticed he appeared rather shaky as he made his way from the room. She followed behind him until they got to the bedroom. She opened the door and stood back for Anthony to go in behind him. "I'll be waiting in the kitchen if you need any assistance with the dressing." She closed the door and went to the coffee pot to pour another cup to calm her nerves. She felt so guilty over the whole episode, and realized she should have given him the first whole day to rest.

Carter lay on the bed resenting the fact that he was depending on Dr. Delasko for help with his leg, but it was still better than going to the hospital, he supposed. He could see the doctor had deep feelings for Emma, which would cause him to resent Carter in turn. He felt relieved when the cast was off, though he had to admit the pain was more severe where the bone had splintered from the shell fragments.

The doctor pressed all over the area where the leg had been injured, and Carter winced each time the sorest place was touched.

"I'm afraid there's a new problem here, Carter. My guess would be either a bone splinter that hasn't reattached, or shell fragment working it's way out. If you're willing, we can have you admitted to the hospital tomorrow, and I can remove whichever is causing the problem rather easily. You'll need to stay there several days until the new stitches heal."

Carter closed his eyes and shook his head, his fears becoming a reality. "I guess I don't have much choice. I'll just have to pray harder for fast healing."

Anthony opened the bedroom door and called Emma in. He showed her the problem, and explained what he would need to do.

"Carter, I am so sorry! It probably happened from the catastrophe this afternoon."

"Not necessarily, Emma," Anthony said. "It could be either a bone or shell fragment that's been working its way out, and if so it would have happened anyway sooner or later. I should be able to take care of it tomorrow. If you'll help me get the new dressing on his leg, he should just stay in bed until you can bring him to the hospital tomorrow morning. I'll set up the admission and surgery schedule."

Their task finished, Anthony pulled a blanket over the bandaged leg and patted Carter's arm. "We'll get you shaped up soon so you can get back to Illinois."

Carter woke early in the morning, sat up and reached for his crutches, moaning when he felt like someone had beaten him all over. Yesterday's trauma must have used a lot of muscles he hadn't put into play for awhile. He made it to the bathroom and back and wanted nothing more than to crawl into bed and sleep for a week. Instead, he had to go to a hospital room—again—have another surgery, and lay there for several days just staring at the ceiling. Then he remembered what soldiers were going through all over the world at this very minute, and felt like a whiny baby.

Sorry, Shakespeare. I'd trade places with you if I could. I'd rather you were in the hospital healing and waiting to go home to your wife and baby, and I was laying six feet under. Thankfully, my soul would be in heaven then, where I know you are right now.

He managed to get dressed and hobbled to the kitchen where Emma and her mother were making bacon and eggs and brewing coffee. "That sure smells good, ladies." He pulled out a chair and sat down, his leg stretched out in front of him.

"The coffee will be ready shortly, Carter, but I don't think you can have anything to eat. Anthony called earlier and said he has a room set up for you, and the surgery for one o'clock. That means you can't eat until after the operation and you're awake again," Emma said.

"Oh, that's awful," her mother said. "You should have told me, Emma, and we wouldn't have cooked anything until after you'd gone."

Carter chuckled ruefully. "I'm sure I'll survive on just coffee, Mrs. Tanneyhill. You go ahead and eat something, Emma. It might be awhile before you get anything else."

Emma sat in the waiting room outside the surgery. She knew Anthony was one of the best surgeons around, but she still blamed herself for Carter's new problem. She sipped the coffee she'd brought from the cafeteria, deep in thought. Soon she stood and paced the room, worrying about how things were going in the operating room. It was harder being on this side of the door than on the other side; at least she was in the know when she assisted the surgeons.

Hours later, Anthony finally came out.

"It went well, Emma. The shell fragment was wedged under a bone splinter that kept it from fusing to the femur. I removed both, so the bone should heal more quickly now. The nurses will be taking Carter back to his room, and you can see him there. Meantime, why don't we get coffee in the cafeteria."

Emma would have rather just rushed to Carter's room to help get him settled comfortably, but she knew she owed the time to Anthony for taking care of a problem she caused. "Sure, Anthony. My coffee grew cold long ago."

Walking through the halls brought back memories for Emma of the months she'd spent in the hospital as a nurse for Anthony and the other hospital doctors. She knew from Anthony that some of the younger doctors were now in the service, and she wondered where they were stationed and what they might be facing. "Have you heard from any of the doctors who enlisted?"

"Only Adam and Timothy. They're both in war-torn countries and haven't written any good news. I guess I should be thankful I couldn't pass my physical. Here we are. If you want to take that small table over by the window, I'll go get our coffee."

Emma sat and watched him walk away. He was such a good man, and handsome besides. Why was it that she had no deep feelings for him, but cared so much for Carter? She could have the best of everything married to Anthony, and could still be a nurse in this hospital to continue her own career.

Did she really have any chance of ending up with Carter? Especially since she would be going back to Hawaii in less than two weeks, and he'd be going home to Illinois.

She saw Anthony headed to the table with a loaded tray. "What is all that?"

"I haven't had much to eat yet today, and I figured you most likely haven't either. So I brought soup and crackers, and cinnamon rolls for dessert. Dig in."

The sight of the food stirred her hunger, and she eagerly did as requested, digging into the soup and crackers. They both ate silently until the rolls and coffee.

"So what is the plan regarding Carter?" Anthony asked. "He'll be here several days, but I imagine he's getting anxious to go home to his family."

"He'll most likely rest at our place a couple more days, and Kevin and I will drive him to Illinois after that. Then it won't be long before I have to return to Hawaii. Now that I've come home, I'm not really looking forward to going back, even though Hawaii is a choice assignment in this war."

"How much longer do you have on your enlistment?"

"At least a year and a half." She finished the roll—it was delicious—and drank the remainder of her coffee. "Thank you so much for everything, Anthony. Thanks for dinner, but most of all for doing the surgery on Carter's leg. I still feel it was my foolishness that brought it about, but you're probably right that it would have happened sometime in the near future any way. In that case, I'm glad you were the one to do the surgery."

He stood and pulled out her chair. "You're more than welcome, Emma. You know I would do anything for you. You only need ask." He took her hand and leaned over to kiss her cheek before walking away.

Emma watched until he went through the door, and then she made her way quickly to Carter's room.

He opened his eyes when she touched his arm. "Are you still here, Lady? You don't have to hang around, you know, though I always enjoy your company."

"Carter, I'll be hanging around as long as you have to be here. When you're able to go back to my parents' home you can rest up a few more days—no boat rides, I promise—and then Kevin and I will drive you home."

"Dang, I was really looking forward to rowing that boat again." He squeezed her hand, and they both laughed.

Chapter Forty

Allie woke up and looked around the white room, confused about where she was.

"Hello. I'm glad to see you're finally awake."

Allie tried to turn her head, but realized it was confined by something around her neck. "Where am I?"

A young woman in a nurse's uniform leaned over to look down into her face. "You're in the hospital. You've been in an auto accident. Do you remember anything about it?"

Allie thought back, and suddenly she remembered. "Oh, no! We were on our way back to the mission when a bus drove on our side of the narrow road and pushed us over a cliff. We turned over several times, but that's the last I remember." She suddenly thought of the baby and tried to move her right hand to touch her stomach. It was strapped to some kind of board, so she moved her left one up. It hurt, but at least she could move it to her stomach. "My baby! Did I lose my baby?"

"The baby seems to be doing well so far, but we'll need to keep you here for some time to be sure; plus, you have some healing to do yourself."

"What about my husband, Daniel? Is he okay? And why isn't he here with me?"

The nurse brought a cup of water and helped her to drink. "Your doctor asked me to let him know when you wake up. Then you can talk to him about your husband and baby. I'll be back after that, and I'll help you eat when you're ready."

Allie was suddenly frightened, and wondered about the injuries she might have—obviously her neck and left arm for starters. She moved her legs one at a time and, though they hurt, they didn't seem to be broken.

There was a knock at her door and Dr. Ambrose walked in. "Mrs. Martin, I'm glad to see you're awake. I believe the nurse told you the baby is doing well. You, yourself, have a badly sprained neck and a broken right arm. You will most likely be here at least a month until we're sure the baby is continuing to thrive, and that you have no other complications from the accident."

"But what about Daniel? He must have been hurt too, or he would be here with me right now."

The doctor hesitated, fooling with his pencil and tablet. "Mrs. Martin, your husband was a very brave man. When the rescue team went to get you out of the vehicle, they reported that Mr. Martin had flung himself over you face down and held tight to the sides of the seat to protect you and the baby. I'm sorry, but he was already gone when they pulled him out of the vehicle. They were amazed that you were still living, and they believe that was due to his fast thinking."

Allie stared unseeingly up at the ceiling, wishing she could at least shake her head in denial. Daniel—the great planner, who promised to take care of her and the baby the rest of her life—could not be dead! *No God! Not Daniel, who said I was his life, who brought me to Mexico so we could serve you together. Not Daniel, who flung himself over me as we went over the bank in order to protect me and the baby. No, no, no!* She began to sob aloud, hyperventilate, and then began to choke.

Dr. Ambrose rushed over to lift her head and back up, placing another pillow behind her and ringing the bell for help. The nurse rushed in and he ordered a syringe with a sedative to calm her down and hopefully put her to sleep. That done, her eyes soon closed and she lay still again.

"Doctor," she whispered without opening her eyes.

"Yes, Mrs. Martin?"

"Will I be able to see my husband?"

He laid his hand on hers. "After you rest a little longer, we'll wheel you down to where he is."

"Thank you." And she was asleep.

✿

When Allie woke again, her memory was foggy until she focused on the terror of the bus hitting them and sending them over the bank. Then she remembered Daniel flinging himself over her right before they rolled, and she knew nothing after that. Now she felt dead inside and couldn't believe she actually was alive. She didn't want to be. If the God in heaven cared anything at all about her, he wouldn't have allowed this to happen to Daniel.

She reached for the bell attached to her bed and the nurse was soon beside her. "I'd like to be taken to see my husband now."

"Give me a second to get help and a wheelchair, and we'll wheel you down."

She soon returned with the chair and a young man to help lift Allie from the bed to the chair.

Allie stifled a moan when they moved her, but the pain meant nothing, and she wondered if anything in life would ever mean something again. They wheeled her into a room she supposed was the morgue. An older man quickly pulled a sheet over someone on one of three litters. "Is that Daniel?" she asked.

The man turned to her. "Are you here to view Daniel Martin?"

"Yes, my husband."

He moved over to the litter beside her. "No, he's here. I'll lower the litter so you can see him from your seat." After cranking it down to her level, he slowly pulled the sheet down to Daniel's chest. "As you can see, he has few facial or upper body injuries, mostly due to his protecting you and gripping both sides of your seat so tightly. When the vehicle came to a final stop, the left side of his head hit the metal above the passenger window, giving him the blow that caused an aneurysm and bringing about instant death."

She lifted her left hand and touched his face before turning away. "What am I to do about his funeral?"

The nurse behind her put a hand on her shoulder. "His sister and brother-in-law have been notified, and so have your parents. They should all be here by tomorrow morning to take over whatever plans need to be made."

Allie nodded and glanced over at Daniel's face one last time. "I'd like to go back to my room now."

When the nurse and young man took her back and moved her from the wheelchair onto the bed, she closed her eyes and shut out the world. The numbness came over her, and she was grateful to escape into a deep sleep.

Chapter Forty-One

Carter was thankful when he was released from the hospital three days after surgery. Not that he had minded the rest or the boredom, since Emma spent most of the days keeping him company. Her parents and Kevin stopped by each evening, so he was ready for sleep by the end of the day. He had to admit he was beginning to feel like part of the family, and he liked it.

Dr. Delasko dropped by quite often when Emma or her family were there— supposedly to check up on him—but Carter was of the opinion that Anthony considered himself part of the Tanneyhill family too and wanted Carter to know it.

He checked Carter's leg one last time and had the nurse wrap it. "I'd say you're on the road to recovery, Carter. I'm sure you're anxious to get home to your family. He gave him a meaningful look when he stressed the words 'your family.' "

"I should be home within the week, if you feel I'm able to travel."

"You should be fine as long as you take it slow. Are you planning to go by train?"

Carter tried not to let his anger show through. "Most likely." Emma and her father walked in. "Hey, Emma and Dennis. You're certainly a welcome sight. The good doctor here has given me the okay to go, so I'm ready when you are."

Emma said "hello" to Anthony and turned to smile at Carter. "The car is right outside. Let's get you into your chair and wheeled out of here."

Dennis wheeled the chair over, and Anthony walked to the door. "I'll be out sometime tomorrow to check up on our patient." He made sure to catch Emma's eye as he said it, and Carter felt like there was a challenge meant for him in that look.

It was a lovely day, and Carter was relaxing on the deck at the Tanneyhills' home, enjoying the nice breeze coming off the lake.

Anthony showed up each evening, and in Carter's opinion he was acting possessively towards Emma. By the third evening he declared that Carter should be well enough to make the trip home the next day.

"Kevin and I are planning to drive him home the day after tomorrow. He talked with his family and they are happy to have Kevin and me stay with them for a few days. That way I'll be sure Carter's doing well before I have to head back to Hawaii."

Carter noticed the crestfallen look on the doctor's face, and realized the man's pain over losing Emma was very real to him; he couldn't help but feel a pang of sympathy for Anthony. It brought back the pain Carter had suffered in losing Allie, and he was glad he'd gotten past the worst of it. He hoped she was happy in her life with Daniel as missionaries in Mexico, and for the first time he truly meant it.

He looked back at Emma, and felt a surge of feeling rush through his body, knowing he could be happy building a life with her if only they could make that future happen.

When Kevin came home from school the next afternoon, he and Emma helped Carter into the boat again and took him out for a short ride within close radius of the house—with Kevin rowing this time. Carter leaned back against a pile of cushions feeling like the sultan he'd read about when he was in high school. That must be the life!

"You and your folks have a great place to live. This has been a perfect holiday for recuperating. I want to thank you both for all you've done for me."

Kevin grinned as he continued rowing. "It might have been even better if a certain person hadn't dumped you and your cast leg into the lake in the middle of a storm."

Emma smacked him on the head with a pillow she was holding. "Be nice, brother. Just remember I'll be leaving again soon and you might not get to see me for another year."

"Now Emma, what kind of brother would I be if I didn't pick on you?"

"I guess you have a point. I wouldn't want any brother but you, Kevin. And I think I just heard the dinner gong ringing, so I guess it's time to head back. We'll have to be up rather early to head for Illinois."

Carter realized how blessed he was to have met and become a part of the Tanneyhill family, and smiled when he thought of his brother Joey and Kevin running around in the woods together back home. He hoped Emma and Kevin would feel as comfortable there as he felt in their family home.

The three left at 4:00 a.m. with Kevin driving, Emma in the front passenger seat, and Carter settled in the back. Emma was concerned that traveling this soon after surgery might be too much for Carter, but Anthony had assured them both the night before that he should do well.

Of course, she recognized that Anthony wanted Carter out of her life as soon as possible, but being the good surgeon that he was, she didn't think he would say it was okay if he had any doubts. She wished Anthony would find someone else he'd want to share his life with instead of focusing all his dreams on her. At this point she realized she saw him only as a friend—and not even a particularly good friend.

"Are you ready for some coffee, Kevin? I know I am."

"Sure, sis. Pour me one. And how about one of those cinnamon rolls you and Mom made last evening?"

"Sounds good to me. Coming right up."

"How about the same for the man bumming a ride in the back, young lady?"

She looked around and saw Carter sitting up. "Sure enough, soldier. I thought you were asleep."

"I was half-dozing until I heard the words 'coffee' and 'cinnamon rolls.' "

Emma handed him a cup of coffee and one of the rolls. "We're moving right along since we started so early. And there are more rolls and sandwiches we can munch on as we drive, so we should make good time."

A Bridge to Somewhere

They pulled onto the dirt lane leading back to Carter's home early that evening. Before Emma had stopped in front of the house and turned off the engine, a man, woman and boy came running out of the house.

Kevin jumped out and opened the back door to help Carter stand to greet his family. Emma also went around to the opened door to be sure he could stand without any problem after the long ride, and he didn't need her assistance.

"Carter, oh my son. Thank the Lord you're still alive and in one piece," his mother said through her tears, and she tried to hug him carefully.

He handed his one crutch to Kevin and held his mother closely. When she stepped aside his father took Carter's hand before clasping him rather tightly. "Son, we've been praying for you constantly since the day you left. We're sorry you've had to come home injured, but so thankful you're home to stay."

Finally Joey moved got his turn with his big brother. "Hey, it's so great to have you home again," and he squeezed him tightly around the waist. Joey looked around at the two strangers. "I imagine this is Emma and her brother Kevin." He grinned and held out a hand to each of them.

"Goodness, I'm sorry, Emma and Kevin," Carter's mother said. "We don't mean to be so rude. We're so grateful for everything you've done for our son, Emma. And for you too, Kevin, driving them from California to Minnesota, and then here today. Thank you."

Kevin grinned. "Emma helped with the driving, too. She's better at driving a car than rowing a boat, but that's another story Carter can tell you about later."

Carter's dad clapped Kevin on the back. "That sounds like a story Joey and I might like to hear. But Marge has supper ready with turkey and all the fixings. Kevin and Joey, how about you two bringing in the luggage while I make sure this son of mine makes it to the house okay after that long trip?"

Marge turned to Emma. "I'm sure the boys can handle the suitcases. Why don't you come in with me and wash up a little while I get the food on the table?"

Emma turned to Carter, so used to making sure he wasn't having any problems, but she realized his father could handle anything that would come up.

Carter smiled at her. "See you inside shortly. I just want a minute to look around the old homestead and thank the Lord that I've come home."

She nodded and followed Mrs. Benton into the large kitchen. Breathing in the aroma of the turkey in the oven made her realize how hungry she was.

"There's a bathroom off the kitchen to the right. Take your time freshening up, and the meal will be ready by the time the men come in."

"Thank you, Mrs. Benton. I shouldn't be long, and I'll be glad to help you out."

"Just call me Marge, dear. All my friends do."

Carter's family seemed so friendly, and they reminded Emma of her own. She hoped once more that one day the two families could be one big, happy family with her and Carter united in the middle as husband and wife.

Chapter Forty-Two

*A*llie woke the next morning to a hand on her left arm but—still unable to turn her head—assumed it was the nurse. Then the person leaned over to look into her face and she saw it was her mother.

"Alice Marie, oh, honey. I'm so sorry."

Allie saw the tears streaming down her mother's cheeks, and felt nothing except that same emptiness she had faced since she woke yesterday and learned her whole world had been torn apart.

"No need to cry, Mother. It won't bring Daniel or my world back to where it was just two days ago. I'm now as dead inside as he is physically, and I don't think I'll ever be able to feel or weep again."

"Alice, that doesn't sound like my girl who lived and worked so hard for the Lord most of her life."

"And look where that got me."

"But think of the baby, dear. The doctor and nurse told me the baby is doing well, and they expect him or her to make it full term. That's something to live for."

The nurse came in with a tray. "Are you ready for breakfast, Allie?"

"Thank you, but I'm really not hungry."

"You need to eat for your baby and to regain your own strength."

"What's the use? The baby and I should both have died with Daniel, then we'd all be in heaven together."

"I understand that life seems hopeless for you right now. But you'll need to be here a few more weeks and, in that time, if you don't eat on your own, we'll have to feed you intravenously."

"Now Alice, I'm sure you don't want that to happen," her mother said in a coaxing voice as if to a small child, which irritated Allie.

"Sit me up, nurse, and I'll eat every bite to satisfy everyone. Meanwhile, Mother, why don't you go to the cafeteria and eat something yourself to keep up your strength. It seems like you might be here awhile if you plan to stay until I can leave."

When Allie was sitting with a tray of food in front of her, her mother walked to the door and looked back sadly before leaving.

The nurse moved to the door too. "Allie, I know you're suffering. Just remember that your mother had a long trip down here with your husband's sister and her husband, too. They're all tired, grieving and they still have to discuss the details of your husband's funeral arrangements with you."

Allie was beyond worrying about anyone else's feelings right now, and answered the prying nurse shortly. "They can do whatever they want. He belonged to them a lot longer than he belonged to me. I just don't care anymore."

The nurse just shook her head and left.

Allie concentrated on eating every bit of the food on the tray to keep everyone from nagging at her. If she had her way, she'd never eat another thing and just lay there until she died of malnutrition but—as the nurse said—they wouldn't allow that to happen.

The best plan would be to get strong as soon as possible so she could go back home. At that point she could decide if she wanted to go on living and—if not—how and when she would end it all. She had to be sure she never versed that thought to anyone, though, or she could end up in a home for the mentally insane.

After the nurse took the tray—praising her for eating all her food—her mother came back, followed by Eileen and Arthur. Eileen walked over to Allie and gripped her left hand, weeping.

"Allie, I'm so sorry. I know how much I'll miss him, but I'm sure your sorrow goes much deeper. They told us how he shielded you and the baby with his body. That is so like Daniel. He loved you so much, and when he wrote about the baby he was so excited that the words almost bounced off the page. That was unlike the calm brother I knew who was always planning ahead."

Allie tried to drum up an expression of sympathy from within her now-frozen heart, but very little came to mind. She shrugged. After all, Eileen's life would go on as usual with her husband and two children, but it was Allie's life that was destroyed right along with Daniel's. "I'm so sorry for your loss, too, Eileen and Arthur. I know how much you both cared about Daniel. The nurse said you wanted to discuss arrangements for his funeral. They tell me I'm to be here at least a month; so whatever you plan, I'll be unable to attend anyway."

Arthur stepped closer. "We've discussed this with David and Joyce White from the mission. We've considered having a service here in the hospital chapel. David offered to do the eulogy. That way you can attend the service. We can either have Daniel shipped back to be buried beside his and Eileen's mother, or taken to a cemetery of your choice in your home area, whichever you'd prefer."

Allie's mind felt as dead and blind as her heart, so she closed her eyes for a moment before speaking. "I think Daniel would prefer being buried beside his mother. When I'm able to travel, I'll go there to visit the graves, but I think that's the right choice."

"If that's what you're sure you want, I'll go ahead and make the arrangements," Arthur said, and Eileen nodded her head in agreement.

When they left, Allie turned to her mother. "Where are you staying?"

"David and Joyce gave me the use of your room, if it's okay with you. Arthur wanted me to ask you if you want him to take Daniel's clothes from the room before they leave."

"Yes. He can keep any he wants and give the rest to the mission to dole out. I believe Daniel would have liked that. How long are you planning to stay down here, Mother?"

"As long as you're here, Alice. I told David and Joyce I'll assist them at the mission when I'm not with you. That will help them until they find a couple to take your place."

"That's good of you. I'm sure they'll appreciate it. I really need to sleep. Do you have a way back to the mission?"

"Yes, Arthur and Eileen are staying there too, and he rented a car while they're here." Her mother squeezed her hand lightly. "Have a good sleep, dear. We'll be back in the morning and will know more about the funeral arrangements by then."

When she left, Allie lay back with a sigh. After six months of marriage, the arrangements to end it all would take only a moment to resolve and a few days to make it like it never happened. But she knew in her heart she would never again be the same.

The funeral service was only an hour away. Allie would be thankful to have it over with and Daniel's family gone. She had tried to pretend she was doing better than she was for their sake, but she was tired of the pretense. They would be flying back—taking Daniel along in the casket they had chosen—to have another service in their church and a burial beside his mother.

Allie's mother and Joyce helped Allie put one of the larger maternity dresses on over the broken arm after they were able to get it down over the neck brace. Her mother brushed her hair gently. The nurse came to push her to the chapel in a wheelchair, and Allie was upset when she rolled her up front by the casket.

Allie wanted to scream, "No, I don't want to see him. I saw him once, and once was all I can take." Instead, she clamped her mouth shut and looked at him lying so peaceful and handsome in the brown suit she had chosen from the three Arthur had brought to her for a decision. She forced back the tears that finally threatened to come, and willed her heart and mind to turn as blank as they had been since she awoke after the accident.

Her left hand reached out of its own volition to touch his hand and then his face. They both felt cold and almost rubbery, and she quickly jerked her hand back and laid it in her lap. The nurse wheeled her back beside the first row of seats as David White began the eulogy. She sat as though deaf, and her body felt as cold and rubbery as Daniel's had. She retreated into the darkness of her mind until the entire horror was over and Daniel—the main part of her life for the last six months—was forever taken from her.

Chapter Forty-Three

"The meal was delicious, Mrs. Benton," Emma praised.

"I'll second that statement," Kevin stated.

"It's been a while since I've eaten your great cooking, Mom, but I will definitely third what our guests said."

"Thanks to all of you, but cooking a decent meal is the least I can do to welcome our guests and my oldest son home with us again. And Emma, remember I told you to call me Marge. Now, why don't all of you relax in the living room, and I'll be in shortly. I'm sure you'll be ready to sleep soon after that long trip."

"Marge, I've been sitting enough. Please allow me to help with the dishes."

"Okay, Emma, if you're sure. The men can talk in the living room, and you and I can get acquainted while we work."

Marge asked how Emma and Carter had met. Emma explained that Carter's unit had been stationed at Schofield for intensive battle training, and told her they'd done a lot of sightseeing together on his days off. "When he left for Guadalcanal, we wrote back and forth. Then came the day I had dreaded might happen; he was brought back to base after being wounded, along with his friend Shakespeare. Carter was devastated when Shakespeare passed away."

Marge nodded. "He wrote to us about that, and also about how he's to take some of Shakespeare's belongings to his wife. From what he said, I don't think he is looking forward to that day."

"Yes, he's brought that up several times to me as well. If I could only stay in the states longer, I could go with him to see her. I admired Shakespeare too. He was such a good Christian man who was always ready to encourage anyone who was afraid or feeling down."

Marge dried the last dish and put it in the cupboard. "Well, let's join the men for a few minutes, and then we can get you all settled in for the night."

The men were laughing when the women entered the room. "What did we miss?" Marge asked.

Joey was doubled over, still giggling.

"I'm sure it wasn't that funny when it happened," Kevin said with a grin, "but Carter and I were telling them about his and Emma's rowboat trip; it was right after we'd warned him about Emma's rowing abilities. Lightning struck a tall tree on the bank and it fell across the lake almost on top of them! They had to dive into the water and drag themselves to shore, with Carter's cast full of water. Then, by some miracle, the tree falling in flipped the boat upright again; Emma swam out and brought it back to shore. Carter rowed them home where we were all worriedly waiting for them."

Marge looked horrified. "Joey, that's not funny at all! And Amos, how could you have laughed? What if Carter had drowned after surviving being shot in Guadalcanal and making it back to Minnesota?"

"That's what I kept saying," Emma spoke up. "I felt it was my fault for taking him that far when I knew how quickly a storm could brew up on the lake."

"But remember, Emma, the Lord was watching over us, and Dr. Delasko said it was good that the accident caused the bone splinter and shell fragment to move out close to the side of my leg where he could easily remove them."

"Well, we need to praise the Lord for bringing you both through it safely. Which reminds me, do you three plan to go to church with us tomorrow?" Marge asked.

"I do," Carter said. "I have a lot of catching up to do. What about you two?" he asked Emma and Kevin.

"I wouldn't miss it," Emma said, and Kevin stated it sounded great to him.

"In that case, why don't we get you three to your rooms since we'll be up rather early in the morning. Kevin, do you mind bunking in with Joey?"

"No, ma'am. We'll try not to talk all night."

"Carter, we put the cot in here for you to use until you can manage the steps more easily," his father said. "Emma, I believe Joey put your bag in Carter's room upstairs."

Emma hadn't realized how exhausted she was until she lay down in Carter's bed. Just the thought of all the years he had slept in it made her feel warm and snugly.

Carter woke up early the next morning and smiled to think that Emma was sleeping upstairs in his room—in the very bed he had slept in most nights from his youth on up to adulthood. *Would there ever come a day when they would be husband and wife and share that room when they came to visit?* It was nice to think about. He sat up and made his way on the crutches to the downstairs bathroom, where he washed up and got ready for church before anyone else got up.

Later, everyone was dressed, had eaten, and were driving in Carter's car on the way to church. "You've certainly kept my car in topnotch shape, Dad. Thanks a lot."

"It wasn't just me, son. Joey was always wiping off any smudges and cleaning it inside and out. He said when he's old enough to drive, you would probably let him use it once in a while if you saw how he cared for it, so he needed to keep it looking good."

"Good thinking, Joey. Do you have any good-looking girls eyed up yet to ask out on a date when you get to drive?"

"Nah, Carter. The girls my age are already checking out the older football players hoping one of them will ask them out."

"That's the way it works sometimes. But just wait, one of these days a cute one your age will notice you and start following you around."

"I'm in no hurry. What if that did happen, and just when I was really liking her, she up and dropped me for another guy? I don't what that to happen to me."

Carter knew how that felt, and exactly what girl Joey was talking about. Feeling his face flush, he glanced over at Emma, but she was studiously looking straight ahead. Apparently Allie's rejection of Carter and hasty marriage to another man had affected the family, too, and not just Carter.

"Joey, that's enough talk about girls," their mother said in a sharp tone.

Fortunately, they were pulling into the church parking lot right then.

Carter prayed he wouldn't run into Allie's parents.

Greeted warm-heartedly by many church members, Carter's spirits lifted, and he made his way into the sanctuary on his crutches. When they were finally filing into a row halfway up the aisle, he looked around and was glad he didn't see Allie's parents anywhere. They must be traveling this weekend.

After the offering was taken, the preacher stood at the pulpit. "I want to first and foremost welcome Carter Benton back with us from the war front at Guadalcanal. Although he sustained injuries that will keep him from further serving our country's mission, we're delighted that he is healing and to have him back with us safe and sound. Welcome back, Carter!" Everyone gave a hearty round of applause, and get well wishes and thanks were murmured from all over the congregation.

The minister continued, "It is with a heavy heart that I to make a second announcement today about one of our members. Many of you were here six months ago when Alice Preston married Daniel Martin. Soon after, they went to Mexico on a mission trip and were asked to stay out the year." He paused to gain control of his breathing.

"Several days ago, Daniel and Alice were returning from a check-up for Alice at a local hospital when a bus hit their car head-on. The jeep was pushed over a long embankment, turning over several times. Daniel died at the scene, and while protecting Alice from harm. Alice was taken back to the hospital unconscious, with a broken arm and injured neck. The baby she is expecting survived the accident, and they have high hopes he or she will make it through to the end of the pregnancy. Dorothy Preston is in Mexico with Alice at this time. Please pray for the entire family."

Carter sat rigid from the first mention of Allie's name as it was linked with Daniel's. While the preacher discussed the accident, Daniel's death, and Allie's injuries and the baby she was carrying, Carter felt he might hyperventilate. Everything he had gone through was paled by comparison to what Allie was now experiencing.

This was *his* Allie suffering. He sensed Emma glancing over at him and knew his face must appear visibly shaken, but he couldn't remove his thoughts from Allie's plight.

When the congregation stood for the first hymn, Carter rose woodenly, unable to sing a note. How he wished he could be by Allie's side to comfort her, but he knew all he could do was pray for her.

Chapter Forty-Four

*E*mma felt Carter's pain from the first mention of Allie's name, and she wanted to weep openly for him and Allie when the preacher relayed what had happened. She wondered what was going through his mind, and if he would ever be truly over her and ready to move on to a new relationship.

She thought the sermon would never end so they could leave and he could get away, breathe some fresh air. On the way out, she heard others discussing the sadness of what happened in Mexico with Daniel and Allie. Few people were stopping Carter to talk, since they most likely knew his relationship with Allie before he left for the war, and found the situation awkward at best.

Then a young couple came up to him, and the woman was crying. "Oh, Carter, I'm so sorry about how things turned out between you and Allie. Now, with her life to have come to such tragedy, and you being wounded in action, I just don't understand how things like this happen to good people. I feel awful for both of you."

"Thank you, Anna, I'm at a loss myself right now. I don't know what to say or even think. I need some time to process all that has happened." Carter gave Anna a hug, and introduced her and Jesse to Emma. "Let's get together this week for dinner. Give me a call so we can work out what night works best for everyone."

"We will, Carter. We'll be praying for you, and also for Allie and the baby."

Marge heated up the leftovers from the evening before, while Emma set the table. Carter walked outside and hobbled to a bench that faced a field and woods behind it. He needed time alone and space to begin to figure out what went wrong in his life, and how he could fix it.

Marge patted Emma's shoulder. "Just be patient and pray for him, dear. He had deep feelings for Allie for years through high school and beyond. When she refused his ring and soon after married Daniel, he was heartbroken, as were we. In his heart and mind, he had come to grips with the fact that she was lost to him forever. Now his heart must be in a turmoil, between feeling her pain and wondering if there is anything left for the two of them down the road. But, I've seen how he looks at you, and how much you care for him. Don't give up. The good Lord knows who should be together and who shouldn't."

"Thank you, Marge. I am in deep with my feelings for Carter, you're right, but the fact that I'll be going back to Hawaii in a week and will be away for the next year greatly reduces my chances of being 'the one.' When Allie returns home, who knows what will happen, and whether their feelings for each other will reignite while I'm gone."

"Just pray, Emma, and let the Lord take care of it all. That's really all you can do at this point. Now, if you could give a dinner call to the men outside, the meal is ready."

When Carter was called in to dinner, he wished he could ditch the crutches and run across the field to lose himself in the woods on the other side. *Lord, where do I go from here? My leg needs to heal before I can make any kind of life decisions. When I knew Allie was out of my life and Emma became so important to me, I felt I could see a future for the two of us. Now Allie is injured and Daniel is gone, and my feelings are tumbling over one another. At this point, I don't know how to interact with Emma or what to say to her. Please help me, Lord.*

His father ambled solemnly over to him. "Son, I know you're broken up over the news we heard this morning about Allie and her husband. Right now you can only take one step at a time and try to trust the Lord to lead you. Dinner is ready, and you may not feel like eating or being around people, but going into the house and sitting at the table is the next step at this moment. So come on, son. Let's face this together."

Carter nodded and put the crutches under his arms and took a step toward the house and people inside who cared about him.

❦

Given the circumstances, Emma didn't know whether to stay the time she and Kevin had planned on, or leave the next morning. She decided to play it by ear until she saw if Carter seemed to want her there, or if he pulled away, preferring to be alone.

When everyone was seated, Mr. Benton asked the blessing and began passing around the food to the family and their guests.

Emma noted that Carter took smaller portions than usual and ate quietly. She followed his example, since her appetite had also fled with the dour announcement that morning in church. She was sad for Allie and what she was going through, and heartsick for Carter in his pain and mixed-up feelings. But she was also heavy at heart for herself, knowing that the change in Allie's circumstances would most likely take away any chance she might have ever had with Carter.

"Mrs. Benton, the food tastes every bit as good as it did last evening. Could I have some more stuffing, please?"

Emma glanced over at her brother and noted his plate was already empty. Leave it to Kevin to have a taste for food no matter the circumstances. "Kevin, your appetite is as huge as always. The Bentons won't have a thing left in the refrigerator by the time we leave!"

"Sorry, Mrs. Benton. This stuffing is just great and makes a growing boy want more." He grinned.

"You just eat anything you want while you're here, Kevin." She passed the stuffing, potatoes, and more turkey over to him. "And don't you worry…there's plenty of food in this house."

He smiled again, dug into the dishes in front of him, and spooned out second helpings onto his plate.

Emma glanced over at Carter, and saw he had finished his food and was reaching down for his crutches to leave the table.

"Thanks again for the good meal, Mom. If no one minds, I'd like to go outside and get some fresh air." He made his way around the table and to the door without a response from anyone.

Kevin and Joey kept eating while the three adults just looked at one another. Marge finally stood and took her plate and Carter's. She repeated her earlier advice, as if she knew Emma needed to be reassured. "I'm sure he just needs time to think, Emma. Give him a little while, maybe he'll get his mind straight."

Emma helped clear the table and wash the dishes, and then straightened up the kitchen. The boys headed outside to pitch a ball around, and Mr. Benton went to the basement to tinker in his tool room. Emma didn't know what to do with herself when the work was done. "Do you mind if I go out the front door and take a walk along the road, Marge? I need the exercise, and I don't want to disturb Carter's thoughts."

"That's a good idea, dear. The traffic isn't very heavy along this back road. I think I'll bake a couple more apple pies. They seemed to go rather quickly with the boys."

"They were great. I can stay and help, if you'd like."

"No, no. You go for your walk. You haven't gotten much exercise since that long trip cooped up in the car. And helping Carter has kept you tied to the house too. Take a break. I like to bake when I'm upset, and I think each of us has a lot to think about today after hearing the message this morning."

Emma headed toward the living room and paused. "You must have known Allie well, since she and Carter dated for some time. He talked to me a little about her, and I know he was hurt deeply when she broke off their relationship and married Daniel. Do you think her feelings for Carter changed that quickly, or was it the draw to the mission field instead?"

Marge shrugged her shoulders. "I've pondered that question myself for awhile. When they were together they seemed so in love, and I assumed she cared as much for him as he did for her. Then she changed after the night of his going away party; I thought she couldn't face his being away so long, and the possibility that he may never come back. But then before I knew it, she was getting married and going off to Mexico with Daniel. She had classes with him for several years at college, so maybe she cared more for him than anyone realized. I just don't know."

"I've thought over a lot of the same things after what he told me. I guess only the Lord knows for sure. Well, thanks for being honest with me. I'll be back in a while." Emma went through the living room and out the front door. She hurried to the road so Carter wouldn't spot her if he was anywhere nearby. One thing she knew for sure; she had a lot of praying to do herself and some decisions to make.

Chapter Forty-Five

Carter turned in time to see Emma walking up the road. He wanted to call her back and weep in her arms, but he felt that wasn't fair to her. He was aware she had feelings for him, and he shared those feelings too, although they'd never really discussed it. She must feel as confused as he was since she had to return to Hawaii and would be going without any assurance of a future with him.

He knew he would miss her when she was gone. They had grown close before he was shipped to Guadalcanal, and even closer when he was injured and transported back to Schofield. She could have refused to fly back with him, and she certainly hadn't needed to take him to her home, or drive him here to his family. He had the feeling that she would leave tomorrow if he didn't open up to her today.

Lord, what should I do? Before he'd finished the question, his answer had come to him, as clear as day. Emma was a good Christian woman, and they didn't come any better. They needed to have an open and frank discussion when she returned. How he wished he could toss away the crutches and run after her.

Emma had prayed hard for guidance on her walk. On the way back, she had finally decided to leave tomorrow if Carter kept his distance. Turning into the Benton's driveway, she saw Carter sitting on a bench watching her. She walked over to him slowly. "Carter, I'm so sorry. I don't know what else to say regarding Allie's accident."

He moved over on the bench. "Sit here with me, Emma."

She sat down facing him, and searched his blue eyes not knowing what he might say. His eyes were such a fathomless shade of a perfect sky blue—she felt she could drown in them.

He slid closer and put an arm around her shoulders. "Emma, you've been such a close and understanding friend from the first day we walked the beach together on Waikiki. You seemed to understand my pain over losing Allie, and your friendship helped to ease the hurt. You supported me as a pen pal and friend when I heard she married Daniel, and little-by-little the longing for what would never be began to ease. Finally, the day came, without me even realizing it, when you were the one on my mind and in my heart. Not Allie." He looked away.

"Until this morning, right, Carter?"

He turned back to her and pulled her even closer. "Yes, until this morning. At that point I couldn't help but wonder if God had meant for her and me to be together, and I was thrown into a deep confusion. When I saw you walking down the road, it was as if you were walking out of my life, and I couldn't bear that to happen either.

"I don't know what God has planned down the road for us. I just know I don't want our friendship to end, and if God deems for it to mean more when you're back in the states, I believe we could have a good life together serving Him. That is as far as I've progressed in my thinking so far. Could you share with me where your thoughts lie right now?"

She hesitated, and then leaned over and kissed his lips softly. "Carter, I know I care more for you than any man I've ever spent time with. I pray for God's will in both our lives. If it means we'll be together in the future as man and wife, you can count on me to be there. If not, I'll be praying for your happiness whatever you end up doing."

He kissed her then. "You're certainly the kind of woman any man would be proud to call his wife, Emma. Let's promise to write back and forth, keep in touch, and let the Lord work His will in it all."

She smiled—though she felt tears in her eyes—and cupped the side of his face with her hand. "That sounds like a mature decision to me, Carter."

He took her hand in his. "Hey, what do you say we go inside, play a game of checkers, and have a nice, cold glass of iced tea?"

"Sounds like a little slice of heaven to me."

Emma and Kevin stayed two more days. She drove Carter's car while he showed her the town and pointed out all his boyhood haunts. They stopped by Annie and Jesse's house for dinner and had a great time playing with Nathan.

Emma couldn't help but note how good he was with children. Which, inevitably, led to thoughts of Allie and her baby. If he and Allie renewed their friendship, Emma could see Carter wanting to spend time with her little one, which of course meant all three would be spending time together. She pushed those thoughts away, remembering the promise she and Carter had made to let the future up to the Lord. She had to trust that His plan would be what was best for all concerned.

Kevin was in the driver's seat the morning they were preparing to leave. Mrs. Benton had packed a large bag of food for them and filled their coffee thermos.

Emma stood outside the passenger door, drawing close to Carter. "I'm going to miss you," she said, tears in her eyes as she contemplated leaving him.

"Same here, lady." Carter pulled her to him in spite of the crutches that were in the way. "Call when you get home so I know you made it safely."

"It might be the middle of the night. If it is, I'll call in the morning. You take care of yourself, Carter. Let me know when you can get around without your crutches. I'll miss you so much."

"And I will miss you, more than you'll ever know." He kissed her, and she was surprised at the tears in his eyes. He held the door for her to get in, and leaned down to look over at Kevin. "Drive carefully, young man. No falling asleep at the wheel."

Kevin grinned. "Hey, you have to admit I'm a pretty good driver. I got you from California to Minnesota and from there to here in one piece, didn't I?"

"Yes, I have to agree you did. I hope to see you both really soon. Thank you again, for everything. I'm grateful to you both."

Emma stared back at him in the side mirror—as he stood in the driveway—until they turned onto the country road and headed toward home.

Chapter Forty-Six

A few weeks later, Dr. Ambrose walked into Allie's room with a smile. "Well, Mrs. Martin, if you're sure you're up for a plane ride back to Illinois with your mother, I believe the day after tomorrow we can get you released and on your way."

Her face lit up at those words. "You really mean it?"

"You're doing much better, and walking around with no apparent problems. You say your neck no longer hurts, and the brace is gone. Your arm is healing nicely, and the baby is active and growing. I see no reason for you to stay here any longer."

"Thank you, Dr. Ambrose. Those are the best words I've heard since my arrival here. Was my mother able to get the plane tickets?"

"I gave her the news yesterday, so she was able to make the arrangements for you both to fly home. I'm sure she'll be in soon to discuss all the details. You've been a good patient with everything you've been through, and I wish you nothing but the best in your future plans." He squeezed her hand in comfort and encouragement, and left the room.

"Thank you, Lord," she spoke aloud and lay back on her pillow. It was then she realized those were the first words she'd spoken to the Lord since the day of the accident, when she'd screamed for help as the jeep rolled down the embankment. She realized her anger at God was very real, and she wondered how to go on with her spiritual relationship after the way her life had been turned upside down; everything she'd thought was following his path had been taken from her. What way did she turn now?

Allie was relieved when they finally pulled into the driveway of her childhood home. It felt like years instead of just months since, as a newly-married woman, she had left with Daniel to stay at his apartment, and from there travel together to Mexico. The flight back had been rough, and she had been glad to hug her father when he met them at the airport and drove them home.

She had grown to feel safe with Daniel and believed him when he said he would take care of her and the baby. And then such a short time later he was dead and she was in the hospital, wishing she too had gone with him to heaven.

Now all she wanted was to curl up in her own bed and let her parents take care of her. She didn't ever want to leave the house, and she didn't want people hugging her and telling her they were sorry, with that look of pity in their eyes. When Daniel died, her life died too. At this point, she wasn't even sure that she had any love or feelings left to give her baby when he or she arrived, and she had healed to the point where that worried her.

Walking into the kitchen seemed strange—like even the house didn't welcome her—and she wondered if she would ever feel at home anywhere again. "I'm really tired, Mom. Do you mind if I go up to my room to rest?"

"Of course not, dear. I feel rather disoriented myself since I've been away nearly a month. You go rest and your father and I will go for groceries. I'll let you know when dinner is ready later. Would you like a cup of tea? I'll bring you one up before I leave."

"That would be great, Mom. Thanks."

Her father came in carrying her bags of clothing from the mission. "Do you want these up in your room, Allie?"

"Please, Dad. I'll get them sorted and organized after I rest."

He followed her up the steps to her room, set the bags by the closet and moved over to hug her as she stood by the bed. "I love you, sweetheart. I can't even begin to imagine how you must feel after what you've been through. Your mother and I will be here to help you in any way we can. All you need do is ask."

"That means a lot to me, Dad. Thanks. I think I mostly need a safe place to heal right now, and for that there's no place like home, right?" He held her closely, his arms letting her know he'd do his best to be that safety net for her.

She stood by the bed until he was gone. Looking around, even her room seemed cold and bleak, and she escaped again into the familiar blankness of her mind. Right now she owed life to her baby, and after that she would decide what direction to take. At least she would know her mother would take good care of the child if she herself were no longer around.

She had changed into a nightgown and climbed under the covers when her mother knocked on the door.

"Allie, honey, I've brought your tea."

"Come in, Mom."

Her mother placed the mug on the nightstand beside the bed along with some cookies she'd baked before leaving the mission. "Here's a snack too in case you're hungry. Your father and I won't be gone long and we'll check on you when we get back. Just try to rest, dear. Tomorrow we'll give Doc Wilson a call so he can come over and make sure the trip didn't cause you or the baby any problems."

"Okay, Mom. I'll be fine. Please don't worry about me."

She heard her parents leave and was glad to be alone in the house. In the hospital there had always been someone hovering over her, checking or testing this and that, or urging her to eat. Now the total silence was all she needed.

Allie awoke the next morning to sun shining through her window and a new tray of tea and food on the stand beside her. There was a bowl of dry cereal, a small pitcher of milk, and a bran muffin still warm from the oven. She picked up a card that lay by the food.

Allie,

We're so glad to have you home, but so sorry about the circumstances that brought you here. You were in such a sound sleep last evening when dinner was ready, that I didn't wake you. Enjoy your breakfast, and let me know if you need help with your bath because of your arm. Doc Wilson will be over around 2:00.

Love, Mom

Allie sat up and ate the food—mainly for the baby's sake—because as far as she was concerned, she could care less if she ever ate again. She managed the bath by herself, though a nurse had always helped her in the hospital. It was time she became more self-sufficient, just so there wouldn't always be someone hanging around expecting her to make conversation or trying to cheer her up. What could they possibly think she had to be cheerful about?

She carried the dishes down the stairs and put them in the sink. Her mother was outside in the back yard working on the vegetable garden her father must have put in while they were in Mexico. The day was warm, so she went outside to sit in the sun and watch her mother hoe between the rows.

"Good morning, Alice. I'm glad you had a refreshing sleep last night. I thought that was probably more beneficial than waking you for supper."

"Yes, I appreciated that, thank you. I haven't gotten any true peace in months. I needed that. It looks like Dad got the garden started while you were away."

"Yes, he did. It was a nice surprise for me. You know how I like working with vegetables and flowers. Is it okay that Doc Wilson is coming over this afternoon to give you a check up?"

Allie nodded. "I imagine he'll be the one to deliver the baby here at home, so now's a good time for him to see how the pregnancy is progressing. I know one thing, he or she is certainly becoming more active."

Her mother stood and took off her garden gloves and walked over to sit at the table with Allie. "Have you thought of any names for the baby?"

Allie looked down at the large dress she was wearing and picked at a piece of fuzz she noticed. "Of course it will be Daniel, if it's a boy. If it's a girl, I've heard of someone who named a girl Danielle. What do you think of that?" She looked over at her mother who smiled.

"I think that would be quite a tribute to Daniel, in either case. I love that. Why don't I bring us out some iced tea. Something cold to drink would go nicely right now, what do you think?"

"Sounds great, Mom. This sun is sure feeling good about now too."

Doc Wilson knocked at the door after lunch. Allie stood to greet him with a hug. He had been the doctor who delivered her, and took care of every illness and accident throughout her childhood—not only for her but half the county's other youth and young adults. He had a way with young and old that instantly made them feel heard and understood. Just seeing him here raised her spirits a notch.

"My dear, there are no words to say how I feel about what you've been through. I'm sure the Lord had a reason for you and the baby surviving the accident, and I will do my best to get you both through the birth in good health. Now if you could sit on the daybed, I'll listen to the baby's heartbeat and check you both over to be sure everything is going well. I'll also take a look at the medical records you brought back from Mexico too. You're in good hands, Allie."

When he finished, he looked up at her and smiled. "That sure is an active little one you're carrying, Allie. All your vital signs are checking out well. Why don't you come over to my office next week and we'll x-ray that arm to see if the cast can come off soon?"

Allie again felt emotionally drained when Doc left, though he was one of her favorite people. At this point every person she came into contact with cause her more emotional trauma because she had to pretend she was OK; she needed to just spend time alone. She admitted to herself that she also resented his statement about the Lord having a reason for her and the baby to survive the accident; she didn't think she would ever believe that.

Chapter Forty-Seven

Carter was sitting in Doc Wilson's office discussing the war and how bad things had been in Guadalcanal. Doc had just taken off the leg brace and x-rayed the bone that had been damaged.

"The x-ray's looking good, Carter. How does it feel when you put weight on it without the brace?"

Carter stood to test it. "Still sore in spots and numb in others. Do you think it's safe for me to get rid of the crutches?"

"Only if you're willing to use a cane for awhile. Treat it like you're just learning to walk all over again; don't overdo it, and as soon as you start to feel pain, rest. If you injure it again, it could take a lot longer to heal. Try out those canes in the corner to see which one fits best, but don't get rid of the crutches just yet. Your leg will tire quickly in the beginning and you'll still need to use them from time to time."

Carter limped over slowly and tried a couple canes for size. "I think this one will do, Doc, thank you." He used it to take pressure off his leg as he walked back to the chair he had been sitting in.

Doc leaned back in his chair. "Have you seen Allie since she got home?"

Carter shook his head. "I've considered it, but I have no idea what I would even say to her, or if she'd even want to see me. Jesse and Anna stopped to visit me a couple times, and Emma and I had dinner with them. Annie had gone to see Allie, but said she didn't seem to want company. They said her baby's due in less than two months. Have you been taking care of her?"

Doc nodded. "I checked her over the day after she got home. She's in good health and the baby's quite active, but I'm concerned about Allie emotionally. She's definitely not the lively young woman we all knew before. It's like she's living in another world mentally, and refuses to go out anywhere, even to church."

"I've been going to church with my family and have seen Mr. and Mrs. Preston there, but was surprised that Allie hasn't come with them. The Prestons spoke to me a few times and asked how I was doing and we exchanged just the general niceties. When I asked about Allie, their answers were short, saying she still needs a lot of rest. I haven't felt welcome to drop by and see her."

Carter thanked Doc again and stood to leave, taking the crutches in his left arm and holding the cane with his right. His mother was in the waiting room reading a magazine and stood when he and Doc came out.

"Doc says I can use the cane part of the time so—hopefully—when the leg is a little stronger I should be able to drive the car again and use the brake safely. I still have that trip to make to Alabama to take some things to my buddy's wife," he explained for Doc's benefit, since he didn't know the story. "She should have had their baby by now. When he knew he was dying, he gave me all the songs and poems he had written while in the service to give to her, and let her know that his last thoughts were of her. He was a very special man who really loved the Lord and reached out to others ever chance he got. I need to honor his last request as soon as I'm physically able to do so."

"Well, he must have thought a lot of you too, Carter, to have given you the honor and duty that is normally bestowed only upon the best of friends and compatriots."

"Yeah. We became like brothers from the minute we met in the barracks at Fort Lawton, Washington. I think of all the men I got to know during my short stay in the army, and pray for them daily, wondering if they're still alive, dead or wounded. It makes me value each day to the fullest, yet my heart is still haunted with thoughts of these brave men, and what they're going through for our country and our freedom."

He stared at the floor briefly before looking back up at Doc. "Thanks, Doc. Hopefully, my leg will soon be back to normal. If so, maybe they'll let me go back into battle."

Doc shook his head. "I wouldn't count on that, Carter, from what I saw on the x-ray. That leg will always be tender, and a fall or sharp blow could undo what repairs have been made. I think you had a couple excellent surgeons for it to be as healed as it is now. So take care of yourself while you recuperate, and don't do anything foolish."

At the car, Carter put the crutches in the back and slid into the front passenger seat with the cane. "Well, Mom, this should be the start of my living a normal life again, though I can't help but feel guilty being here when I know what so many are going through on all the battlefields. Doc's words made me feel both relieved that I couldn't go back, and guilty that I was leaving my friends on their own."

She started the car. "Well, honey, you did what you could do in the war, and you need to think first about protecting your leg in your activities from now on if you want to be able to keep walking on it. Right now that has to be your top priority."

"Yeah, Mom, I hear you. But so often in my head I hear bombs exploding, guns going off, and men screaming and dying; it's hard not to feel the guilt."

She patted his hand. "I know, son. I thank the Lord every day that you've come home to us; I too feel sad for all the men and women out there fighting, and for all the mothers and fathers whose children won't ever come home."

They rode in silence to the grocery store in town. "I need a few things for supper. Do you want to go in and look around for something you'd like, or would you rather wait in the car?"

He opened his door. "I'll go in. This is a chance to try out walking in public places with just the cane. I've also had a hankering for some of that good chocolate ice cream they sell here. I'll get that for our dessert tonight."

His leg got tired much faster with the cane, and it was harder to get up over the doorstep to the store. Once inside, he valued something as normal as looking around at all the food choices, after the little they'd often had to eat in the field. He made his way back to the freezer section where they kept the ice cream. He noticed a woman with light hair like Allie, but she was much heavier than Allie had been. He walked up and waited behind her to pick out the ice cream.

She turned around then, and he heard her say "Carter?"

He stepped back in shock and almost lost his balance when pain shot up his leg. "Allie! I'm surprised to see you here. I've heard you seldom leave your parents' house."

"And I heard you almost lost a leg in a battle. How are you doing?"

"I was at Doc Wilson's today, and he says I can graduate from crutches to this cane. I heard about your accident. I'm so sorry about Daniel, and the injuries you sustained."

"Life takes some strange turns, doesn't it?"

"I guess only the Lord knows the end from the beginning. I had written to you about my friend Shakespeare who wrote poems, songs and stories. He was wounded when I was, and died beside me in the hospital. His wife was expecting their first baby that he too will never get to see."

"Stories like theirs and mine make me wonder if God cares at all how things turn out for us on earth. I'm glad to see you made it home, and can at least walk again, Carter. I hope your future holds better things for you."

She turned and walked away while Carter stared after her. Was that the same Allie who broke off the relationship with him so she could go serve God wherever and however He wanted her to? Her words and expressions spoke of a deep bitterness, a matching anguish to the way he had felt when Shakespeare died. He saw the depression that Doc had mentioned, and he too worried whether Allie would make it out to the other side.

Chapter Forty-Eight

Carter spent the next week walking more each day to get his leg strong enough for the drive to Alabama. He had written to Shakespeare's wife, Marietta, to see if he could visit within the month, and she had answered that she looked forward to their meeting since Rodney had written so much about him. Hearing Shakespeare referred to as "Rodney" was strange to Carter, but apparently that was the name his wife knew him by. According to her, the baby had been born the same day Shakespeare died, so it would always be a bittersweet day as she celebrated each year. It was a boy, and she'd named him Rodney James for his father.

Carter searched through the words in her letter trying to get a feel for her attitude regarding her husband's death, but found no bitterness there, and he wondered why it was different for her than for him or Allie.

That took him back to his meeting with Allie for the hundredth time, contemplating her attitude change toward God. It was almost as if they had switched opinions about the decision to serve the Lord. After all the horror he had seen and experienced, he now knew he wanted to definitely follow the Lord wherever He would lead. But Allie had gone the opposite way, sinking into depression and disbelief instead. His heart broke for her.

In order to move forward with his new life goals, he had decided to start Bible school at Moody Bible Institute in September. His mother had driven him to the school to sign up for his first semester's courses, and she expressed how proud she was of him, both in what he'd done in serving his country, and now making the decision to serve the Lord.

Marietta had sent directions to Huntsville, Alabama and where she was now living with her mother on a small farm not far from the town limits. Carter was finally on the road and surprised at the feeling of freedom that surged over him. Since he joined the Army and went for basic training, there was always someone else telling him what to do and when to do it. After being wounded in Guadalcanal his life had been in the hands of someone else until he finally got home. Even then, he was constantly at the mercy of others to take him any place he wanted or needed to go. Now that his leg had healed enough to drive, he was finally free to travel anywhere on his own.

In thinking about it, he realized that even during the years he and Allie were dating, most of his free time had been spent doing what he felt would please her. That thought, however, brought back the nostalgia and familiar ache of that relationship loss, though the Allie he had run into last week was far from the determined woman he had offered a diamond ring to.

But if Allie's bitterness was due to trauma from the accident and Daniel's death, would the real Allie resurface after the baby was born? And, if so, would she remember what they had together and want him to share a life with her and the baby—along with any children they could have together?

Realizing that line of thinking was useless at this point, he turned his mind to Emma. Sweet, beautiful Emma, who had been a best friend to him almost from the time they met, and all his emotional aches soothed. They had been writing letters back and forth several times weekly, and he could tell from the tone of her words that she missed him as much as he missed her. He knew life with her would be good, wherever they ended up.

He talked to the Lord at that point, asking his blessing on Emma and her family. Then he prayed for Allie and the bitterness she appeared to have regarding her change in circumstances, and her need to blame God for it.

His leg was tiring, so he stopped for gas and a light meal inside the small, attached restaurant. Later he stopped for the night at a motel to give his mind and his leg the rest they deserved.

He crossed the state line into Alabama the next afternoon. When he

A Bridge to Somewhere

entered the town of Huntsville, he laid out the paper with the directions to the farm. He found the place out in the country by four o'clock, said a brief prayer and took a deep breath before getting out of the car.

A big hound dog lumbered off the porch and down the four steps to greet him, long ears swaying as he walked. "Hello there, buddy. Are you the official greeter?" Carter petted the dog and went up onto the porch. He heard the cry of a baby when he knocked, and figured he indeed had the right place. A woman answered the door and he recognized her from the picture Shakespeare had shown him. He offered her a smile and held out his hand to embrace hers.

The woman smiled. "Well, you have to be Carter. Come right on in. My Mama's out milking the cow, but dinner's in the oven, so come on in and rest while we talk."

"Before we sit, I've been carrying this duffel with me ever since Hawaii, waiting to be physically well enough to make the trip to deliver it to you. Shakespeare entrusted it to me, and I will feel much better when it's safely in your hands." He pointed to the bundle that contained Shakespeare's writings and photos he'd brought to the door with him.

"I'm much obliged, Carter. He thought so much of you. Knowing Rodney, I'm sure he wanted you to hand-deliver his things so we could talk in depth about all that you two and your unit went through—from the meeting in Fort Lawton to the day you were both wounded. He would have wanted me to know it all, and I'm anxious to hear what happened to I can feel some peace and closure around the loss of my beloved husband."

Carter carried in Shakespeare's duffel bag containing his friend's special belongings. He was thankful Marietta appeared to be in a calm frame of mind after all she'd been through—being notified of Rodney's death, receiving his body returned to her, and then going through the funeral and burial soon after having the baby.

"Bring it into the living room, Carter. We can spread it around in there without getting in the way of cooking or dishes."

He set the bag beside the couch where Marietta indicated. The baby was beginning to fuss. "Would you like me to hold him while you begin sorting through what your husband sent?"

"You wouldn't mind?"

"It would be my honor, and help me feel close to Shakespeare again. My friend back home has a young baby boy, Nathan, and I hold him every chance I get too. I look forward to being a father one day. Are you calling him Rodney, or Junior?"

"His official name is Rodney James Gruber, Jr., but I've been calling him Jamey."

"Jamey it is, then." He took the squirming infant, wrapped the blanket around him more securely and rocked him back and forth in his arms. The baby looked up at Carter with eyes that reminded him of his father, and he mourned for the loss the baby would someday understand. He blinked a few times, peered up at Carter as if deciding whether to trust him, and then went to sleep.

Marietta smiled. "I can see you'll make a great father some day, Carter. Why don't you get more comfortable on the rocker in the corner now that Jamey's asleep? I've been spoiling him by rocking him to sleep more often than not, so he's gotten used to the motion of the rocker. With the loss of Rodney, every moment with Jamey is even more precious to me, and I enjoy spending as much time holding him as I possibly can."

Her eyes filled with tears as she turned away, and Carter wanted to cry with her over the loss of their mutual friend. He rocked back and forth holding the baby close, feeling the same nearness to Shakespeare that Marietta obviously felt when she held him like this.

He heard the kitchen door open and knew Marietta's mother must have returned from milking the cows. The hound that had greeted him on the porch sauntered into the room and flopped onto the floor by a piano.

"That's our dog, Raunchy. So named because he came up on our porch a couple months ago and made himself at home. Unfortunately, he smelled really bad after rolling in either a dead animal or manure. We gave him a good bath, and he's hung around here ever since. So the name stuck, though he spends most of his time now on the porch or in the house and hasn't rolled in anything gross since."

Carter chuckled. "He's certainly friendly enough. Maybe Shakespeare sent him to look over you."

"Hi, there. I assume you're Carter," the older woman—who was obviously Marietta's mother—said a bit gruffly as she entered the room.

"In person. I guess you're Marietta's mother and Jamey's grandmother, but I'm sorry, I didn't get your name yet."

"My full name is Marie Alena Alden, but you can just call me Marie. I've never gotten used to being called Mrs. Alden, and I'm not thinkin' of starting now. Unfortunately, now that Marietta's father passed a couple of years ago, most of the chores around here have fallen to me and Marietta. At least milking's taken care of for the day."

"Well, it's certainly nice to meet you, Marie. Your son-in-law and I became very good friends while serving in the same unit. I miss him a lot, too."

"Rodney was such a good man. He loved the Lord and wanted to serve Him in any way he could. As a Christian, it's still hard sometimes for me to understand why the good Lord takes ones like him home so soon."

"I was angry myself when I knew he was going to die, but he kept telling me the Lord had his own plan for each life and knew what He was doing. I would have gladly given my life for his, but the Lord obviously doesn't work that way."

She simply nodded and turned to her daughter. "I need to care for the milk, Marietta, and I'll have supper ready soon. You just stay here and see what Rodney sent, and talk with Carter; I'm sure he has much to tell you. Why don't I put Jamey in his crib, Carter? He'll likely sleep there through our meal. And if you'd like to use the bathroom, it's right over here." She pointed the direction of the washroom, and then walked over and gently picked up her grandson, kissing the top of his head.

"I enjoyed holding him, Marie, but if you think he'll sleep awhile, I believe I will take the time to wash up a little."

"Help yourself to a washcloth and towel in the closet to the right of the sink."

"Thank you." He stood and spoke to Marietta. "I'll be back shortly and will be glad to answer any questions you might have and go over what happened with you."

Carter realized how tired his leg was as he all but dragged himself over to the bathroom. He was glad now that he had come, and knew his fears had all been in vain about how hard it would be to meet Shakespeare's wife. She was everything, and more, that his friend had said she would be.

Chapter Forty-Nine

Carter enjoyed the ham, okra, and yams Marie served for supper, along with homemade biscuits, and shortcakes that were served for dessert with fresh strawberries and home-churned whipped cream. "Great meal, Marie. How about I do up the dishes for you while you relax from your long day's work?"

"Now, Carter, you're a guest. You and Marietta just head back to the living room and talk the rest of the evening. I'll get the dishes taken care of in a jiffy, and when my grandson wakes up I'll have time to enjoy him."

Marietta stood and took Carter's and her dishes to the sink. "Are you sure, Mama? Carter and I can do them quickly together, and you can work in your garden the way you enjoy in the evenings."

"Yes, Marie, please. I've done a lot of dishes in my lifetime," Carter joined in.

Marie looked uncertain. "Well, if you're sure. I did have some weeding that needed done. Just be sure to tell me when Jamey wakes up, and I'll come in and take care of him."

They reassured her, and Carter started washing and rinsing the dishes while Marietta put the food away and dried dishes in between. Soon they were back in the living room with Marietta continuing to go through the things her husband had sent to her.

"Oh, these two songs on top were ones he didn't get to mail to me after he wrote them." She read them aloud and hummed through them the next time. "Do you mind if I play them on the piano?"

"Of course not. I probably didn't get to read or hear them either. He must have written them the evening his group was in camp for an overnight break. He was wounded the next afternoon when Sonny and I went out to gather intelligence and send back a report. When I saw him get hit, I emptied my gun into the enemy troops, and was wounded right after him; the next day we were flown back to Hawaii with three other injured men from our unit."

She sat down at the piano and began to play the music to the first one, singing the words too on the second run-through. It brought Shakespeare to life so vividly he had to force back the tears that wanted to flow. He could picture his friend singing the lyrics himself, with his other musician-friends backing him up.

The next one was such a personal message to Marietta that she stopped in the middle of it and wept aloud. He moved to sit on the piano bench beside her and encircled her in his arms. "I'm so sorry. I know how much I miss him, so it must be much harder for you. I wish I could ease your pain."

Just then the baby cried out, and she stood to go care for him.

Carter stayed on the bench reading over both songs again. *Lord, I know you're in charge and have your reasons for everything that happens in the lives of your children. Please comfort Marietta, and as Jamey grows older, let him come to know his father through the writings he left behind.*

She returned shortly with Jamey hiccuping against her shoulder. She sat on the rocker with him, softly humming and kissing him as she swayed.

Carter went to the couch. "Why don't I tell you about the things Rodney and I did together after we met? It will probably be better for you to go through what he sent after I leave."

"You're not planning to leave too soon, are you? I really want to hear and visit with you as much as possible before you go home. I'm so grateful for this visit from you, it feels like one of my last remaining ties to the man Rodney was."

He heard the panic in her voice and sought to soothe her. "I don't want to overstay my welcome, and I need to get back before the fall classes start at Moody Bible Institute. And, I don't want to become a burden on you and your mother."

"You could never be that, Carter. I was hoping you would stay at least a week. We have the guest room upstairs ready for you, and you're welcome to stay as long as you like. I wanted to take you to some of the places Rodney and I went together even as teenagers. We began dating in eleventh grade, you know. Many of us teens in church were in the same grade and active as a group. One day we were playing softball and I ran into Rodney at first base and knocked him over. Suddenly, we noticed one another in a whole new way."

She smiled at the memory, and Carter leaned back to relax and listen to the stories she told about their dating years, going to a Bible college together afterward, and then marrying following graduation.

Marie came in before darkness had settled. "Oh, Jamey woke up and you didn't call me!"

"Sorry, Mom. He went back to sleep while we talked and I rocked him. He'll be awake again soon. Why don't you go ahead and have a relaxing bath until then? When you're ready to take the baby, Carter will most likely be ready to turn in for the night."

Marietta turned to him. "You should bring in your luggage before it's totally dark, Carter. Your leg has to be tired after driving the last two days."

"I hadn't thought about that. I'll go get it right now." He took the bag with his clothing and toilet articles out of the trunk of his car, and tried to decide if he should take the cane. His leg was complaining loudly, but if he could make it up to the room he would be using, he could swallow a couple aspirins before going to bed.

Marie was soon down and asked if he wanted anything to eat or drink before going upstairs.

"Thanks, but I'm still full from that amazing meal we had earlier. I'm much obliged for your hospitality. If you don't mind, I'll go up and settle in for the night."

"You just make yourself at home, young man." She seemed to be warming up the longer he knew her, and she went over and took the baby from her daughter's arms.

Marietta stood and gave over the rocker. "I'll help you upstairs with your luggage, Carter, and make sure everything is out that you might need."

She reached for his bag, but his hand closed over hers. "I'm not so disabled that I can't carry my own belongings, Mrs. Gruber."

She put her hands in the air. "Sorry, soldier. I know how independent you men can be. I'll go up first and make sure the guest room is in order, if that won't insult your manhood." She laughed and ran up the steep steps.

Carter chuckled, but held on tightly to the right handrail, dragging his bag up with his left hand. He turned to the room where Marietta was taking down the bedcovers and opening a window to let in the fresh evening air. "This is a nice room, thank you," he said, taking in his surroundings.

She opened a closet and pulled out some hangers. "Just hang any clothes in here you want to keep from wrinkling. And I've put extra towels and washcloths on the stand, besides the ones in the bathroom closet. If you don't see something you need, just dig around in closets, or ask." She moved over to him and gave him a hug. "I'm so thankful you came, Carter. Your visit should do more than anything to help me come to terms with Rodney's death, and the last days of his life that I didn't get to be a part of. This means so much to me. Good night."

He lay awake in the comfy guest bed, amazed at how mature and kind Marietta was. She reminded him so much of Shakespeare, and he could understand how two such wonderful souls found and were drawn to each other. He felt foolish that he'd been so afraid to come here, and he was so glad he did. He fell asleep with a smile on his face, for the first time in a long, long while.

Chapter Fifty

*A*llie lay in bed, staring at the moonlight shining through the window. She couldn't stay in one position very long since it seemed to make the baby uncomfortable, and he or she wouldn't stop kicking and go to sleep. She wondered again—as she had wondered so often—how her well-planned life had turned into such a nightmare.

What happened to the carefree days she and Carter had enjoyed together? In her visions of youth she had pictured the two of them getting married somewhere in the future after she finished the Bible Institute. She dreamed that he too would have wanted to go to a mission field to serve the Lord, and they would go together.

Then the war came along and he joined up, and now she realized she had been afraid he would either be gone for years, or die in battle. How ironic.

Apparently it was instead Daniel who had grown to love her and had dreams and visions of his own of them marrying and going to the mission field together following graduation. His dreams must have been stronger than hers, for his came to fruition; before she knew it, she was walking down the aisle of her church to become his wife—and off to Mexico they went. The first couple months of their marriage, she had resented her impulsive decisions and thought often of Carter.

Then she and Daniel grew closer, and when they discovered they were going to have a baby, any thoughts of Carter became nothing but brief reminiscent clips of their special times together.

She still couldn't believe she ran into him in the grocery store in town the other day. She seldom left her parents' home, because she didn't want to see people who might ask questions she didn't want to answer. But there he stood, big as life and twice as handsome, blue eyes looking into hers, and asking silent questions. He was already home from war, and her fears of him being gone for years or dying hadn't come to fruition.

Who was the pretty woman her mother said was with him at church several weeks ago? Where was she from, and what did they mean to one another? Jealousy spread through her like hot lava, and she absently noted that she was actually feeling something again, although it wasn't a positive emotion. *What did that mean?* Since Daniel's death she had done well closing out anything that resembled feelings of any sort—wanting her heart and mind to just feel empty and as dead as Daniel was.

The baby kicked extra hard and she turned to her back, willing sleep to come and erase all the things she could no longer deal with.

❦

Emma took her lunch out to the table under the tree where she and Carter had so often shared iced tea and long talks during his stay at the Schofield medical center. Sitting back on the chair, she closed her eyes and tried to remember the last talk they'd had there before leaving to go back to the states. She thought of how excited he was to hear she would be accompanying him as his nurse for two weeks. That trip together felt almost like a honeymoon to her, though nothing indiscreet had happened between them.

She took out the last letter she'd received from him. He was planning to leave for Alabama the next day to meet Shakespeare's wife, Marietta, and their newborn baby. He said he was still edgy about the trip and the meeting, though her letters to him didn't appear to exhibit anger or resentment toward God over Rodney's death.

Carter wrote about how freeing it would be to take off on his own and driving off into the sunset, resting when he wanted to stop, and moving on when he was ready. She smiled remembering how he had resented having to accept any help from others during his recuperation.

Reading about him registering to go to Bible College excited her. It obviously meant he was preparing to move ahead to serve the Lord in any way he was led. Her year and a half remaining enlistment time seemed eons long, because her greatest desire was now to go back to take biblical studies herself, in the hopes that she and Carter could one day serve together.

Then she read that he had run into Allie in the grocery store a few days before, and how bitter Allie had sounded regarding the Lord as the drastic ending to her marriage and missionary service. She couldn't believe that God would allow things like that to happen to His children.

> *I'm praying her bitterness is only a reaction to the trauma she has been through and not an opinion she'll carry the rest of her life. Please pray for her too, Emma.*
>
> *According to your letters, you and the other nurses are busier than ever with the wounded coming in. Please let me know if any of our buddies show up. I haven't had a letter from Sonny and the others in our unit for some time now, so all I can do is pray for all of them often.*
>
> *I also pray for you daily. Take care, pretty lady.*
>
> *Love, Carter*

She wished an "I" and "you" had been attached to his ending. As time went on, she'd come to know in her heart that she loved him deeply, but kept her letters to him in the same manner as the ones he sent to her—good friend to good friend.

His references to Allie caused jealous twinges to her heart, knowing that after a period of time since Daniel was gone, Allie might do a turnaround and head back to Carter again. *And here I am, thousands of miles away—too far to make any permanent moves of my own. Lord, all I can say is, your will be done.*

Chapter Fifty-One

Carter woke rather late to a baby crying, and was confused until he looked around the bedroom in Marie and Marietta's home and remembered where he was; he smiled, thinking of the great afternoon and evening he'd had after arriving yesterday.

Then sadness overwhelmed him—Shakespeare should be the one here instead of him. He'd been a lucky man, and it was a shame that he didn't get to experience fatherhood and family life. He would have really loved this.

His leg ached when he got out of bed. Apparently the trip had overdone it. He rubbed the area that hurt the most and dressed before heading to the bathroom. From the top of the steps he heard Marietta's voice talking soothingly to Jamey, "Now, now honey-boy, there's nothing to cry about. You've been changed and fed, and Momma's right here to cuddle you."

Carter liked the gentleness of her voice; it reminded him of the way his mother had soothed him as a child when he was upset or hurt. He was thankful once more for the great parents he'd had; he knew there were so many others who were less lucky than he was.

While shaving, he also thought of Allie's parents, and how good they had always been to her. Yet she had been very headstrong in her character since the day they had noticed one another and begun to date. She had certainly been determined about going to the mission field after graduating from Bible College, so it made it difficult for him to understand why she had apparently turned against everything she had decided to do for the Lord. He understood her bitter feelings, but he was surprised she had given up all her dreams so quickly.

It was hard for him to picture her having a baby, especially to another man. He'd often dreamed of the day she would be married to him and the children they might have together, but those dreams had fallen by the wayside, that dream had died for him.

He slowly made his way down the stairs holding tightly to the rail with his right hand. The last thing he wanted to do was to take a tumble and get the two women upset and fussing over him.

Marietta smiled at him as she rocked the baby and crooned one of Rodney's songs. Carter grinned and waved, not wanting to wake Jamey again.

She stood and whispered, "I'm going to put him in his bed, then we'll have breakfast."

He nodded and walked to the kitchen where he could smell coffee perking. Marie was frying sausage and making pancakes. His stomach suddenly felt empty and ready for some country cooking.

She smiled, seemingly in finer spirits today. "Good morning, Carter. Did you sleep well last night?"

"Like a log, Marie. The bed was so soft and comfortable, I don't think I moved all night."

"Pour yourself a cup of coffee and have a seat at the table. Breakfast is just about ready."

Marietta came into the kitchen then and poured herself a cup of coffee before carrying over a steaming plate of hotcakes. Marie brought over the sausage. "Carter, would you like to ask the blessing over the food?"

"Yes, ma'am, I sure would. Precious Lord, thank you for the food Marie has prepared, and for the safe trip you provided for me this week. Thanks, too, for this sturdy young man who arrived safely into this world. Bless him and his mother and grandmother, and watch over their safety each day. Amen."

He saw Marietta wipe her eyes before handing him the pancakes, and wished once more that he and Shakespeare could have traded places after what happened in Guadalcanal. It should have been their Rodney sitting here. His appetite had suddenly waned, but he forced himself to eat so the women wouldn't get upset.

"I have plans for us today, Carter, if you're up to it."

He smiled over at her. "What might those plans be?"

"I'll drive our truck and take you around to all the places Rodney and I used to spend much of our time. He wrote poems and stories about many of them."

A Bridge to Somewhere

"I just bet I'll remember some of them from the songs when I see them for myself. That sounds like a good plan to me. Are we able to take Jamey along?"

"No, no, young man," her mother said. "This is my day to have that boy all to myself. Marietta doesn't go much of anyplace any more, except church or the store when we need something. A day out will do her some good. You two go and enjoy this beautiful weather and a little freedom."

"Best not to argue with my Mama, Carter. We can leave any time you're ready."

Marietta drove first through the countryside to an area by a stream. "This is our old swimming hole; we have a lot of great memories here, and it's still used a lot by the teens in the area."

Carter grinned. "Looks just like the one we have back home—rope swing and all."

"I'm surprised there are no kids here today. School will be starting back up in a few weeks. Maybe something else exciting is going on. Are you up to getting out and walking around a little?"

"Sure thing. Give me the grand tour." He got out of the truck using his cane in his right hand and holding to the door with his left.

They walked a path through the woods along the stream and stopped by a large oak tree which sported a huge limb that jutted out about seat level. It would make a perfect place to perch and listen to the stream gurgling by.

"This is where Rodney brought me on our first date senior year. We must have talked for hours that day, and I guess we never stopped talking one way or another from then on." She gazed off into the distance. "I guess that's what I'll miss the most—I took for granted that I would always have him to talk to."

She turned sad eyes back to Carter, and he took her hand. "I'm not great at talking, Marietta, but I'm a good listener. Anytime you want to talk, give me a call, write me a letter, or bring the boy up to Illinois for a visit."

She patted his hand. "You're a kind man, Carter Benton. I'm glad you were with my Rodney at the end. I can see why he felt you were so special." She pulled away and moved on.

"Rodney wrote me a poem that night of our first date. It was so unique—romantic and funny at the same time. I framed it and kept it hanging in my room. Still do. We came here the night he asked me to go steady, and here's what he did that time." She moved over to another tree and ran her hand over a large heart carved into the bark with M & R forever in it. "Unfortunately, forever didn't last as long as we hoped."

"It seldom does, I guess. There's a tree in the woods on Allie's farm where I carved our initials one day, too, thinking it was the beginning of our forever together; that was also short-lived."

"Rodney kept me up on all you were going through with her. It must have been painful when she married someone else."

"It was, but I guess you don't know what has happened to her," and he went on to explain.

"Oh, Carter, how awful for her, and now she'll be raising a baby on her own like me. Is there any chance you two might get back together?"

"I doubt it very much, Marietta." Carter leaned against the tree. "I ran into her in the grocery store in town recently, and she sounded bitter against God now, after what happened. What's strange is she broke up with me because she didn't feel I would want to serve God on a mission field with her. Now I doubt if she'll ever want to go back to one herself."

"Who knows what the Lord has planned, Carter. I was so sure Rodney would make it back safely from the war, and we could go on with whatever plans the Lord had next for us." She shrugged. "Who knows what each day will bring. Why don't we go into town now and have lunch at the Soda Shoppe?"

They were both silent on the way to town, each deep in their own thoughts.

She found a parking spot close to the building, and they went in and found seats. "What a neat place," he said, looking around. "My treat, please. What will you have?"

"My usual—hamburger and fries, and a cherry coke, please."

"Coming right up!" He limped to the counter and placed the order, paying for it there. He put a couple nickels into the jukebox and punched the numbers for *By The Light Of The Silv'ry Moon*, and *We'll Meet Again*, two of his favorite songs.

As he seated himself at the table, she smiled over at him. "Good song choices. Rodney and I used to sit outside on moonlit nights and listen to those, as well as some others on the radio that we plugged into a socket through the kitchen window."

"Did he play a guitar and sing the songs he had written?"

"Oh, yeah. Some days the memories of him singing and playing are so poignant I wonder how I can go on without him."

"At least you have such great memories to help you along the way, although I understand in some ways that makes it even more painful. And he left a part of himself behind, in his son and his writings."

"I keep reminding myself of that over and over. Oh, here comes our food."

Carter asked a blessing, and they ate silently—each lost in their own thoughts of love and loss.

After eating, they visited some of the local shops. Carter bought a unique vase with flowers from a floral shop. "Do you think your mother will like these?"

"Carter, you shouldn't spend your money on flowers. Mom grows all kinds in her flower garden."

"I bet she doesn't have any of these. And besides, when these die, she can bring in some of her own to put in the vase—bringing cheer into the house. Will we be visiting Rodney's grave?"

"That's the next stop."

"What were his favorite flowers? I'd like to put something on it for him."

"He loved lilies—they reminded him of Jesus being referred to as the Lily of the Valley."

Carter went back to the desk and ordered some lilies in a special vase he could push into the ground for the cemetery plot.

The visit to the cemetery was hushed. There was a cross and a tombstone; Carter placed the lilies between them and stood with hands behind his back contemplating the memories he had of his special friend. How hard it must be for Marietta to go on without the companionship of the unique person that he was.

"Are you ready to go, Carter? It's probably time we gave Mom a break. Jamey can be a handful when you're the only one caring for him all day long."

Carter stood tall and gave a final military salute in goodbye to one of the greatest friends he'd ever have.

Carter stayed two more days with Marietta showing him around the area; he felt they parted as good friends, and he was glad he made the time for her. "You're welcome to bring Jamey and come up for a visit any time, Marietta. My parents have heard so much about your husband they would be glad to have you come."

"Thank you, Carter, for the invitation, and for coming here to share so much about the last months of Rodney's life with me. It was invaluable, and helped me feel like I was there with him during his final days. I'm glad you're going to a Bible College; Rodney would be so proud of you for it. Please take care, and come back any time—perhaps with one of your lovely ladies," she teased, as her way of saying goodbye, giving him one last hug.

He drove the entire distance in one clip this time, and got there after dark. The time had passed quickly, while he thought over the many sad and funny stories Marietta and he had shared about the person they both missed.

Chapter Fifty-Two

*A*llie was only a month away from the baby making his or her arrival, and she was dreading everything about it. The only good part would be the kicking would end soon. If the baby was anywhere near that active after birth, she didn't look forward to trying to keep up with it.

She realized she needed to get out of this house, before she was really driven insane. She decided to go visit Annie and Nathan while Jesse was at work.

"Mom, do you mind if I drive the car over to see Annie?"

"Goodness, no, dear. It's time you start getting out to spend time with someone else besides your dad and me. I could drive you over if you want. You haven't been driving much since you came home."

"I'd rather try on my own, thanks. I have to get back to my life sometime. If I can fit behind the wheel I should be able to drive." Her mother handed her the keys and she made her way slowly to the five-year-old Ford in the driveway.

She pushed the seat back as far as it would go and got in, but then her feet could barely reach the pedals, so she moved it up a little. She finally got as comfortable as she could get, made it out of the driveway, and arrived at Annie's successfully ten minutes later. She and Nathan were out playing in the yard and came over to greet her when she pulled in.

"Allie, it's great to see you out and about finally! I've been wanting to stop over again, but I felt you weren't up to company the last time I was there, and I wanted to give you time to mourn and heal."

Allie made her way out of the car rather clumsily. "It's been really rough for me getting through all the changes of the past several months, Annie. I mainly just hung around the house, reading or helping Mom with cooking and cleaning. I knew if I went anywhere I would run into someone who would ask a lot of questions, and I didn't want to put myself through that."

"Well, I won't ask you anything personal. If there's something you want to talk to me about, I'll always be ready to listen. Let's go in and have a cup of tea and a piece of apple pie, freshly baked this morning."

"Sounds good, except I don't need to gain much more weight according to Doc Wilson. But I won't pass up just a tiny piece." She was surprised how good it felt to talk to someone her own age, and comforting to know she wouldn't be asking any questions.

Allie glanced down at little Nathan who already looked a lot like his daddy. For the first time she wondered if her baby would be a boy or a girl, and whichever sex it was, would it look like Daniel? "Nathan's getting big, isn't he? And he's already starting to resemble Jesse."

"And don't think that doesn't make Jesse proud when someone says that." Annie carried Nathan into the house and held the door open for Allie. "Have a seat at the table and I'll put on a pot of water for tea." She removed Nathan's jacket, put him in his highchair and gave him a cookie to chew on.

"The fall leaves are beginning to turn already, aren't they? They're so beautiful when all the colors are out and blending. I've been trying my hand at painting lately, and Jesse says I'm getting rather good." She laughed as she filled the teakettle with water. "Of course that's a husband for you. He'd say it was good even if it was the ugliest thing ever, at least if he's smart. Didn't you used to draw a lot in high school? I remember the art teacher sometimes putting your pictures up on the wall and praising them. Do you still do much of it?"

Allie shook her head. "No, I haven't had an urge to draw or do much else since my world got turned upside down."

Annie put teabags in a lovely teapot and stood waiting for the water to boil. "I would think drawing might be rather therapeutic after what you've gone through." The kettle whistled and she turned the stove off and filled the teapot. "Do you take sugar and milk in yours?"

"Yes, please." Annie's statement had her thinking and wondering why she hadn't turned to drawing again while sitting at home these last few months. Part of her hoped she died in childbirth, and then she wouldn't have to face life ever again. Maybe that thought was what kept her from doing much of anything. Maybe she was waiting to see if that happened, and if it didn't, what would be her next plan for her failed life?

"Allie, are you okay?" Annie had placed the cup of tea in front her of along with a spoon and the milk and sugar.

"What? Sorry, Annie. You had me wondering why I haven't been drawing."

Just then Nathan laid his face on the highchair table. "Oops, I think it's time for someone's nap. Give me a second and I'll put him to bed and be back out to get the pie."

Chills swept over Allie when she watched how lovingly Annie took her son from the highchair and cuddled him closely while carrying him from the kitchen. *What kind of mother will I be? Right now I feel nothing but regret for the child in my womb. Would I feel differently if Daniel was still living, or if Carter was the father?*

Annie returned to the kitchen and took out a delicious-looking pie that made Allie's mouth water. It was then she realized that food was the only interest she had at present. No wonder Doc Wilson was scolding her about her weight. It was sadly her only comfort.

Annie placed the plates and forks on the table and sat down to join her friend. "The boy's all tucked in, so it's time for mama to relax and enjoy some girl talk."

"Does Jesse know where he stands as far as the draft goes?"

"So far, so good, thank the good Lord. Did you hear that Earl Donnelly was wounded in the Battle of the Bulge and is in a hospital in Austria?"

"No! He and Jesse and Carter were great buddies all through school. In fact, I sort of had a thing for him before Carter and I started dating. How badly was he wounded?"

"I hear he lost some toes and has a lot of shrapnel in his leg. He's to be sent home too when he's healed enough."

"I guess Carter was wounded badly in his side and leg."

"Yes, but he's worked hard at healing, and now he's going to Moody Bible Institute."

Allie's fork clanked onto her plate. "What! When I suggested he go there when I did, he wouldn't even consider it. And what about that woman he had at church several months ago? Is she still in his life?"

"She was the nurse he met in Hawaii. She took care of him there, and when he was healed enough to come home, she was given two weeks to accompany him back. After that, she had to return to Hawaii for the rest of her term of enlistment. I don't know much more than that since we haven't seen him very often either."

Allie realized that staying so much to herself, she was way behind on the local news. Now she had much to mull over in her mind. She couldn't believe that Carter was now attending Moody Bible Institute. It was like they had flips sides; she turned away from God and Carter turned to Him!

"Why don't you stay for supper, Allie? Jesse will be home soon, and he'll be glad to see you. We pray for you every night when we have our devotional time."

"Thanks for the invitation and for the prayers, but my mother would worry if I'm not home in time for supper." She stood and carried her plate and cup and saucer to the sink. "The pie was wonderful, Annie. I wish I were able to cook like that. But then, I never tried very hard to learn when I was growing up."

She hugged her friend goodbye and went out to the car, squeezing herself into the driver's seat. She backed out the long driveway and onto the road, suddenly hearing the loud squealing of brakes and then the crash of metal crunching metal. Her body was crushed against the steering wheel and she felt pain ripping up through her body. *No, not again!*

Chapter Fifty-Three

Allie was in a daze when a man knocked on her window. "Ma'am, are you okay?"

Annie came running up to the door too, just as Jesse pulled into the driveway. "What happened?" Annie screamed at the man, while trying to get Allie's door open.

"I was just driving by and she backed out right in front of me."

The door was jammed, and both of them kept trying to get it open. Jesse ran over. "Is she okay? What happened?"

The man explained how she'd pulled out in front of him and he couldn't get stopped. Jesse kicked on the spot where it appeared to be stuck, and then yanked it open. "Allie, are you okay?"

She turned glassy eyes to him. "I'm in a lot of pain. Do you think my baby is trying to come?"

"Let's get you out of there and into the house. We'll call Doc Wilson and have him come right over." But the seat had shoved her up too tightly against the steering wheel, and Jesse couldn't get her out. She started to panic in earnest then.

The other man went to the passenger door and crawled in, trying to reach the latch from that side while Jesse comforted her. "It worked!" Jesse yelled. "Now, let's get her out and into the house."

Annie ran ahead to open the door, and the two men practically carried Allie after getting her out of the vehicle. In the house, they helped her to the couch where she laid back, moaning and holding her stomach tightly.

Annie ran to the phone and called Doc Wilson and Allie's mother.

"Doc and your mother will both be here soon, Allie. Can I get you something to drink?"

She shook her head. "I just want the pain to stop. You don't think it's the baby, do you? I'm not due for another month."

"Doc should be here soon, he should be able to tell. Meantime, Jesse and the man who hit you are moving the vehicles off the road."

Annie pulled a chair over and sat holding Allie's hand. "I'm so sorry this happened."

"It was my fault. I should have been looking for any cars that might be coming. All I needed was another accident, after what I've suffered over the last one." Then her face registered fear. "What if the baby dies because of my stupidity?"

"Both you and the baby are in God's hands, Allie. Just trust in Him."

"Yeah, right. I trusted in him in January and married Daniel. Look how that all turned out! No, I don't think I have much trust left these days."

Annie heard the door open and Jesse talking to the doctor. "She's on the living room couch, Doc. This way."

"Well, young lady, what happened now?"

"I wasn't paying attention, Doc Wilson, and now I'm in trouble again. I'm having hard pain. Do you think the baby's going to be born early?"

"Let me check things out and see what's going on." He used his stethoscope and listened to the baby's heartbeat. "It's faster than usual, but he or she seems to be as strong as before." He pressed her abdomen. It doesn't feel like a contraction yet, but the accident could bring on an early birth."

Her mother and father came into the room. "Oh, Allie, I should have driven you over myself. Doc, what's the prognosis? Is she hurt, in labor?" Her mother turned to the doctor. "Is she well enough to move to our house, or does she need to go to the hospital? I'm sorry, I'm panicking and I can't stop asking questions!"

"Let's all just calm down. I think she can go home, Dorothy. If we can get her back there and into her bed, I can examine her more thoroughly to see if there could be an injury that's causing the pain. Let's try taking her in my car since it's a little larger."

Allie's parents helped her out to the doctor's car, with Jesse and Annie following behind. The man who had hit her car had already gone, leaving information as to where he could be reached.

"Hang in there, Allie. We'll have you home soon." Doc Wilson pulled out slowly and drove safely, but faster.

The Prestons left the car until later, pulling the truck into their driveway beside the doctor's car and rushed over to help get Allie out. She was gasping and moaning. "I don't think we can get her upstairs to her room, Doc. We'll put her into our bedroom downstairs instead." Dorothy rushed ahead to open the doors to the house and the bedroom, and quickly threw a heavy sheet over the bedspread for Allie to lie on.

They got her settled back onto two pillows, and she suddenly screamed.

Doc Wilson pressed a hand on her stomach and nodded. "Well, I guess that tells us the little one has decided to make his or her entrance right now."

Dorothy ran for towels and managed to get her daughter undressed and covered with another sheet.

Allie was sobbing and holding her hands on her stomach. "If my baby dies, it will be all my fault!"

The doctor listened to her abdomen with his stethoscope. "The heartbeat is as strong as ever, Allie. I think this baby is determined to make its debut into the world."

In a very rushed birth, with a few more labor pains and loud screams from Allie, the infant made its way out into the world, screaming louder than the mother. The doctor checked the baby over. "You have a very healthy daughter, Allie. My guess is she'll be as determined as her mother. So what will you name her?" Doc wrapped the baby in one of the towels and laid her in Allie's arms.

"Her name will be Danielle, but why is she so wrinkled?"

Her mother and the doctor both laughed. "Many newborns, especially early ones, often look wrinkled at birth. Your mother can wash her off now and dress her in the newborn clothes you must have stored upstairs."

Allie's mother took the baby. "I'll get her more presentable, Allie, and your father can bring the cradle in here. I'll be back to get you cleaned up, dressed, and the bed changed. Doc, why don't you go out to the kitchen and help yourself to a cup of coffee. I had put a fresh pot on before Annie called about the accident."

"Sounds good to me, Dorothy."

He turned to Allie. "Now young lady, you've just been through yet another traumatic experience. I know you're still hurting, but I want to tell you that the accident brought the birth about much faster and less painful than it would have been normally, so I guess that's something to be grateful for. Your mother will be back shortly, and she'll get you settled so you can rest a while."

He went out and Allie wanted to scream and cry herself. She thought all mothers felt instant love for their child when it was born, but just then she felt nothing for the wrinkled little person who had made her arrival so unceremoniously today. *What if she never connected with Danielle?* She certainly owed something to Dan to take care of his daughter.

Her mother soon returned—thankfully without the baby—and bringing a basin of soap and water, clean clothes and fresh bedding. She quickly set about cleaning up her daughter and the bed. Allie breathed a sigh of relief when she was comfortably dressed in a cotton nightgown and between clean sheets.

Her mother kissed Allie's cheek and gathered up the soiled laundry. "Now you just rest, dear. Your dad left the cradle in the kitchen. I'll take care of little Danielle while you sleep. When dinner's ready I'll bring you in a tray."

Allie's mind slid gratefully into no-man's-land again, where she once more felt nothing, and she welcomed sleep.

Allie jumped when a hand touched her face.

"I didn't mean to frighten you, dear, but you missed supper, and Danielle's been crying for some time. Doc Wilson checked in on you before he left, and also examined Danielle. He says she seems fine, and is probably crying because she's hungry. Your father's walking the floor with her now, so do you think you can sit up and eat something yourself before feeding her?"

"Feeding her?" Allie panicked. "What am I supposed to feed her?"

"Breast milk, dear. Surely you've heard women talk at some time regarding breastfeeding their baby. It might take both of you several tries before it works out okay, but she has to eat. Can I bring in some supper for you now?"

"Yes, please. I'm suddenly hungry too." Anything to put off trying to feed the baby from her breast. She had watched women nursing their babies at the mission, and it looked disgusting to her. *What if it doesn't work for me?*

She dragged out her meal until her father pushed the cradle into the room and placed it beside the bed. Her mother followed carrying the baby, who was thankfully no longer crying.

Her dad patted Allie's hand and took her tray. "You did well, honey. I'm sure Danielle will settle down and sleep quite a while after she eats."

Allie wanted to scream again. *Why did life take such strange and horrid turns?* She wasn't ready to be a mother, and certainly not ready to breastfeed an infant. "Don't mothers sometimes feed babies milk in a bottle these days?"

Her mother smiled. "Only if mother's milk isn't available. It's much better for infants than cow's milk or bottled milk." She placed a pillow under Allie's left arm and positioned the baby in the crook of her elbow. Danielle soon found what she was looking for. "Oh, that's great!" her mother proclaimed. "Especially for an early infant. You may not have any trouble nursing at all, Allie."

Allie looked down at the small wrinkled being who seemed to know what she was doing, but Allie felt little love or compassion for the infant.

Allie's mother tried to teach her to burp the baby in the middle of feeding, but Danielle screamed and then emitted a loud burp before going back to nursing, seeming to know instinctively where to latch on.

Danielle soon fell asleep and pulled away from feeding, for which Allie was totally grateful.

Her mother took the infant and laid her in the cradle. "Try to sleep more now while you can, Allie. When she wakes later she'll want to feed again. They nurse every two hours in the beginning months of life."

At that point, Allie wished she could just sleep the rest of her life away. Remembering her plans and dreams from her teens and the years at Moody Institute, she realized now she had only wanted to be a missionary, never a mother.

Maybe that was why she'd refused Carter's ring—he'd talked about marriage and raising children together, and that wasn't her dream. So must have subconsciously married Daniel thinking their lives together would just be as missionaries, not parents; how naive she had been, in what felt like that lifetime ago.

She should have taken proper precautions to make sure this didn't happen—but it wasn't something much talked about at home, and it hadn't even crossed her mind to use protection. *Everything in her life seemed to be too little, too late,* she thought as sleep claimed her again.

Chapter Fifty-Four

Carter had a month in at Moody Institute and was rejoicing in what he was learning; it went so much deeper than anything he could gain from just sitting in a church service every week. *Why didn't I come here after graduation from high school like Allie did? Would she have accepted my ring then and married me if I had done that?* But the past was the past, and he could only go where and how the Lord would lead him.

He was headed home for the first time since he'd come to the institute, so he threw in his dirty clothes to take home and wash while he was there. He could run them through his mother's wringer washer and hang them outside to dry. It felt good to look forward to seeing his parents and brother Joey again, and sit down to a home-cooked meal with his family while they caught up on one another's lives.

Driving his car again lifted his spirits, as he headed down the road to home, talking with God and singing along with the radio. He felt free again! Pulling into the driveway, Joey came excitedly running and shouting, "Carter's home!" His mom and dad were soon out the door as they came to greet him.

Carter jumped out and Joey flew into him, clamping his long, thin arms around Carter's waist. Carter hugged him back, lifting him up and swinging him around. "Hey, little brother, you're heavier than the last time I picked you up. My leg must be getting stronger."

When he put Joey down, his brother punched him lightly. "Uh-uh. You're just weaker because you're not exercising much these days."

Carter turned to his mother and held her tight, and moved to shake his father's hand. Instead, his dad hugged him hard. "We're so glad to have you here for a few days, son. How are things going at the institute?"

"Just great! I wish I had gone right out of school." He put an arm around his mother's waist as the three walked to the house.

A Bridge to Somewhere

"How's your leg doing, Carter?"

"Some days I still need to use the cane, but I keep doing the exercises Doc Wilson told me to do each day. I'm hoping the time will come when it's totally well, but I'm thankful I survived to come home, unlike some of my buddies. I had a letter from Sonny Hawkins saying both Randy and Johnny died in one of the battles. Our little friend, Ryan, was with them and apparently tried hard to save both their lives. He was such a timid young man, but Sonny says he's become quite the brave fighter."

Entering the house, Carter sniffed, the aroma of a wonderful dinner permeating the air. "The aroma tells me you made my favorite roast beef meal, Mom. Does it also include your great mashed potatoes and gravy?"

"Just the way you like 'em, dear, and my canned green beans too. For dessert I made two apple pies, and your dad cranked up a freezer of vanilla ice cream to go with the pies."

"Wow, sounds like a little taste of heaven." He squeezed her around the waist. "Like I always say, Mom, you're the best!" He turned to his dad and brother. "And so are you two, Dad and Joey. I thank the Lord every day for the family He gave me. I'll just wash up and help you carry the food to the table, Mom."

When he came out of the bathroom, the food was already on the table and his chair pulled out. His dad asked the blessing, and they sat down to the feast.

"What's new around here?" he asked as he filled his plate with the food that was passed. "Was Jesse drafted yet?"

"No, but he and Annie just made the decision that he should sign up. Both their parents are upset, but Jesse felt he should be out there with the rest of the soldiers doing his part."

"I hate to see him do that, but maybe by the time he goes through basic training and is sent somewhere, the war will be over. I'll stop by in the morning to see them."

"There was an accident in front of their house two weeks ago," Joey piped up.

His mother gave him a stern look, and he glanced down at his plate and started to shovel mashed potatoes into his mouth.

"Was anyone hurt?"

His mother and father looked at one another, and she laid down her fork. "It was Allie. She went over to visit Annie while Jesse was at work.

When she went to leave in the late afternoon, she pulled out in front of another vehicle that hit her car and shoved her against the steering wheel. Jesse got home just then, and he and the other driver were able to get her out of the car and into the house. They called Doc Wilson to go over to check her condition. She was having severe pain. Her parents came and they and Doc got her over to their house. She had the baby soon after, a month early. It's a girl, and she named her Danielle for the father. From what we've heard, she and the baby are doing well."

That news shook Carter so much that he laid down his fork too. "Do you think she would welcome a visit from me?'

"I heard that so far Annie is the only one she's agreed to see, but it would be worth a try to go knock on their door."

Carter spent the evening playing checkers with Joey after insisting on helping his mother with the dishes. He was up early the next morning to start his laundry, but his mother was soon beside him.

"Now, Carter, why didn't you just give me your clothes last evening and I would have had them done this morning."

"Mom, I'm not a kid anymore, and need to be able to take care of myself."

"I know, dear, but a mother sometimes gets joy from still being able to do something for her child, even if he is grown. I'll do these while you have breakfast. I know you want to visit Jesse and Annie, and try to see Allie today too."

He hugged her and kissed her cheek. "Okay, Mom, if it gives you joy, I'll take you up on your offer. Because I know it doesn't bring me any joy to do it!" He grinned and tugged on her hair. "I'll be sure to get back this afternoon to spend more time with all of you. I also have some homework and studying to do before I head back Monday morning."

Carter stopped over at Jesse and Annie's place and was greeted by Nathan running up to him as he stepped in the door. Carter picked him up and swung him up in the air, enjoying the boy's giggling and big smiles. He held him in his left arm and shook Jesse's hand and hugged Annie. "How are things in the Hayford family?"

"So far, so good. We decided I'm going in next week to sign up for the

Army. After seeing you injured, I put it off for awhile, but then decided I had as much responsibility as the next person to take part in the war."

"I'll certainly be praying for you, Jesse. It was really hard for me to visit my friend Shakespeare's wife and son after he died in battle. He never got to see his son. Jamey will be growing up without a father, and Marietta without a husband, unless she remarries at some point."

He glanced over at Annie, whose face had turned pale as she stared at Jesse. "I'm so sorry, Annie. I shouldn't have brought up all of that with you two deciding Jesse would join up and take his chances."

Annie gripped her husband's hand tightly. "We've gone over all the ins and outs of the whole decision, Carter, so don't feel bad bringing up the possible consequences of Jesse enlisting. We hear it on the news daily, too. We know what we could be facing, and we'll try our best to let it all in the Lord's hands. By the way, did you hear about Allie?"

"Yes, my mother told me about it over dinner last evening. I'm hoping Allie will let me stop in for a short visit. I hear you're the only one she's let in so far. Do you think she'll be upset if I drop by?"

Annie shrugged her shoulders. "I certainly couldn't say, Carter. She's been distant from everyone since she returned from Mexico, and I was amazed when she stopped to see me the day of the accident. I went by the next day to see how she was doing and was surprised Allie had the baby, and that she wanted me to go into her room and talk awhile. Danielle is an adorable little girl with a rather loud voice who lets Allie and her mother know when she's unhappy and wants to eat." Annie laughed. "I think Allie will have her hands full with that one as she grows older. The strange thing I noticed was that Allie seems more annoyed than loving with the dear little thing. I'd say stop by, and hope for the best."

Carter stayed for lunch with the Hayfords and enjoyed their company before finally getting up the nerve to stop at the Preston house. Henry opened the door when Carter knocked.

"Come in, young man. I've been wondering if you'd stop by. How are things at the institute?"

"Going great, Henry. I wish I had gone there much earlier. How are Allie and the baby doing?"

"The baby's just a little thing, but she has a bit of a temper. Allie seems to be having a hard time adjusting to motherhood. She and the baby are in the living room. Come on in. I'm sure she'll be glad to see you. Maybe you can cheer her up a bit."

Allie was absorbed in a book at the end of the couch and rocking the cradle beside her with her right hand.

"Allie, you have company," her father said.

Her head jerked up, brows pulled together angrily. "Oh, it's you, Carter. I'm not used to having visitors, except Annie. Since you're here, you might as well sit and talk a few minutes."

The Allie he was facing appeared nothing like the girl he'd known and loved. He sat in a chair across from her and searched for something to say. "I was sorry to hear about your accident, but glad that both you and your daughter came through childbirth safely."

She closed her book and laid it aside. "It was my stupidity for not looking behind me before backing out. Doc Wilson said the accident made the birth much faster and less painful than it would have been normally. Of course, being a man, he's never had a baby and couldn't possibly know how painful it was or can be."

Carter cleared his throat and sat up straighter, wondering what he should say to that. He chose diplomacy, and said, "Annie told me you named her Danielle. She seems to be sleeping well for you."

Allie sneered. "Yeah, momentarily, if I continue to rock the cradle. If she wakes up before you leave, you'll be sure to hear her, believe me."

Carter couldn't resist standing to walk over to look at the baby he had once hoped would be his. She was certainly tiny, with black ringlets all over her head. Annie had to be wrong. How could any parent resist a little one who looked like that? "She's beautiful, Allie. A daughter you can cherish."

"She looks more like her father than me. I was hoping her hair might be blond. So, tell me how school's going at the institute. I was shocked when I heard you were going there. I remember trying to get you to go with me, and you refused; so what changed your mind?"

"The Lord. It would be hard engaging in a war and not drawing closer to God. Shakespeare—the man whose poems I sometimes sent you—was so close to God that we all drew to him and the love he emanated, knowing he was an example of the best of humanity."

A Bridge to Somewhere

"Pooh! I once thought I was as close to God as anyone could be, and look what happened to me!"

"I know you've been through a lot, Allie. I'm sure it hurt to lose your husband that way and suffer the injuries you endured. But at least you and your baby lived through it all. God must have had some future plan for you and her. Shakespeare's wife had her baby the same day he died; she's also still hurting."

Anger crossed her face. "And I'm supposed to feel better because someone else went through a similar experience?"

"That's not what I'm saying. I'm just pointing out that bad experiences can either turn us away from God or draw us closer to Him. I remember the girl who told me she wanted to be a missionary and serve the Lord wherever He sent her. I also remember she felt that staying home and having a family was like walking over a bridge to nowhere. Those words stuck in my mind so that the Lord has made me see what you meant; now I definitely want to walk over a bridge that takes me where He wants me to go."

Just then the baby woke up with a loud wail. "Now look what you've done," Allie said. "Your loud talking woke her up, and her being awake isn't much fun at all."

"Sorry!" He reached into the cradle and picked up the tiny bundle in the small blanket, cuddling her in his left arm and moving her slowly back and forth. Her wailing stopped, and she opened her eyes and gazed up at him with curious and innocent eyes. She looked like a beautifully perfect doll, and he was immediately mesmerized.

"Well, you must have the magic touch, that might tell you whatever bridge you cross, a family will be waiting on the other side. If you'll excuse me, I need to feed her."

Carter handed the little one to her mother, and the baby wailed immediately.

"Thanks for stopping, Carter. I hope things go well for you in your studies, and that you will one day get the blessings you believe God sometimes hands out."

He walked to the door and turned back to her. "I'll be praying for you and Danielle daily, Allie, and that you will one day get back the strong beliefs you once held in God's love."

When Carter left, he was concerned about Allie's personality changes and the resentment she seemed to emanate toward her daughter. He thought of Marietta, remembering her love toward her son, and determined to phone her when he got home to see how she and Jamey were doing.

"Jamey, Mom and I are making it through one day at a time, Carter. Rodney's music, poems and stories are uplifting. I've been talking to one of our college professors, and he feels we can work together to get them all published into a book."

"How exciting! I'll look forward to getting one when they come out." He told her about Allie and the baby. "I wish you and Jamey could come for a visit soon. My family looks forward to meeting you, and you might be able to encourage Allie in some way."

"It sounds like it would also be uplifting for me too, Carter. When would you be home for a few days that we could come up?"

"I'm planning to come home one weekend a month, so if you know what weekend would suit you, I'll make sure to be home during that time."

"I'll make the plans, Carter, and write a letter to you at college. Thanks so much for calling. Hearing your voice was uplifting in itself. Bye, now."

Chapter Fifty-Five

Time moved by quickly for Carter as he took his classes seriously and spent long hours studying. He also worked in the library and cafeteria to help finance his schooling.

Marietta had written that she was planning a visit in three weeks if it suited him and his family, so he decided to go home Friday evening to work out the details with his parents. He also felt a push to stop by Allie's again on Saturday to see if her attitude was changing toward her baby and God.

He was home Friday in time for supper, and his parents and Joey were happy to hear that Marietta and baby Jamey would be coming in a few weeks. His mother planned to get Carter's room ready for them, and he could bunk in with Joey.

Carter stopped by Jesse and Annie's the next morning. Nathan was still sleeping, so Carter had coffee with them and they shared with him that Jesse was to report for Army training Monday morning. "I'll sure be praying for you, buddy. Maybe the war will be over by the time you're through training." They discussed basic training and what Jesse could expect when he got there, and then Carter switched topics.

"Have you seen Allie lately, Annie?"

"Only once. She wasn't in a very good mood, ranting on about how you felt everything that happens to us will either draw us closer or push us further from God. She wasn't happy about it. So if you plan to stop by, I'd suggest you tone down your rhetoric on God for now until she's ready to hear it."

"Thanks for the warning. I don't think I said those actual words to her, but I did say I'd be praying she'd get back the strong feelings she'd once had for God."

He finished his coffee. "I think I'll go over there now and try to mend a fence or two." He gripped Jesse's shoulder. "Please stay safe for us, friend. I'll miss you and I'll be praying for you."

When Carter knocked on Allie's door, he heard the baby crying loudly. Allie answered with a scowl on her face. "This isn't a good time, Carter. Of course, it seldom is if Danielle's awake."

He opened the door wider and stepped into the room, walked to the cradle and picked up the baby. She immediately stopped crying and hiccuped a few times, teardrops still clinging to her long, dark lashes. "Hi little one. There now, you don't want to cry and get upset," he crooned.

Allie came at him in anger. "Between you and my parents, I'll never get her trained to cry herself to sleep. Even if I pick her up, she just keeps crying."

"Maybe she senses your anger. Why are you so angry, Allie?"

She got into his face. "Why am I angry? My life has been totally turned around from what I planned. Now I have nothing left to live for!"

The baby jumped at the loudness of her voice and screamed again. Carter stepped back and soothed Danielle with soft tones, then reached out a hand to Allie, touching her arm. "Allie, I'm sure the Lord has another plan for you."

She brushed his hand away. "And don't you touch me or talk to me about God. If you had gone to the Bible institute when I wanted you to, maybe we would be missionaries together right now, and hopefully be childless for a long time."

He stepped back again, rocking Danielle in his arms. "Allie, I'm sorry if you feel I spoiled your plans for your life. Hopefully you will one day appreciate the beautiful daughter you have and find new plans that include her and bring you happiness."

The baby had fallen asleep while Carter soothed her. He laid her in the cradle, covered her with a blanket, and walked to the door.

"Don't bother coming back, Carter!" She slammed the door behind him as he walked down the steps.

Carter returned to school on Sunday after church, still upset over Allie's anger and attitude toward him, her precious baby, and God. He worked, studied and prayed hard for the next three weeks, and left early

Friday afternoon to be home before Marietta and Jamey arrived. He knew they had beat him there when he saw the green Ford truck in his parents' driveway. He pulled in, grabbed his books and laundry and headed quickly into the house. He saw Jamey napping in a crib in the living room, and smiled when he heard Marietta and his mother talking in the kitchen. He laid his books on the corner desk and set his laundry bag beside the cellar door.

"Hey, ladies, it's so great to see and hear you both gabbing like old friends already!" He walked over and hugged Marietta first. "Well, Marietta, it looks like you made good time. How did Jamey do on the way up?"

"He was an angel and slept most of the way."

"That should have made the driving more pleasurable then." He went to his mother and hugged her. "I guess I'm too late to make introductions, Mom."

"Yes, you are, we've been talking nonstop for an hour. I'm trying to convince her to stay longer than just the weekend."

"Sounds like a great idea to me, Marietta. Then you and Mom can do some more sightseeing while you're here."

"I'm considering staying a few more days, Carter. I've felt uplifted already. Getting away for a bit might be just what the doctor ordered."

Jamey slept through dinner, but woke up just as they finished eating. Carter enjoyed holding him and talking to him while the women took care of the dishes. He seemed such a happy little guy, and Carter wanted to weep at the thought that his father would never hold him or experience the joys of fatherhood.

When Joey got home from playing football with some friends, he took over entertaining Jamey while the adults talked. Before long, Jamey was yawning and fussing, his bedtime now overdue.

Carter carried the small crib upstairs to his room, and Marietta said goodnight to the family and went to care for the baby; she planned to turn in early herself, the toll of the long drive making her more tired than usual.

After breakfast the next morning, Carter's mother suggested that he and Joey entertain Jamey while she took Marietta shopping.

"I know what we'll do, Carter, let's take Jamey over to see Nathan and Annie," Joey smiled hopefully at his big brother.

Carter laughed. "Sounds good, but I know you're thinking about the awesome desserts Annie always has around."

Joey grinned. "I don't remember you ever passing them by when she gets her treats out."

"You got me there, kiddo. Off we go, then, to playtime and dessert!" They left shortly after the women walked out the door.

Annie and Nathan were outside. She was raking leaves, and Nathan was "helping." As soon as she had a pile raked together, he jumped into the middle of it and got back up giggling, leaves clinging to his hair and clothing. It was a warm fall day, so they stayed outside to visit. Carter sat on the swing with Jamey, and Joey helped to rake and jump in the leaves with Nathan. It was close to noon when Annie invited them in for lunch and dessert. Joey couldn't stop smiling as he shoved two slices of apple pie with ice cream into his mouth.

They arrived back home just before Marietta and his mother walked in, chatting away. "How was your day out, ladies?"

"It was great," Marietta exclaimed. "We had a nice lunch in town and looked through the unusual little shops you have here. I found a nice gift for my mother."

Jamey started fussing. "I'm sure he's ready to be fed. I'll just take him upstairs, if it's all right."

"Make yourself at home, Marietta," Carter's mother said.

Marietta and Jamey came back down an hour later, both looking rested, and Jamey smiled and giggled at the faces Joey was making at him.

"Carter, did you want to try a visit with Allie now?" Marietta asked.

Unsure, he glanced over at her. "I guess if we're going to try getting it in, now's as good as ever," though Carter wasn't sure of the reception they would receive after his last visit.

⁂

They were soon knocking at Allie's door. She opened it and looked surprised to see Carter standing there beside a woman and a baby. "Carter! I guess you're home for the weekend. Who are your friends?"

"Hi, Allie. This is my friend Shakespeare's widow and baby, Marietta and Jamey. I told you about them earlier."

"Yes, please come in. Danielle just recently went to sleep in her cradle." She led them into the living room, wondering if Carter was trying to take the place of his dead friend with the widow and baby, but she pushed the pain of that thought from her heart.

"Can I get coffee or tea for either of you?" she asked when they were seated.

"No, thanks you," they both replied.

Allie sat on a chair facing them as they took a seat on the sofa. The baby was squirming around, so Carter reached for him and soon had him giggling. Allie was always surprised at how well Carter seemed to be with children. "Did you drive up from Alabama, Marietta?"

"Yes, it was a great trip, and I was blessed that Jamey slept most of the way."

"How long are you staying?"

"Several days, at least. Carter's mother's been urging us to stay longer. I'm so sorry to hear about your tragedy in Mexico. It had to have been quite an ordeal."

"Yes, it was," Allie stated, looking down at the floor, then back to the woman. "But I've heard about your tragedy, too, losing your husband in war before he ever got to see his son. I'm sorry."

"It was heart-wrenching, for sure. But the Bible doesn't tell us that all of life will always be good. At least I know he's with the Savior, as is your husband."

Allie looked away toward the window. "Yes, I'm sure that's where Daniel is, but it doesn't ease our loss to remain behind on our own, taking care of a child."

"You're right about that. I suppose we're both fortunate to have parents to help carry our burden. My father died several years ago, so my mother's also glad for my help on the farm, and Jamey cheers her up a lot."

"My parents dote too much on Danielle," Allie said. "They think she should be picked up the minute she cries, and Carter's the same way when he's here. One wail and he picks her up and cuddles her." She looked at him and was momentarily dazed by the blue eyes that had always made her breathless. Then Danielle woke up with a loud wail.

Marietta took Jamey from Carter. "Maybe he can hold her now, Allie. I'm looking forward to meeting her."

"May I?" Carter asked, looking over at Allie.

"Be my guest. She's in the dining room, Carter."

He left and soon returned with the little one bundled in a small blanket and blinking up at him as he cooed. "Well hello there, little lady with the dark curly hair." He sat down by Marietta and Jamey. Jamey reached out to the baby with a gurgle, and she smiled.

They talked a while longer, and Allie actually was sorry to see them leave. "It was nice meeting you, Marietta. Why don't you come back for a visit before you head home?" Allie was surprised to feel drawn to the woman who had also lost her husband recently. She felt like she finally found someone who understood what she'd been going through. She also was curious to find out if there was any kind of relationship kindling between her and Carter.

Chapter Fifty-Six

Carter was surprised to see Allie and Danielle at church the next morning with her parents. She came over to him and his family afterward and spoke to his family and Marietta before turning to him. "Are you leaving this afternoon to go back to college, Carter?"

"Yes, Mom's planning an early supper, and I'll leave shortly after."

"Have a safe trip back, and I hope your studies are going well." She turned to Marietta. "Would you and Jamey like to come over for lunch tomorrow? I'm sure we have lots to discuss."

Marietta turned to Carter's mother. "Marie, do you have anything special planned for tomorrow?"

"Just laundry day, Marietta. So you go and have a good visit. I'll do any clothing you need washed while I'm taking care of ours."

"If you're sure you don't mind." She turned to Allie after Marie. "It sounds good to me, Allie. What time do you have in mind?"

"Noon should be good. I'll look forward to seeing you then." She said goodbye to Carter and his family and went out the door with her parents.

Carter watched Allie walk away and was surprised again at the change in her attitude since the last time he'd seen her. He couldn't help but hope meeting Marietta had been the impetus she needed to get past her pain and build a new life.

Carter left for Moody soon after supper, wishing Marietta a safe trip, and hugging her, Jamey, Joey and his parents goodbye. "I don't think I'll be back before the Christmas break, Mom and Dad. I have a lot of catching up to do getting ready for finals this semester."

He had much on his mind on the way back to Chicago: Marietta and Jamey, Allie and Danielle, and Emma, who was never far from his thoughts. How he wished she were close by so they could talk about life, and all the twists and turns that had taken place for both of them the last few years. He missed his best friend, and wondered when he'd get to see her again.

⁂

Finally, Carter's first semester of college was over, he'd passed with flying colors, and he was headed home for the ten-day stretch over Christmas and New Years. He felt happier and more content than he ever had before, and he was ready to celebrate life this holiday season. He had shopped in town for gifts for Joey and their parents, for Annie and Nathan, and for Marietta, Jamey and her mother, too. At the last minute he also bought a drawing pad for Allie—hoping she might get back to the artwork she used to love—and a small rubber doll in a yellow outfit that would go with Danielle's coloring. He had mailed quite a few gifts to Emma two weeks early to be sure she got them in time and had something to unwrap on Christmas Day.

Joey beamed when Carter arrived with his arms full of packages and his usual bag of dirty clothes. "'Bout time you got here, big brother. I have the saw ready and the tree picked out for us to cut for our celebration."

Carter grinned. "And what if I don't like that tree and want to pick a different one?"

Joey looked thoughtful. "Oh, well, since you weren't here to choose last year, I guess I can give you first choice this year."

Carter laughed. "No, squirt, I'm teasing you. I'm sure whatever you picked out will be fine."

The whole family was busy the two days before Christmas preparing for the special day. Christmas Eve they went to church together and sat with Annie and Nathan, praying that wherever Jesse was, he would be safe.

Carter was glad to see Allie and her parents file into the row in front of him, with Dorothy Preston carrying the baby. He hoped that meant Allie was feeling better and coming more regularly now.

There was a program given by the teens and children, and uplifting songs by the choir, though Carter's eyes kept drifting to Allie in the row ahead. From the back, her hair looked like the same golden curls of the Allie he remembered, and he was encouraged that she'd smiled at him before sitting down; maybe they were friends again.

The young adults were invited to Annie's place after the service. Carter dropped his parents off at home, and he and Joey drove over to Annie's, where Carter enjoyed getting reacquainted with some of his old friends from the youth group. When he stepped into the living room later, Allie was in deep conversation with Carl Thomas. Carl's family had a farm on the other side of the Preston's eighty acres, but Carl had been five years ahead of Carter and Allie's class—at that time he hadn't paid much attention to the younger kids. Carter decided to join them.

"Good evening, Carl. It's good to see you home in one piece." He reached out to shake hands. "I don't know if you remember me."

"Oh yes, I remember you, Carter. I hear you were wounded on Guadalcanal. That's supposedly a tough place to get stationed. I'm glad you made it out of there."

"Is there any place that's not tough during a war? Where is your unit stationed?"

"Actually, I'm afraid I've been medically discharged like you. My unit was in England, and I lost part of the calf of my left leg in one of our campaigns. I spent most of the past year in a British hospital having several surgeries and healing."

"Wow, I'm sorry to hear that. What are you planning to do now?"

"I'll work in one of the plants making war supplies until the war's over, then see what becomes available after that. I hear you're going to Moody Bible Institute. What do you plan after your degree is finished?"

Carter shrugged his shoulders. "Whatever the Lord leads me to do."

Allie snorted. "I just hope his plan for you works out better than mine did."

Carl looked over at her. "Allie, from what I remember of you growing up, you were always talking about the Lord, and of someday becoming a missionary. I know you had a bad turn of events, but sometimes bad turns can make us stronger and more able to go on with what we had planned, or point us to a different purpose or program."

"That's good advice, Allie," Carter said. "And I believe it's time to get Joey and head home. I'll stop by sometime this week with a gift for Danielle, if that's all right."

"I hope it isn't a stuffed animal. She already has enough of them, but I guess one more won't matter so much, so come on by. I know she seems to enjoy you holding her, for whatever reason."

Carter saw the surprise on Carl's face at her harsh words, so he put a hand on Carl's shoulder. "Have a good Christmas, Carl. Let's get together sometime this week and compare war experiences."

"I look forward to it, Carter. Give me a call."

"I could take you home, Carl, if you need a lift." Allie volunteered.

"Thanks, Allie, but I have my Dad's truck. I'll be in touch with you sometime this week, if you'd like to go to lunch a day."

"That sounds good, Carl. It helps to get away from the house once in a while."

Jealousy moved through Carter's being, though he realized what she really meant was getting away from the baby for a time, and it made him sad on behalf of Danielle, too. He hoped her mother could heal and learn to value her child before Danielle was old enough to understand what was going on.

Carter stopped by Allie's the day after Christmas. Their tree was decorated artistically as Allie had done each year that Carter had been dating her. "You did a great job, as usual, Allie. I brought a gift for you too." He handed her the wrapped drawing pad.

She looked rather stunned. "You shouldn't have gotten me a gift, Carter. I certainly didn't get anything for you." But she sat down on the couch and opened it. "A drawing pad! Thank you. I've been thinking about getting back to drawing again. Maybe this will encourage me."

He handed her the wrapped box with the doll for Danielle. "This is what I got for the baby." He grinned. "And it's not a stuffed toy."

"Thank goodness." She unwrapped it and took it out of the box. "It's great, Carter. She won't be able to hold or play with it for some time yet, but I'm sure she'll like it a lot in a few more months."

He stood, suddenly feeling awkward. "Well, I guess I'll be going now. I told Annie I'd be over for lunch with a gift for Nathan."

She got up and walked him to the door. "Thanks again for the gifts. I appreciate you continuing to be my friend, even though I've rebuffed your kindness time and again. I'm hoping the new year will bring out a new Allie. God knows I'm ready to let this current one go!"

❦

Carter enjoyed the rest of his holiday at home and spending time with so many old friends. He thought of Emma often, and wished she were here to meet his friends and just relax with. He had lunch with Carl Thomas one day, and they compared war horror stories. Then Carl abruptly changed the subject. "Carter, I know you and Allie had a serious relationship before she broke it off and married Daniel from the institute. I've admired her from afar since she was young, but now she seems as if she would consider going out with me. Would you be upset if I dated her?"

Carter almost choked on his coffee, though he had expected the question would come up after what he's seen at the Christmas party. "We have no ties presently, Carl, and I know she needs a friend. I pray daily that she will turn back to the Lord, and I would want for her what the Lord wants. So be her friend, and try to encourage her to turn back to God. I wish you the best."

Chapter Fifty-Six

*E*mma was taking a break with a glass of iced tea under their favorite tree to read over Carter's last few letters. One had just come today and she was anxious to go over it several more times. It sounded like Allie still held a bad attitude toward him, though he had obviously been trying to befriend her and the baby. Now one of her neighbors, Carl Thomas, might be interested in her. Emma wondered how Carter really felt about that. It wasn't obvious from his letter, and she was trying to read between the lines.

"Hey, Emma. I thought I might find you here," Dr. Sanford said. "Mind if I join you for a break? Things have calmed down in there for a little while." He sat in the chair on the other side of the table and took a long swallow of his iced cola. "Mail from home?"

"Yes, each of my family writes once a week. Carter and I keep in touch too."

"How's he doing? Is his leg holding up?"

"Yes, he says it's doing quite well, and the limp isn't as noticeable anymore. He's been attending Moody Bible Institute since last September, and hopes to go straight through the summers so he'll be out much sooner."

"Does he plan to be a preacher?"

"Possibly. He's trusting the Lord to lead him where He wants him to be."

"You and he are both rather religious, aren't you?"

"I don't think either of us considers it being religious—just trying to live for the Lord."

"That's interesting. Are you and Carter a couple?"

"Not in the sense of planning marriage or being engaged, at least not at this time. We're just good friends." Though Emma wished she could say it was more than that. She pictured herself flashing an engagement ring from Carter, and she imagined how happy she would be if that dream came true.

"I really need a day away from here, Emma. I know you have tomorrow off, too; would you like to go into Honolulu with me for dinner and a movie?"

She hesitated. "You know what, that sounds good. I could use a day away from here myself. I look forward to it."

❦

Emma enjoyed her day out with Dr. Sanford, or Joel as he insisted she call him. He was a good conversationalist, and asked her a lot of questions about her beliefs, and she was glad to share her spiritual ideals with him.

They started spending their day off together in activities or sightseeing, which helped take their minds from the daily horrors of the war that had taken over their medical center. She worried that Joel might be developing feelings for her, while her heart and mind remained steadfastly with Carter.

"Do you have anyone special back in the states, Joel?" she asked one day.

"You mean as in a special girlfriend?"

"I guess that is what I'm asking. If there is someone special, I can't help but wonder if she might not appreciate us spending so much time together as friends."

"I was engaged for a couple months, and we were planning a wedding until the war began and I joined up as a doctor. We wrote back and forth frequently, and then one day I got a letter stating she was marrying one of the older doctors whose wife had died the year before. She had been working in his office as a nurse. When he asked her out, she accepted, and not long after agreed to marry him. She said she was lonely, and wanted to have children soon. So that was that. Another relationship lost due to the war."

Emma touched his arm. "Joel, I'm so sorry. I'm sure that was quite a blow to take."

He smiled. "As you can see, I survived. And right now I've been enjoying spending time with a very lovely young woman. Speaking of which, would you like to spend some time at the beach tomorrow afternoon? I saw on your schedule that you have the day off."

She nodded. "I love the beach. I'll round up some food for a picnic."

He squeezed her hand gently. "I'll meet you around ten, then."

Whistling, he made his way out the door of the building.

Oh, Lord, I don't want to give Joel the wrong impression about my feelings for him. I've just been so lonely, too, and it has been good to spend time with someone the past few weeks. I don't want to lead him astray.

※

Back in the states, Carter was ending his second semester and had planned to go home for two weeks before the summer term began, but he was offered a job cleaning the buildings with several other students. He needed the money for college and expenses, so he would just have one weekend for a quick trip home to visit his family.

His mother made special meals and did all his laundry, sending him along to go visit his friends on Saturday. Jesse had been in the service for four months and was still stationed in the states. Carter prayed the war would be over before his best friend was sent overseas. He stopped to visit Annie and Nathan, and couldn't believe how Nathan had grown in the few months since he'd last seen the boy. Nathan seldom stopped talking now, and Carter could tell he missed his father by the way Nathan hung on him the entire visit.

"Have you seen much of Allie?" He asked Annie.

She nodded. "We get together at least once a week. She's been drawing every day for hours while Danielle's sleeping. Believe it or not, she's been going to church and helping with crafts for the younger kids, and the general store in town has been displaying some of her drawings for sale." Carter smiled, hoping his gift of the drawing tablet had helped change her life for the better. "She's been seeing Carl Thomas on a regular basis, Carter, and they've been coming to church together."

Carter felt like a fist had slammed into his stomach. "I guess that's good for both of them. He asked if I minded if he dated her the last time I was home. I said she needed a friend, and I hoped he could help her turn back to the Lord."

"So how do you feel knowing they're spending time together?"

"I have to admit it hurts to hear it, but she's not the Allie I dated, fell in love with, and planned for a future with anymore. I'm glad she's back to her artwork and taking part in church activities. Maybe Carl is the one for her. What more can I say?"

Carter left soon after, pretending the news didn't bother him, but he had to admit it wasn't so easy to let it go. He spent time with Joey and some of his buddies, taking them swimming in the creek that the area's teens liked to frequent, and tried to take his mind off Allie. But the whole time he was there all he could think about were the times he and Allie had spent at the swimming hole during their summers together. He walked along the bank to the tree where he had carved their initials and traced his finger through the letters. He now knew their "forever" would not be coming true.

Sunday morning in church Carter prepared himself for the jolt of seeing Allie and Carl come into church together. He was glad Annie had warned him, because it happened soon after he was seated. Carl carried Danielle, who was cooing and smiling, and they sat in the row in front of Carter and his family.

Carl turned to shake his hand. "Carter! It's good to see you again. Are you home for the summer?"

"No, I'm taking classes the summer term too, and working at the school, so I have to go back this evening."

He turned to Allie. "Hi, Allie, how are you? I hear you're doing a lot of drawing, and teaching the kids. I'm so glad to hear that!"

"Yes. Thank you for the drawing pad that got me started again. I'm also taking lessons in oil and water painting. How's school going for you?"

"Well, so far. I see Danielle has grown a lot in the past few months."

"Yes, and she doesn't cry nearly as much as she did in the beginning. Things have gotten a lot better all the way around. Now she's even enjoying the doll you gave her for Christmas."

Carter smiled, and pushed back his thoughts that it should have been him sitting beside her and holding their baby instead. Those days were over.

Chapter Fifty-Seven

*I*t was hard for Allie to see Carter looking so well and seeming so content in his life, when she was still struggling in hers. She thought not for the first time that their roles had reversed, and he was living the life she'd always wanted for them. Yet, if she was honest with herself, she was much more content with her artwork than she had been with the mission work. And through her art she could also reach out to others for the Lord. She had finally come to realize that mission work was not the only way to serve, and by opening herself up to what really brought her joy, she could more adequately serve God than by forcing herself to be something or someone she wasn't.

She glanced over at Carl as he held Danielle, and she was thankful for his influence in her life. He was so good with the baby, and she herself now felt the love for her daughter that had seemed to be missing in the beginning.

Carl apparently enjoyed the farm life, and worked along with both her father and his dad wherever and whenever help was needed. But she had to wonder how deep her feelings were for him, or his for her.

How could she know what was the right path after all that had happened to her in the past two years when she'd thought she was following God's will? She was afraid to trust her decisions. First she had felt she was in love with Carter, but wanted to serve the Lord in ways he wouldn't. So she decided to marry Daniel and go to the mission field with him, even though her feelings hadn't gone as deeply as his had seemed to.

Then his death and her pregnancy had been more than she thought she could bear, and she now realized she'd turned away from God, blaming Him for what happened. She needed to live day-to-day until the Lord showed her a clear path and she wasn't conflicted about her decisions. Just then the preacher read: "Show me your ways, O LORD, teach me your paths." She almost looked up toward the ceiling to see if Jesus was looking down at her as the words were spoken.

When the service was over, Carter's mother fussed over Danielle while his father talked to Carl. Allie looked around for Carter and saw him talking to some of the girls from their high school class. She turned away when she experienced a jolt of jealousy, and was glad he would be away at school through most of the summer.

Carter left to go back to school shortly after the evening meal. His appetite had diminished since he saw Allie and Carl together in church this morning. His mother had complained about the small amount of food he ate at lunch, so he made sure he piled more on his plate at supper and forced himself to eat it.

"Carter, I packed a lot of leftovers for you to take along for this week. I put them in a container with a block of ice, so it should be okay for a couple days at school," his mother said.

He hugged his parents, and gave Joey a light punch on his arm when he walked out to the car to say goodbye. "Joey, thanks for all the help you give to Mom and Dad. I'm proud of you, too, for the good friends you pal around with. From what I can tell, none of you are drinking or smoking." He looked into his brother's blue eyes. "You aren't, are you?"

Joey put his hands in his pockets, looked down and scuffed his shoe in the dirt before looking back up. "Of course not, Carter. I hope you trust me more than that. A couple of them have tried giving me cigarettes and sometimes a beer, but I've always refused them. You're my role model, and I want to serve the Lord and my country when I'm out of school, just like you're doing."

Carter hugged him then. "Those are words any older brother would be proud to hear. I hope to always be there for you any time you need help or brotherly advice from me. Take care now, and write me letters. I probably won't be back for a few months. Maybe not until Christmas."

He drove off thinking of the lonely days ahead, away from his family and close friends; but he looked forward to making progress toward his goals and building a brighter future for himself.

Lorena Estep

Carter made a few male friends from his work in the cafeteria and cleaning at college, and talked to some of the young women in passing who attended the institute. He especially enjoyed conversations with a couple around age forty, Joan and Samuel Orner, who were in their last year at school. They planned to go to Brazil and work with missionaries in the field, taking over for an older couple who would soon retire back to the states. They said more workers were needed in that area if Carter was considering the mission field when he graduated.

He thought of Emma often, and wrote her at least a page every night before he went to sleep. When he had four pages he'd send them off and start the next missive. He wrote extensively about the couple that was planning to go to the mission in Brazil the end of next June, telling her they were always in need of more support there. He wondered if it was something that would interest her, and waited excitedly for her response. Could this possibly be something they could do as a couple?

When Emma received Carter's letter about Brazil as a mission field, she also grew hopeful, since South America was a place she had always wanted to visit—something seemed to draw her there. *Could their path be opening up?* On her next day off, she went into Honolulu and bought a book with a lot of information on South America—especially Brazil—and then bought a second one and sent it to Carter from the post office before heading back to base. He could probably find a lot of information himself in the institute library, but this would be his own book that he could keep in his room and read when he had a little time.

She was scanning through her book on the bus ride to the barracks when she felt the bus swerve and then heard and felt a crash on the left side of the vehicle. She grabbed the back of the seat in front of her, but the bus rolled to its other side and slid along the ground. Emma lost her grip and was thrown to the seat on the opposite side, landing on the male occupant. Her head hit the window and all went black.

Chapter Fifty-Eight

Emma woke up with pain from her head to her feet and tried to open her eyes. Everything was blurry. She tried to sit up, but pain ripped through her body.

"Emma, no! Just lie still."

She heard Catherine's voice, then a touch on her arm. "Where am I, Catherine?"

"You're back in the medical center at Schofield in one of the beds. Do you remember what happened?"

Emma searched through her mind and went back to her last day off. "I remember going into Honolulu yesterday and buying two books, but nothing after that."

"Dear, that was four days ago. You were coming back on a bus when a jeep going in the other direction lost control and struck the bus on the side. The bus rolled and you've been unconscious since then. Are you in much pain?"

"All over. Do I have any broken bones?"

"Just your left wrist, and a fractured skull, which is causing you the most problems. Dr. Sanford has been in to check on you every couple hours. He said I was to come get him when you regained consciousness, so I'll go tell him now."

"Wait! What about my book and purse? Were they found?"

"Yes, sweetie. Some of the pages of the book were torn, but both it and your purse fared better than you did. The poor man you landed on helped to cushion your fall somewhat, but he was trapped until the ambulance crew arrived and got you out first."

"Is he badly injured?"

"A mild concussion and some bruising, but he's up and around and about to be sent back to his unit. You just rest now, while I get Dr. Sanford."

Emma tried to open her eyes wider, but they felt like they were half-glued shut. She began to take inventory of her body. She lifted her right arm, noting it felt bruised and sore. Her left arm was heavier, so she reached across with her right hand and felt the cast from below the elbow to her hand. Just then she heard steps coming toward her.

"Well, young lady, you finally decided to wake up," Joel Sanford said. "Do you remember the accident?"

"Just barely. I was reading when the bus swerved, then there was a crash and I flew from my seat."

"Your wrist and bruising will heal in a month or so, but the skull fracture is something you'll have to guard most of your life."

"Why won't my eyes open wider? Is it from the skull fracture?"

"Some from that and the bruising and swelling on your face. You have two black eyes, so you might not want to look in a mirror for a while." He chuckled. "I know how women don't like having any facial injuries, but I feel sure your impairment will clear up nicely within a month or so. If you feel like eating, the nurses will bring you a light meal." He patted her shoulder. "I'm just so thankful you survived."

When he left, Catherine and Sandra helped her sit up in the hospital bed, though she had to stifle a groan when the pain shot through her. "There were five others on the bus besides the man across from me and the bus driver. Was anyone else severely hurt?"

"No broken bones, just a lot of bruising. They were all soldiers who saw it coming and were able to protect themselves rather well—they weren't reading like some young lady we know. Now what do you want to eat?" Sandra asked.

"Just some tea and toast for now, please," Emma requested. "Let's see how that stays down before venturing further. I wonder if someone can help me by writing a letter to Carter to let him know what happened and that I'll be OK?"

"Sure, I can do that for you. Speaking of Carter, you had two letters from him while you were out, and a couple from your family and that Dr. Delasko. When you're up to reading, I'll open them for you," Sandra volunteered. "Or I'll read them to you, if you like." She snickered.

"Thanks, but I'll give my eyes a day or two to rest and read them in private. It will give me something to look forward to while I'm healing."

Carter received two letters from Emma, and a week later the book on South America and Brazil came. He smiled while he glanced through the book and looked forward to showing it to Joan and Samuel over lunch the next day. He wrote a long letter to Emma thanking her for the book, and saying how he wished she were there to read it with him. Since she'd also gotten one for herself, they could at least share thoughts on the country and what they'd read through the mail.

Joan and Samuel were delighted with it the next day, and pointed out interesting things they had been told the last time the missionary couple was home on furlough. Carter wrote down all they said so he could pass it along to Emma. He realized more each day how much he missed her. She was such a caring and unselfish person—so mature for the young woman she was. He checked the mail each day watching for letters from her, but grew concerned when more than a week passed without any mail from her. Finally, he used the pay phone to call her parents in Minnesota. Kevin answered on the first ring.

"Hello, Kevin. It's Carter calling from Moody Institute."

"Carter! How great to hear your voice. How are things in school?"

"They're going well. I'm calling to see if you've heard anything from Emma lately? I usually get a couple letters a week, but it's been over a week and a half since I've received anything."

"Oh, Carter, I'm sorry. We should have tried to contact you. She was in a bus accident on her way back to Schofield from Honolulu."

Carter's chest tightened like a brick and he could hardly breathe. "How badly was she injured? I pray it wasn't too serious."

"Here's Mom, Carter. She can tell you all about it."

"Carter? Hello. I'm sorry we didn't try to get in touch with you. Dr. Sanford called us after it happened and said she was in a coma, had a broken wrist, and was badly bruised. He called us four days later to tell us she was conscious. She has a fractured skull and is still in a lot of pain. That's all we know for now. Is there a number where we can reach you when we know more?"

"I'll call you from the pay phone every couple days. Meanwhile, I'll write her every day and hope she can soon write back. Thank you for giving me the information. I care so much for your daughter, Irene; I'll be praying hard." His voice broke at that point, so he quickly said goodbye and hung up.

His knees buckled and he sunk onto a nearby chair. *Oh, Lord, please heal Emma completely and quickly. You know how special she is to me, I just can't lose her now; and I know she's special to you and many others too.*

Samuel came by and stopped. "Carter, are you okay?"

Carter stood. "It's Emma. She was in a bus accident in Hawaii and was hurt rather badly. Please pray for her."

"Come over here and sit down. We'll pray together right now."

They sat and took turns praying aloud. When Carter stopped and put hands over his face in the middle of his prayer, Samuel took over, and then hugged him at the end.

"Joan and I will continue to pray for both Emma and you, Carter. Any time you need to talk, you know where to find us."

"Thanks so much, Samuel. It's good to have Christian friends like you and Joan. I hope you both will get to know Emma sometime in the future."

Carter went to his room to work on his next day's lessons, but instead flopped onto his bed, staring up at the ceiling. The news about Emma finally brought home how much he really felt for this woman who'd been a faithful and true friend since the day he met her. He thought briefly of Allie, his first love, and realized they didn't connect very well if he were honest. Even though he would always have a spot in his heart for her, he was glad they hadn't gotten married at such a young age. It comforted him to think how well Carl would care for her and Danielle, and any other children they might have in the future.

Then he pictured the children he and Emma might have together and smiled. *But does she really want a life with me?* After all, Anthony could give her so much more, and he had been a friend to her and her family for years now. Also, if she chose Dr. Delasko, she could continue working with him as a nurse when she got home instead of going to a mission field, if that kind of stability was what she wanted.

Even Dr. Joel Sanford could offer her a better life. Carter remembered the times he'd noticed the doctor watching Emma when they were both in the same room while he was healing, and Emma had hinted at the possibility of Joel having feelings for her in the letters she'd written to Carter.

But what would I have to give her except a deep love? Or what if the Lord leads me to a mission field and she isn't able to go? Or what if I'm led to be a preacher or just a factory worker and she feels she should go to Brazil, or some other country?

At that point he sat up and reached for his Bible. He skimmed through the Psalms and came to Psalm 34:4; *I sought the Lord, and he heard me, and delivered me from all my fears.* Carter's panic faded to the background with those words, and his spirit was calmed knowing God knew where he wanted both Emma and himself to be and what he wanted them to do in serving him. He thanked the Lord for the encouraging words, turned off the light and slept.

The next day Carter received a short letter from Emma's friend and fellow nurse Sandra, explaining the accident and assuring him that Emma was doing as well as could be expected. She told him Emma would write in just a few days as soon as her head cleared a bit and she was able to put pen to paper again, but she hadn't wanted him to worry with not hearing from her for so long.

He was relieved to have confirmation that Emma was going to be OK, but felt frustrated that he wasn't there to help her through her suffering in the same way she had for him. He made a vow that if things worked out for him and Emma to have a future together, he would always be there to hold her and comfort her in times of need.

Emma was feeling much better after a week of bed rest, though her body continued to ache with every movement she made. She was finally able to phone her family, and they told her Carter had been calling them every few days for any new information.

"He told us he cares deeply for you Emma," Kevin said with a teasing chuckle. "According to Mom, those were his exact words."

Emma's heart did a little flip as she smiled. "Really? He said that?"

"Here's Mom, ask her."

"Hello, dear. It's so great to actually hear your voice. How are your head and wrist doing?"

"Feeling better, although I still have a ways to go. My face looks like a raccoon, with two black eyes that are now surrounded by all shades of blue, purple and yellow. I'm still swollen and black and blue over much of my body too. It hasn't been fun, but I'm blessed to be alive and healing. So. Kevin says Carter's been calling every couple of days?"

"Yes he has. And each time he says how much he cares about you and prays for you constantly. Are things more serious than we thought with you two?"

"I could only hope, Mom. He hasn't said those words to me yet, so I've been following his lead. I'm sure he's still confused over Allie being single and in the area again."

"That's not the way he sounds when I talk with him. He goes on and on about you and how he misses your companionship."

"Well, companionship isn't quite the same as love, Mom."

"It sure goes a long way to making a marriage work out. Your father and I have been the best of companions all our marriage—of course we have our arguments and battles, every marriage does, but if you can't be best friends, the marriage will suffer for it."

"Yes, I know. Watching the relationship between you and Dad is what gives me the desire to end up with the same kind of mate—it reminds me of what Carter and I have when we're together."

"Carter will probably phone again this evening, and he'll be glad to know you're healing and making progress. He's been as worried as we were."

"Tell him...tell him I send my thoughts and love."

Her mother laughed. "I most certainly will, dear. Goodbye, and I love you so much."

Emma went back to her bed and re-read the last two weeks of letters she had from Carter, seeking any hidden words that might give her hope. She found more than she'd imagined, and saw some of what he wrote in a new light after talking to her mother regarding his calls and words of concern for her.

She thought back to the letter she had recently received from Anthony, sending his love, too, and patiently waiting for her to be back in the states to work by his side. She felt sorry that he still carried feelings for her, but her heart and life had no room for him, as kind as he was. She was glad she had honestly let him know that she wouldn't be going back to work in the hospital with him, but that she planned to attend a Bible college and possibly go to a mission field to use her nursing ability there.

A Bridge to Somewhere

She placed Carter's letters under her pillow and leaned back and fell asleep, dreaming of a possibility of being Carter's wife one day, and what it would be like to build a life and a family with him, wherever they would be.

Chapter Fifty-Nine

A week later Emma received a letter from Carter telling her how upset he had been when he heard of the bus accident and the injuries she had suffered. He hated that he wasn't there for her the way she'd been for him when he was injured, and he wished he could be there with her.

He ended with, "Do you think you'll be getting a medical discharge to come home? I long to see you with my own eyes to know you're healing, hold you, and tell you I'm sorry you had to go through this. My thoughts and prayers are constantly with you, Emma. I love you. Love, Carter."

Emma read and reread the letter over and over. Was this finally the declaration she'd been dreaming of? It sure seemed to be. This was the first time he had ever signed his letter "I love you, Love, Carter." Tears filled her eyes and ran down her cheeks.

"Are you okay, Emma?"

She jumped and clasped her letter to her chest when she heard Dr. Sanford's voice. She gulped and nodded her head. "I'm fine, Joel. It's a letter from Carter."

He set an iced tea on the table for her and another one in front of the chair directly across from her. "Is it bad news? Has something happened to him?"

Emma wiped the tears from her cheeks before answering. "I'm hoping it's good news; the words I've been waiting to hear for a long time." Then she made a decision and pushed the letter across to him. "Read it and see what you think."

He looked surprised. "Are you sure? I know how private you are about your life."

"Right now I'd like a man's point of view about what he said."

"Okay, if you're sure." He picked up the letter and read it slowly, then laid it down, a thoughtful look on his face. "Well, I'd say the man is in love with you; if he's just now saying those words for the first time, then that is deeply meaningful. Congratulations," he continued, although he looked sad. "For some time now, I've been hoping feelings have been developing between you and me, though you've definitely been keeping our relationship as friends and nothing more. Now I understand why. I thank you for letting me read this and knowing where your heart stands. I wish you and Carter the best, if that is indeed the path that is unfolding before you."

He handed the letter back to her. "I came out to give you a special message. The Colonel is putting in your medical discharge paperwork this week, so you may be seeing Carter again much sooner than you thought. Though I must say, I'll be missing your friendship and nursing ability."

Just then the sound of an ambulance siren came wailing into the compound area. Joel stood. "It sounds like I'm being paged." He clasped her hand. "I think you should tell him how you feel, Emma; I know its Carter you've wanted for a long time, and it looks like those feelings are being returned." He controlled his expression, then hurried off to take care of the ambulance and his new patients.

It made Emma sad to think she may have caused Joel pain by spending time with him, even though she knew she hadn't sent him any mixed signals. She went over the letter again, feeling the thrill it sent through her body, and prayed for the Lord's will in the lives of both her and Carter.

When Emma returned to her room, she found her friend Sandra there, in tears. "What's wrong, Sandra?"

"Sonny's one of the three injured they're bringing in, and they said his leg is shattered below the knee!"

Emma hugged her friend. "I'm so sorry, honey! I like Sonny a lot too, and I know he and Carter are good friends. Let me come help you with him."

"Thanks, Emma. I heard you'll be getting a discharge to go home soon, though; so you need to guard against doing anything strenuous, or it could affect your own injuries negatively."

Emma followed behind, and knew the first one was Sonny when she saw the blood seeping through the bottom of one side of the blanket covering him. She also saw his red hair peeking out at the top, and her heart slammed in her chest. She knew Sandra was fighting back tears as she moved toward the door to guide the medics into the surgery room.

Emma followed her into the operating room to see if Joel needed any help. He led the medics over to the table he had prepared and helped them get Sonny situated.

Joel glanced over at Emma. "You can stay if you're up to it, Emma. I'd appreciate your help with light duties while Sandra covers the rest."

Emma nodded and moved over to where he indicated. She gasped when the blanket was removed from Sonny's leg and saw only blood and strips of skin where the bottom of his left leg had been. She saw Sandra's face blanch at the sight. Joel called out what tools he needed as he moved ahead to cut away flesh and disinfect for any germs. Soon he neatly sewed up the part of the leg that was left below the knee.

Sonny had remained sedated throughout the transport and surgery. Two medics helped by moving him to one of the beds that Sandra had readied in preparation for the newly arrived men.

"How awful for him, Emma. I know he planned to form a new band if he survived the war and made it back home. What will his life be like now?" Sandra asked.

"He still has his arms, hands, fingers, and voice, Sandra. He can still play a guitar and ukulele and sing. He's tough, and won't let his leg keep him back from doing something good with his life. I know he's a Christian, so God must have something special for him to do yet on earth."

"I know you're right, Emma. I wish I had the spiritual strength you do. Seeing all the tragedies we've witnessed here tends to make me question just what our purpose on this earth truly is."

When Carter received a letter from Emma letting him know that Sonny lost part of his left leg below the knee, he dropped to his own knees beside his bed and prayed for his buddy. Then he remembered letters from both Sonny and Marietta sharing that the two of them had been writing back and forth. Since they had never met in person, he doubted there was something romantic between them; but it would be nice for them both if they ended up together, and could continue Shakespeare's musical legacy.

He continued to study, work hard, and pray for family and friends daily. Then one day he got paged to the front desk for visitors. Fearing something had happened to Joey or his mother or dad, he rushed down to the desk and came face-to-face with a lovely brunette and a man on crutches who sported a red shock of hair! He stopped, surprised, before recovering and rushing over to them.

Carter hugged Emma first. "Oh, my goodness! You are a sight for sore eyes! And, you're all in one piece and as lovely as ever!" Then he turned to Sonny, "And my great friend is alive and standing in front of me, too! What an incredible day." He hugged Sonny more gently, not wanting to cause him any pain. "How did you get here, how did all this come about?" In his excitement he couldn't stop asking questions and wasn't even waiting for the answers!

"It's a long story," Emma said smiling. "Is there somewhere we can sit to go over everything?"

He hugged her again. "Yes, let's go to the cafeteria where we can get something to eat and have a very long talk." He kept her hand in his, but slowed his pace to allow for Sonny's crutches.

"How's the leg healing, Sonny?"

"You mean what's left of it?" He laughed. "It's supposedly healed rather well so far, and Doc Sanford said he felt I'd soon be ready for an artificial bottom half to be attached for some use. Looks like you're almost as good as new. I hardly noticed a limp."

Carter got them seated at a table and asked them for their order. "I sometimes wait on tables for special occasions," he said, grinning, "So I know where to get the best food."

"Well, I'm starved, friend. Bring me whatever you think tastes the best," Sonny requested. "You know what I've been eating for years, I'm certainly not picky at this stage of my life! Anything will taste great."

"Same for me," Emma added with a smile. "It's been a long trip from Hawaii, with not a lot to eat along the way. You're our first stop."

"You haven't been home yet?" Carter asked in surprise.

"Neither of us," Emma said. "They discharged us both at the same time to travel together, so we knew you would have to be our first stop."

"I'm sure there are a couple rooms here I can get for each of you to rest up a little. Then I'll definitely take time to see that you both get home safely. Wait until I bring back our dinner, and we can talk as long as we need."

Carter walked over to the food section whistling and with a huge smile on his face. This was the best day ever! He picked up a tray, dishes and silverware, and filled the plates with all the foods he thought they would most enjoy. After he set down the tray and got everyone situated with silverware and dishes, he reached across for both of their hands, sharing a blessing of prayer and thanksgiving over his closest of friends.

As they talked nonstop, Sonny shared, "I've been writing letters to Marietta and she's been answering. So I'm planning to take a bus or train down to meet her and Jamey as my next stop on the way home. She sounds like such a nice person, and wrote about how she and an editor are putting together a book of Shakespeare's songs and poems."

"She wrote to me about it too, and I think it's a great idea—but I just thought of another idea! I could take time off from my work here and drive you down."

"Are you sure, Carter? That would be great if it doesn't mess up your schedule."

"No, I'm ahead on my studies anyway, and I think the school will give me the time off I need."

"That would be super, Carter, but if we go by way of Nashville, I could stop at home to pick up a few clothes."

Carter stood up. "That would work, Sonny. Let me talk to the man in charge, and I'll let you know if it's settled."

He was soon back. "It's all set! We can leave in the morning. It's about 500 miles from here, so we'll need to leave early. I'll call Marietta and run everything by her."

He looked across to Emma. "What about you, lady? Would you like to go along and meet them too? I know Marietta would love to meet you. Then, when we're done touring the country, I'll take you home to Minnesota."

She reached over and took his hand in both of hers. "Are you sure, Carter? Would Marietta and her mother feel all the company was too much? If not, I'd love to go, but I'll need to call my family and let them know I'll be a few days later getting home."

"Since we're through eating, why don't I call Marietta, and then you can call your family and get things settled with them. I'll also find rooms for each of you."

Carter phoned Marietta first and shared the idea with her.

"Carter, what wonderful news! I'd love to see you and meet Sonny and Emma. I've been in a down time, missing Rodney, yet trying to keep myself up for Mom and Jamey. We have lots of room, so please, please come on down. When do you think you'll get here?"

"If we leave early tomorrow morning, stop a short time at Sonny's home in Nashville for him to pick up a few clothes, and drive straight through we should arrive tomorrow evening, if that's not too soon."

"Never too soon! Have a safe trip and come on down! We'll have sleeping arrangements all ready for you when you get here!" He could hear the elation in her voice, and was so happy that he could bring her some good news and hopefully some new friends too in Sonny and Emma.

Carter got a room for Emma and took a cot to his room for himself, so Sonny could have his bed. Overwhelmed with joy in all that had come about, he kept praising God all the while.

After taking Emma's luggage into her room, he turned to her and took her hands into his. "Does this mean what I pray it does, Emma? Do you have romantic feelings for me as I do for you? If I'm wrong, please forgive me for jumping to the wrong conclusion. I've valued your friendship for so many years that I don't want to mess up a good thing, but I want you in my life as more than a friend too, if you'll have me."

She was laughing and crying all at the same time, and threw her arms around his neck. "You silly man, I have loved you from before you even left for Guadalcanal! I was so afraid to let you know because of your feelings for Allie, so I just kept my love to myself and hoped one day it would be returned. I guess today's finally the day!"

His arms went around her to hold her lightly. "Coming to know the depths of you has made me realize the meaning of true love between mates. That it's built on not only love, but also friendship, comradery, and shared dreams. I feel all these things for you, and I want to have it all, with you and no one else, if you'll have me. Now, I think we need to try to sleep since we have to leave so early in the morning. We'll have time to talk and make plans once we get to Marietta's. Good night, my love. I can't wait to see you again in the morning." He gave her a tentative and very loving kiss before heading back to his own room.

Carter and Sonny talked into the night until Sonny fell asleep in the middle of a sentence. Carter grinned and praised God one last time that he had his friend and the love of his life back before rolling over to sleep.

Chapter Sixty

Carter woke early as the first glimpse of light came inching through the blinds. He smiled at Sonny's snoring and prayed before getting out of the cot to pack his small bag with enough clothing for a few days.

"I guess it's time to go since your bag's already packed, Carter." Sonny mumbled from the bed.

"Good morning, long lost friend. Let's get a quick breakfast and hit the road." Sonny sat up grinning and swung his legs over the side of the bed with a groan.

"You okay?"

"Better than I was the couple weeks after surgery at the medical center in Schofield. I'd say we were both fortunate to have had Doc Sanford to fix us up, along with all the nice, capable nurses we had taking care of us. I think you got the best of the lot with Emma. So you're finally over Allie?"

"Yes I did, and yes I am. We can over it more in-depth later. Right now let's eat breakfast and hit the road. What about you and Sandra? Emma told me how upset she was when they brought you in and you lost your left leg below the knee."

"We got pretty attached during the time we spent in Hawaii before shipping out to Guadalcanal, but once we were apart we didn't correspond very often. And once I was awake in Schofield after surgery, I could tell it grossed her out that I had lost half a leg. But there are more women where I come from who might want me with half a leg." He grinned and waggled his eyebrows.

Carter laughed and took his hand, helping him to stand and hugging him. "You've still got that sense of humor I've always loved. I'm so glad you didn't lose it through the hell of war. You're right there, buddy, and I'll be praying that the Lord will bring you together with the right one."

They walked to Emma's room and Carter knocked, calling out,

"Breakfast time!"

She opened the door with a radiant smile. "I've been waiting hours to hear those words." She stepped out and closed the door.

Carter couldn't take his eyes from her lovely face. He took her hand and drew her close for a kiss on the cheek. "Then let's get breakfast, lady, and be on our journey!"

After breakfast, Carter put their luggage in the trunk and seated Emma up front in the passenger seat. "Does that give you enough room in the back, Sonny?"

Sonny grinned. "Lots of room to lay down and finish my sleep. You two talk all you want, and I'll try not to eavesdrop."

The couple talked endlessly—trying to cover the lost time of the months they were apart—while Carter drove and Sonny snored in the back. They stopped to get lunch and gas, and spent only a short time at Sonny's where Carter helped him get from the car to the house. His stepmother was the only one home and greeted Sonny with open arms.

"We can only stay a couple minutes for me to grab some clothes, Mom. This is my friend, Carter, who I've told you so much about. We're driving to Alabama to stay with another friend there, but I'll be back in a few days and then you're stuck with me for awhile. Carter's girlfriend Emma is waiting in the car." He grabbed a few things without falling and handed them to Carter to pack for him. They were soon seated in the car and back on the road again.

While riding, Sonny talked most of the way about the letters he and Marietta had exchanged. He was excited to meet her and Jamey and her mom, and see all the music Shakespeare had written over the years.

It was almost dark when they pulled into Marietta's that evening and were greeted by the old hound on the porch, who hobbled down to give each of them a sniff. Marietta rushed out to welcome them.

"Please, come in!" Marietta called and opened Emma's door for her to get out to a huge hug. "You have to be Emma, and you're even more lovely than Carter has told me!" That had Emma giggling and blushing, and Carter made a mental note to give her compliments more often.

Carter was soon out of the car and around to hug her next, then turned to take Emma's hand. "Emma, I'm sure you know this is Marietta, and the woman behind her is her mother, Marie, and she's carrying baby Jamey."

"I'm so glad to meet you all. Marietta, your husband was such a wonderful Christian man, and we all loved him and miss him. He brought joy to every group he joined."

Marietta wiped tears from her eyes before turning to the back door of the car and flinging it open. "And this has to be Sonny back here with the red hair and a huge grin. Welcome, Sonny. It's so great to meet you in person. Here, let me take your crutches out so you can join us. Supper is ready, so we hope you're all hungry, because Momma and me cooked up a storm for you all today."

While Marietta got Jamey settled in his high chair and Marie set the wonderful-smelling dinner on the table, the guests took turns washing up in the downstairs bathroom.

When everyone was seated, Marie asked Carter to bless the food, and he thanked the Lord richly for the safe trip, good friends, and the mouth-watering meal that awaited them. The women had outdone themselves with chicken and homemade dumplings, corn, late squash, and bread from the oven; followed by Marie's special apple pie, made with apples from their own trees.

"Ladies, this meal was beyond marvelous," Sonny said. "Carter can attest to the many 'so-called' meals we had in Guadalcanal, consisting mainly of rice and any canned good we'd been fortunate enough to come across. If I never see rice again…"

"We've heard news on the radio and in newspapers from time-to-time of the lack of rations for all in the military," Marie said. "We're fortunate to live on our farm and be able to raise much of our own food, and try to help others around us who are in need. You all feel free to help yourselves to anything you want to eat any time while you are here. Please, make yourselves at home."

After the meal Emma and Carter carried the dishes to the sink and insisted on washing them, while Marietta and Marie focused on putting the leftovers away.

"We want to show you to your rooms so you can go to bed anytime you're tired," Marie said. "When Marietta gets Jamey to bed shortly, we can relax in the living room and catch up more on each other's lives."

Carter and Emma retrieved their belongings, also taking in the bag of clothes Sonny had in the back seat, along with his ukulele.

Carter was shown to a room that he and Sonny would share with two twin beds. Emma was given the same room Carter had slept in the last time he had visited. There were four bedrooms, Marietta and Jamey had their room together, and Marie had her own.

Going back downstairs Emma and Carter found Sonny and Marietta chatting away at the kitchen table.

Marietta shooed them away. "We're doing just fine here together. Why don't you two go out and take a short walk. There's a beautiful moon tonight. Later we can have some music. I'll play the piano and Sonny can either play Rodney's guitar or the ukulele he brought with him. Meanwhile, Mom will try getting Jamey to sleep."

Carter and Emma headed outside to gaze up at the moon together, both pondering all the times they'd looked at the moon and wished they were with the other. "What a great night for two people in love to share." Carter pulled her close and kissed her gently. "It feels like a night I'd like to remember forever."

She leaned her head back against his shoulder and sighed in contentment. "It's our first time alone after declaring our love for one another. How much more special could it be?"

He leaned down and kissed her again, before leading her to a bench where they could sit with the full moon glowing down around them. How he wished he had a ring to offer her just then, how incredibly romantic that would be. The thought took him back to the ring he had offered Allie and she had refused, and it made him nervous about trying with another woman. Eventually he had returned the ring to the jewelry shop for money towards his schooling. He now knew he'd soon be looking for another one to offer this special woman.

"What are you thinking, Carter? I'm sure you want to finish your courses at Moody. Are you still considering going to a mission field when you graduate?"

He looked down into her questioning eyes, and he pictured their lives together wherever the Lord would lead them.

"Yes, Emma, I want to finish my Bible courses, and I pray the Lord would have us serve Him together wherever he leads. What are your feelings regarding that?"

He saw hope and love in her brown eyes. "Carter, when I look back over all God has done in our lives in the past years, I have to believe he has meant us to serve Him together. So I have to say from the depths of my heart, 'Where you go, I will go; where you lodge, I will lodge.' We both believe deeply in the same true God, and I know we will follow together as He leads."

Just then they heard the house door open and Sonny call out: "We're all ready to make music, if you two lovebirds care to join us."

They both chuckled. "We'll be right there. Save us a seat," Carter answered.

For the next couple of hours the music entranced them all, with Sonny and Marietta's voices blending so well together, and both Emma and Marie harmonizing beautifully too. Carter knew his voice would spoil the notes, so he rocked the baby to sleep and enjoyed listening to the music. Many of the songs he remembered from his time with Shakespeare, and some of them were the ones that Sonny and Shakespeare had collaborated to make, bringing tears to the eyes of all present.

Carter was awakened by the appetizing aroma of sausage and pancakes early the next morning. He hurriedly dressed and washed up in the bathroom. Sonny followed soon after, and when they both went down to the kitchen they were greeted by all three women setting the table and preparing food and drinks. Jamey sat in a high chair putting small pieces of pancake in his mouth and giggling when the men made silly faces at him.

Emma and Carter quickly took over doing the dishes once again when all had been well fed. With the kitchen clean once more, Marie ordered them all out to enjoy the day.

"I'll love having Jamey all to myself," she argued. "Marietta can show you around the area. Have lunch at the soda shop and check out the stores in town. I'll have dinner ready around 6:00 and we can enjoy more music this evening."

The four were soon in Carter's car with Marietta giving directions from the backseat where she sat with Sonny. "Turn left at the next intersection so we can go to the cemetery first. I want to put these flowers from our backyard in the vase by Rodney's grave."

Carter remembered the way from the time he had been there before. It was a beautiful sunny day and he drove up as close as possible to Shakespeare's grave so Sonny wouldn't have such a hard time getting there with his crutches.

When they all stood in front of the marker, Carter felt chills course through his body, remembering the last words his friend had gasped out to him before taking his last breath. In his heart he still wished he could have taken the man's place, but he had to acknowledge that God was the one in control of life and death. Then he felt Emma's hand gripping his, and he had to be grateful he was alive to experience this time with her. He told them all what Shakespeare had said to him in his last moments, and each of them took turns speaking a few words about the ways Shakespeare had influenced their lives. It was indeed like they were having the funeral Carter, Emma, and Sonny hadn't gotten to attend, and it provided them all with healing and closure to the pain of his loss. Even Marietta seemed deeply affected, and thanked them for their love for her husband.

From there they drove into the unique small town to roam around through the shops. In the clothing store the men each bought a new shirt, and Sonny got a pair of jeans that were the perfect length for his right leg, and could be pinned up on his left one.

While the women checked out the ladies clothing at the other end of the store, Carter whispered to Sonny, "I want to go to the shop next door. I remember seeing jewelry in it the last time I was here. I brought some extra money with me in hopes of finding a ring for Emma."

"Go for it, buddy. I'll stay here and try to keep the women looking a while longer."

Carter rushed off and found the jewelry at a locked counter at the far end of the store next door. He looked the rings over carefully, and finally spied a set with both a small diamond and wedding ring that would be perfect. A man came over behind the counter. "Do you see something you'd like to buy?"

Carter nodded. "I'd like to see the diamond and wedding band set in the back, please, and check on the price too."

The man opened the lock and brought out the set, which he placed on the shelf in front of Carter. "I saw you limping a little when you came in. Were you wounded in this war, young man?"

Carter nodded, said "Yes, sir, I was," then took out both rings to look at them more closely. He felt sure they would fit Emma's small hand and wondered if he had enough money along. "What is the price for the set?" he asked the man.

"They're a special price right now for returning soldiers. Where were you stationed?"

"Guadalcanal, sir."

"I've heard that was one of the roughest spots for our men. I'm sure I can give you a good price on this set if you think it would work for your special woman." He stated a price that Carter knew was more than affordable with what he had with him.

"I'll take it, sir," and he counted out the money from his wallet.

"Here comes another wounded one," the man said, and Carter turned to see Sonny walk in the door.

"That's my best friend who served at Guadalcanal with me, but he took a greater loss than I did. We're both grateful to have survived and have the chance to build a life for ourselves now that we're back from the war."

Sonny made his way over to Carter. "Did you find what you were looking for?"

Carter showed the rings to him and Sonny whistled. "You'd better hide them real quick, I think the women are headed this way."

The man smiled and put the ring box in a small bag for Carter to hide in his pocket just as Emma and Marietta came in the door.

As usual, Carter's heart went into a spin just looking at Emma, his heart leapt, and he hoped their wedding wouldn't be too far away. She walked over to him and slid her arm through his. "I wondered where you got to, Carter. Did you find anything special in here that Marietta and I might like to check out?"

He heard Sonny half-choke at those words, and heard him say, "I saw a couple necklaces over along that other wall, ladies, let's go see if there's anything there you'd like."

He led the women over and Carter followed. "Ooh, I like this one, Emma. What do you think?" Marietta asked.

"That color would be perfect for you, and the one beside it would go with the dress I have on. Let me buy the one for you, and I'll get the other one for myself."

Sonny stepped over and took both necklaces from them. "This is the day for men to treat the ladies. I'll get them both."

Carter took the one Emma liked from Sonny's hand. "I'll get this one for my lady. If you want to get Marietta's choice for her, I'll find something else she would like too for all their hospitality."

"If Sonny wants to get this one for me, Carter, I'll certainly be honored for the gift. I don't need two necklaces, so if you'd like to get the pink one for mother, she would love it."

"What a great idea," Carter said, and took both necklaces to the counter to pay for them, while Sonny bought the one for Marietta.

Carter was starting to get the idea that there could be a little chemistry between the two of them, though Sonny would need to go home soon and get his life going in a new direction, and Marietta would still be grieving her husband for some time.

"If anyone else is hungry, why don't we drop by the soda shop for lunch," Sonny suggested.

They were soon in the shop and seated at a table. The waitress took their orders, while Carter put money into the jukebox close by, making sure to pick all their favorites.

Emma smiled contentedly, looking around at her friends, and enjoyed the comradery over a light lunch and some good music. She couldn't wait to spend the evening with them again. It was a magical time, full of light, laughter, and love after all the darkness the war had brought in the last two years. She wanted to remember this moment forever.

Chapter Sixty-One

Carter and Emma were still in the kitchen when the others said their goodnights and went upstairs to bed. Carter took Emma's hand and led her to the door and out onto the porch. "The moon's still out, lovely lady, why don't we enjoy it again?"

She gazed up at its brightness, then turned back to smile up at him. "These two days still feel like a dream come true to me, Carter."

"Believe me, I feel the exact same way. It feels like I've been waiting for this moment all my life. Why don't we sit on the bench for a few minutes again before turning in for the night?" It was a warm night, and Carter couldn't wait another minute to offer her the diamond and ask her to marry him.

When they sat on the bench, he put his left arm around her. "Are you warm enough?"

She snuggled closer to him in response, saying, "Anywhere you are is warm enough for me, my love."

He held her closely for a moment, then took a deep breath, reached into his right shirt pocket, and took out the ring in the small box. He moved to kneel on his right knee in front of her. "Emma Tanneyhill, you are the love of my life, and I am forever grateful that God has brought us together. The last two years getting to know you and love you have brought me such acceptance and a quiet sense of joy. Will you accept this ring as a token of my love, and marry me as soon as our plans can bring it about?"

Emma gasped, put her right hand over her heart and held out her left one toward him. "Yes, Carter, a thousand times yes! I feel like the luckiest woman in the world to wear your ring and become your wife. And yes, please, as soon as we can arrange it!"

He slipped the ring onto her left hand, stood, and pulled her into their first kiss as an engaged couple. He felt tears on her cheeks, and realized they had blended with some of his own. "Well, my darling Emma, I doubt if either of us will sleep too well tonight, but tomorrow I think we'll be discussing plans for our upcoming nuptials." His smile held all his love for her, and she answered shyly with one of her own.

She held him close, never wanting to let him go. "When we get to Minnesota we'll get our ideas pulled together and our families on the same page, and soon, my love, we'll be calling each other husband and wife."

Emma was up early the next morning after tossing and turning as Carter had predicted. She used the bathroom while the others still slept, and was soon dressed with her suitcase packed and carried downstairs.

Marie wasn't far behind her. "Good morning, Emma. You're sure the early bird, but I imagine you're anxious to get home to your family and the lakehouse."

Emma couldn't help but smile. "And now for an even better reason!" and she held out her left hand to Marie.

Marie put a hand over her mouth and gasped. "Oh, my goodness! A diamond ring!" She hugged Emma and grinned widely. "How fortunate you both are that the good Lord brought you together after all you've both been through."

"And a thousand 'AMENS' to that, Marie!" Carter said from the kitchen doorway.

Marie rushed over to hug him too. When she congratulated and released him, he moved over to Emma, kissed her lips, and then her ring hand, before holding it over to the sun shining through the window to show off the sparkle. His eyes beamed with pride.

Marietta came into the kitchen next. "Why is everyone up so early? I know you need to get on the road soon, but I'm missing all of you already."

"Show her, Emma," Marie said with a huge smile.

"Show me what, Emma?"

Emma held out her left hand and Carter moved over to put his arm around her.

Marietta gasped. "Oh, Emma, and Carter! You're engaged! When did that happen?"

"Last night under the full moon when all of you went off to bed!" Emma exclaimed, and moved closer to Carter as they gazed into one another's eyes.

Marietta moved over to hug both of them. "It couldn't happen to a nicer Christian couple. I hope we'll be invited to the wedding. Any idea when and where it will be yet?"

"I'm sure once we get to Minnesota, the plans will start moving along," Emma said, and Carter grinned. "Of course you'll all be invited," he said. "We're like family."

Just then Sonny hobbled into the room on his crutches with his red hair standing out in all directions. "With all the noise down here, it's rather hard for a fellow to get some sleep. What's going on?"

Emma and Carter both laughed and she held out her hand with the diamond. "Whoa, buddy, you gave her the ring! Congratulations!" Sonny puffed himself up. "I was in charge of keeping you ladies out of the store yesterday while he bought it. I did a pretty good job, if I do say so myself." He joked and winked at Emma and Marietta.

He turned to Marietta. "I think I heard a young man singing in his crib before I came down. I think the words sounded sort of like 'Mommy, come get me.' "

They all laughed, and Marietta headed for the stairs while Marie and Emma started making breakfast.

✿

The three friends were on their way to Nashville an hour later, after a sumptuous breakfast that would keep them going for hours.

They reached Nashville early in the afternoon to drop Sonny off at his home. His stepmother answered the door again, hugged Sonny, and greeted Carter who was holding the bag of Sonny's clothes.

"Your father and I have been so excited that you're back in the states, and waiting for you to get back from Alabama." She glanced down at the bottom of the pant leg that was pinned up. "Welcome home, Sonny. Your father should be back from work soon."

She looked over at Carter. "Thank you so much for taking good care of our son. Would you and your girlfriend want to spend the night before finishing your trip?"

"He and Emma just got engaged yesterday in Alabama, Mom. So I think they want to get on the way to her home in Minnesota so they can share the exciting news with their families."

Sonny turned to hug Carter. "Thanks for everything, buddy. I know you and Emma have a long drive ahead of you still. Be sure to let me know when the wedding will be. I'll try my very best to be there." He moved onto the porch and called out goodbye to Emma.

She had the window down as she saluted him. "See you soon, Sonny. Take good care of that leg, and I hope you get a band going again. You're too good to keep all that music to yourself. You've got to share it with the world."

Carter and Emma got back on the road, stopping for gas and snacks in Nashville, and hoped to get to Minnesota before it would be too far into the night to wake her folks to tell them the news.

Chapter Sixty-Two

They arrived at the Tanneyhill home on the lake right as the sun was beginning to go down, and the moon was peeking out a little bit later.

Kevin and Netta were sitting on the deck, and ran out to the car with Netta yelling, "Emma and Carter, you finally made it!" Then Netta turned back to the door of the house and called out, "Mom and Dad, Emma and Carter just pulled in!"

Emma jumped out of the passenger side and embraced both of her siblings, telling them she loved them and missed them, before Carter even got the car put into park and shut off.

Kevin ran over to shake his hand next. "Carter, how great to see you again too. How long can you stay?"

"A couple days. It depends on your sister and parents, how long they want to put up with me." He smiled over at Emma.

Her mother and father came rushing out with hugs and handshakes. "Hello, to both of you! We thought you might not be here until tomorrow. Come on in for some leftovers from supper and something to drink," her mother said, grabbing Emma's hand and leading her in, with the others following behind.

Talk was nonstop while the family wanted to know all of the details of her trip home, Sonny's injury, and their many stops along the way. Irene made roast beef sandwiches which she brought over to the table, followed by homemade apple pie. Emma's father asked the blessing.

When Emma picked up her sandwich and took a bite, her mother called out in a high-pitched voice, "Emma, what is that ring on your left hand?"

Emma and Carter both laid down their sandwiches and grinned while Emma held out the hand in question to show around the table.

"A diamond! Does it mean what I think it does?" Netta screamed.

"Yes it does!" Emma said, and Netta grabbed her hand to look at the ring closely before letting her sister show it to the others.

"Did you set a date and place for the wedding yet?" Her mother asked.

"That's what we have to discuss, because we want it to be soon."

Netta grabbed Emma's hand. "Can I be your maid of honor? Please, please?"

"Who else would it be, dear?' She turned to Kevin. "And you can be an usher. Joey will probably be Carter's best man." She turned to Carter. "Don't you think?"

"I'm sure he'll expect that."

Mr. Tanneyhill just leaned back and grinned, then reached across the table to shake Carter's hand. "Young man, I can't think of another man I've met who I would rather have for a son-in-law. Welcome to the family." Carter's eyes teared up in gratitude for this wonderful woman and her family to share his life with. There wasn't a dry eye around the table after that.

They were all up early the next morning, and Irene and Netta made a huge breakfast that both Carter and Emma ate with gusto.

While eating, Irene looked across to Carter. "So, what are the plans for the wedding, after marriage, and your classes at Moody Bible Institute, Carter?"

"We discussed a lot of ideas on the way up, Mom," Emma said. "We'd like to get married soon, possibly here by the lake, and I'd like to enroll at Moody Institute too. I could take the classes that would be most useful in teaching women and children if we end up on a mission field. I could also use my nursing experience wherever we go."

Carter sat back and put his arm around Emma's shoulder. "Of course, I do hope I have the blessings of both you and Dennis regarding me marrying your daughter, Irene."

"Carter, I already gave you my blessing last evening, and I already know Irene feels the same way," Dennis replied.

"I certainly do. We'll both be delighted to have you as part of our family, and in truth already consider you like a son. I can't wait to meet your parents too. When we're done with breakfast, why don't you phone your family and give them the news and get their response to the wedding plans?"

Carter's mother was ecstatic over the thought of the upcoming nuptials. "I love Emma, Carter, and the two of you together as man and wife is more than I could have ever hoped for. Your dad and Joey are outside, but I know that whatever plans you make, we'll be sure to be there for the wedding."

Carter laughed. "I thought that would be your answer, Mom. I love you, and I should be home in a couple days to let you know what's been decided regarding the wedding."

Chapter Sixty-Three

The weather was just perfect for the wedding—sun shining brightly, with just enough of a breeze to keep the air fresh and small waves rolling in against the dock where the ceremony was held.

Jesse was home on leave, so he and Annie made the trip for the wedding with Carter's parents and Joey. Annie's parents had been overjoyed to be able to have Nathan with them for a few days so the couple could have some time to themselves during the trip.

Marietta drove her truck up from Alabama to pick up Sonny in Nashville and spent a night there in the spare room of his family's home on the way to the wedding. Grandma Marie had been glad to care for Jamey, and Marietta enjoyed her first days away from the baby since he'd been born.

There were a few friends and neighbors invited from the area, and the pastor of Emma's church performed the ceremony. His wife helped Irene set up the wonderful and delicious spread that would be served on the deck and in the dining area afterward.

Emma's best friend, Jennifer, from the hospital in town, was the first to walk from the house while Marietta and Sonny sang an opening song for the wedding march. Jennifer walked slowly across the deck and down to the large dock area in a lovely long gown of azure blue that nearly matched the sky above. She took her place across from where Jesse stood in his uniform as a groomsman for Carter. Joey stood between him and Carter as best man, both wearing light blue suits and a tie. Kevin also wore a light blue suit and tie and served as an usher showing the guests where to stand or sit on the dock.

Next came Netta, as maiden of honor, also in a beautiful gown of azure blue, as she strolled across the deck to stand next to Jennifer.

Dennis stepped out, and stood beside the door to hold out his arm for

Emma, who followed behind him in an elegant antique white gown that had been her mother's wedding dress. It had been stored away and kept in perfect condition for the time when one or both of the girls might want to wear it for their wedding.

Emma put her right hand over her father's elbow as he walked her down the deck steps and onto the dock to Carter, whose eyes never left her face. His were so full of love for this beautiful woman, and she felt like she needed to pinch herself to be sure it was all real, and her dream had come true. Her father kissed her cheek before giving her hand into Carter's, a tear rolling down his face.

Sonny and Marietta sang one of Shakespeare's special love songs before the pastor began the ceremony, and the ceremony itself took only fifteen minutes, yet the emotion and love surrounding it were palpable. Sniffling could be heard amongst the guests, and Carter guessed that most of the female attendees were crying at how very romantic it all was. Even he wanted to savor every moment, and never forget this day.

The guests stood in line to congratulate the couple, including Emma's former boss and one-time boyfriend Anthony. Carter could see the sadness of loss in the doctor's eyes, and could understand how he had to be feeling that the woman he loved had just married another man.

The food was delicious, the cake was gorgeous, and the afternoon went by in a blur of laughter, happiness, and congratulations. Emma and Carter felt like their faces would be sore the next day from smiling so much, and they'd never had a more genuine day of love in their lives. It was perfection.

Many of the guests asked what was coming next for the couple. Emma told them they would be living in a small apartment at the Moody Bible Institute while they both attended classes there. After that, they would follow the path their God and Savior led them down, and they looked forward to every moment of it.

***

Allie had heard from Annie that Carter and Emma were to be married, and she and Jesse would be going to the wedding by the lake in Minnesota. She also told her that Emma had registered to attend Moody Institute, and she and Carter would have a small apartment there.

A Bridge to Somewhere

It had been a major blow to Allie, though Carl had recently asked her to marry him, and she was considering it. When she went back in her mind to the night of Carter's farewell party, when he offered her a diamond and asked her to wait for him, she couldn't help but wonder what would have come about if she had accepted the ring and waited for him.

If he had come back from the war and been determined to take the Bible courses and go to a mission field, how would it have worked out for them as a couple?

Her thoughts didn't linger there for long, however, knowing those days were over and gone. She thought about Carl, and how caring and loving he was with both her and Danielle. If she said yes to his proposal, Carl and his father, along with her own dad, were planning to build a house for them to live in after marriage.

She knew how much she enjoyed her painting, and also teaching a Sunday school class of youngsters. She had been hired as a substitute teacher in the grade school in town, which would help with finances, along with Carl working in a store outside town for farming and garden supplies.

When she thought back to the time she and Daniel had spent at the mission in Mexico, she now realized that the mission field wasn't where her heart was in serving the Lord. She was much more content in the life she was now living.

※

When Carl stopped over that evening and she looked into his eyes and realized how precious he had become to her, she knew he was the one she wanted to share a future with her and Danielle.

She took his hands in hers and said, "I know I love you, Carl, and after much thought and prayer, I would like to say YES to your question from a few days ago. I would be very blessed and happy to be your wife."

Carl's face lit up, he wrapped his arms around her, and held her tightly, cherishing the dream of a family with her. Allie knew in that moment she at last come home, to both God and in her personal life.

As Carter had pointed out after what he'd seen in the war, turmoil could either turn us away from the Lord or draw us closer to Him. She knew now she'd let her turmoil turn her away from God, and she wanted to change that now, start living for Him again.

She remembered when she'd told Carter that getting married and having a family seemed like a bridge to nowhere.

She now knew that was a foolish notion she had drilled into her heart and mind. If we draw ever closer to the Lord, He will lead us over the bridge He believes is best for us; we just have to be willing to trust Him enough to cross over.

Only those who ignore God will fail to notice the bridge waiting to carry them to heaven on earth. Those who take a risk, who follow Him, might discover something rather wonderful waiting on the other side.

Acknowledgments

My brother Clair Edward Montgomery was 18 years old the day I was born. World War II began December 7, 1941, with the bombing of Pearl Harbor by Japanese planes, and a year later he joined the Army and was soon sent overseas.

He ended up in "The Battle of the Bulge" and was wounded, although he didn't lose his life like so many others. He lost two toes, had shrapnel in his right leg, and spent more than a month in an overseas hospital. At the time of his injury, he been in a foxhole with another soldier who was killed in the same attack.

Clair is no longer with us, and this book was not the story of his life, but I wanted to honor him and all those like him who suffered or died in the war. This could very well have been any of their stories.

I want to thank my daughter Tamira Thayne, who designed the book and made it available for you to read. I'm grateful for her tireless efforts in getting it out to the public. I'd also like to thank my friends Linda and Jim Renney, for their help in proofreading and constructive commentary, which I hope improved the experience for the reader.

Thank you to all my readers of *Out of the Mist* and *He Rode a Palomino* for continuing to nudge me for yet one more book. I have appreciated your support.

I've been blessed to have a wonderful family, and I want my children Lance, Tami, and Vince to know that I love them dearly. A big hug and I love you to my husband, Chuck, as well. Thank you for your encouragement and helping me wade through an ever-changing world. I appreciate you.

About the Author

Lorena Estep writes from the mountains of Central Pennsylvania, where she was born and raised. She was blessed to travel extensively throughout her life, and has visited every state in the U.S. (with the exception of Alaska), as well as much of Europe and the Caribbean. She has always held a deep love for the ocean, and spends as much time there visiting the shoreline as she can.

She has had stories published in *Mature Living* magazine, *Writers Journal*, *On the Line* children's magazine, *True Story* magazine, and had meditations published in *Penned From the Heart*, *Cross & Quill*, and *Purpose* weekly paper for adult Sunday school class.

Lorena most enjoys writing novels. *A Bridge to Somewhere* is her third published full-length novel. She also wrote *Out of the Mist* and *He Rode a Palomino*, both available from amazon.com and other outlets. Excerpts of these follow.

Excerpt from
Out of the Mist
By Lorena Estep

Meg quickened her pace as she jogged on the wet sand by the ocean. The eerie fog and mist from the sea caused a vague uneasiness. The cloying density felt like something out of a horror movie, sending chills radiating up her arms and spine. Visibility was limited to a few yards ahead and to either side.

Pounding footsteps sounded behind her seconds before muscular arms lifted her off the ground. Being half-carried, half-dragged across the sand and in the direction of the street, she screamed shrilly, her arms and legs exploding in a rush of elbowing and kicking.

The assailant swore in a guttural voice as her flailing limbs struck their target.

"Help me, Lord!" Meg called aloud.

Voices resounded out of the mist. "Stop! Put that woman down!" Then, "Sic him, Drake!"

She heard a fierce growl and felt a thud against her captor. He went down to his knees, taking Meg with him.

He cursed again, pushing her aside when a huge, gray beast latched onto his leg.

Now facing the assailant, Meg saw he wore a ski mask and black sweats. She scrambled to her feet and ran toward the man and woman who materialized out of the mist.

The dog's master commanded, "Drake, come!"

Before Drake released the man, a huge fist slammed down on the dog's head like a sledgehammer. Drake fell to the sand, tearing off a chunk of black sweatpants, and the attacker fled into the mist.

Meg ran ahead of the owners to where the dog lay whimpering. "Oh no, Drake, are you all right?" she asked softly.

"Don't touch him," the man cautioned. "If he's confused, he could bite you." *Want to read more? Available from Amazon.com or other outlets.*

Excerpt from
He Rode a Palomino
By Lorena Estep

Tillie stood frozen to the spot, her arms trembling from the weight of the rifle and the fact that she had just sicced her dog on a person she felt she had no reason to fear. She wasn't sure what to do next, but knew she couldn't leave him on the ground forever with a hundred-and-twenty-pound dog on top of him. "Come, Rolf!" she commanded.

Rolf looked back as if to be sure she meant it.

"Come," she stated again firmly. The dog reluctantly moved off his prisoner.

Tillie lowered the gun to her side. Impressed with the calm way Abraham Webber stood, took off his cap and brushed the dirt, grass and twigs from his clothing with it, she felt she should apologize. After all, he was a preacher and obviously wanted to offer friendship. But it was necessary to keep her distance from everyone.

"By now you should realize you aren't welcome here. So you'd best be on your way and don't ever come back. The next time the results could be more dire."

"Believe me, your warning was well taken. But if you ever need help in any way, you can find me at my home on top of the mountain about ten miles from town. Follow the main road here to the first dirt road to the right."

"Thank you, but I'm well able to take care of myself. And I have Rolf. You've seen how well he defends me, so I can't see that I'll ever need any help from you."

"Good day then," he said and strode back the walkway and through the gate, mounted his palomino gracefully and raised a hand in farewell before galloping away, the German shepherd watching his every move.

Tillie's eyes followed until man and horse were out of sight.

Want to read more? Available from Amazon.com or other outlets.